SACHA DUMONT'S EURO-MYSTERIES

AMSTERDAM

SACHA DUMONT'S
EURO-MYSTERIES

AMSTERDAM

BLACK
APOLLC
PRESS

First published in Great Britain by Black Apollo Press, 2012
Copyright © Bob Biderman
A CIP catalogue record of this book is available at the British Library.
ISBN: 9781900355438

Cover design by Kevin Biderman

Thanks to Tineke Smit, Don Munzer and Sue Ulrich

Chapter 1

THERE IS SOMETHING you learn immediately about England as soon as you take to the air. It still has a feudal geometry. Seen from a hundred feet above, the patterns on the ground tell of a thousand years of shifting boundaries, inch by inch, a parcel here, a parcel there, till lines become curves and curves become squiggles and squiggles become fantasies of errant knights and dragons.

I hunched back in my seat, second class, of course (Global Media is global on the cheap when it comes to travel expenses and per diems), and thought about the shallow ditch below, now coming into view, that separates England from the rest of Europe. From the air, you feel you could almost reach across and touch the outstretched hand of Pierre, Marie or Joop Van der Something basking on the other side. It seems you could skip a pebble across without even half a try.

That's from the air. Actually, I prefer taking the ferry from Harwich to the Hook, boarding a rusty boat in the morning chill of grey and then launching queasily into the vapid mist, the smell of brine, the current heaving in your belly. Then the mainland of Europe is so very far away.

(The other way to cross is by Napoleon's dream: the Channel Tunnel. Close your eyes at Ashford and after a moment of darkness, stolid British rail transforms itself into sleek Gallic speedway. Suddenly it dawns on you that, for better or worse, Britain is no longer an island. But from the sky or on a ship, island it is and island it will always be - till the next ice age or other geological disaster comes along again to change things.)

The story proposal I had sent to Tompkins - which he then, mindlessly, shuffled upstairs - was one of those 'try it on' jobs which you never expect will see the light of day. In other words, it hadn't a hope in Hell - which is what I told Marijke when she called. But sometimes things come together in ways you could never conceive at the start.

Probably the very factor which rankled my intestines - the tabloid mentality which had, like a voracious tape worm, eaten through the stomach of the broadsheets till the only remaining perceptible difference was size - curiously worked in my favour this time.

'You want to write a story about a Dutch artist who murdered a prostitute?' Tompkins had asked with a note of disbelief.

'Accused of murdering,' I replied.

Tompkins's ample shoulders seemed to sag like someone carrying a very heavy imaginary bundle up a hill and now was showing signs of extreme exhaustion. 'Tell me there's more to it than that,' he sighed.

'There probably is,' I replied.

'Such as?' He used his hand to prompt me, like a tired director who had wanted to do Shakespeare but had settled for Christmas pantomime.

'Use your imagination,' I said.

He rubbed his forehead, wearily. 'I want to retire,' he said. 'I want to go to some little town in Italy and drink wine and eat cheese and sleep till noon every day and learn to play the mandolin. Do you think people still play the mandolin, Dumont?'

I shrugged. 'Maybe. It depends on how far south you're prepared to go.'

Tompkins closed his eyes. I had the feeling he was going very far south indeed at that very moment.

'About the story...' I prodded.

He opened his eyes and looked at me, half expecting - or hoping - that I wouldn't be there when he did. 'I'll give it some thought,' he said.

Marijke on the other hand had pleaded. 'I really need your help and he was your very good friend...'

'Of course I'll come,' I had told her. 'It's just that I'd be able to stay longer if I could get the paper to send me in some official capacity.'

'Would you have to write a story?' she asked with a bit of trepidation.

'Some sort of story. But then I'd be in a better position to help...'

It's a thin line you tread when you're a journalist. The myth is that you're supposed to be objective. In fact, the only objective reporter I ever met was dead. But what's really not on is going to your editor and asking to do a story because you want to help a friend.

So you learn to couch things in more appropriate language. The prostitute was an immigrant woman, one of the thousands who've been pouring in from the old Dutch colonies over the past twenty years. The artist was the son of a Dutch couple who had hidden some Jews during the war. There was implicit irony and contradiction here. Which, I suppose, is what caught the eye of Lord Fontleroy when he called me in.

'I wanted to discuss the story proposal you sent to Tompkins...'

Tompkins was the senior editor. In days past he never would have sent a story proposal upstairs. He would have had it costed in accounting and maybe had a budget discussion or two and then would have given thumbs up or thumbs down. The only way it would have been sent upstairs was if the legal boys had spotted something fishy. For Tompkins it was a matter of pride and of honour that the power of decision making rested within his ink-clogged fountain pen. Or so he said. And so we believed.

Now, it seemed, Tompkins had about the same decision making power as a plastic Cupie doll.

'It says here,' Tompkins's young superior went on, paging slowly though a file which sat like a heavy lump on his huge, mahogany desk, 'that you were born on V.E. Day. Is that true?'

'Are those my personnel records?' I asked.

'Yes. It also says your mother was German and your father was French...'

It was a fat dossier he was perusing. Clearly it contained more details than I had ever written into a C.V.

'... and you were born in England the very day war ended. That makes you a rather perfect European.'

'I'm not sure I know what you're getting at,' I said.

A polished metal cylinder glistened blue like the veins in his hand as he reached out to grab a pencil from its contents. 'The old Europe died the day of your birth,' he said, starting to scribble something on one of the papers. 'Now, after fifty years of gestation, a new Europe has finally started to emerge. It's that new Europe which Global Media, PLC is trying to gear its message to....'

Tossing aside his pencil, he swung around in his chair, stood up and walked to the window overlooking the river which snaked through the City like a serpent with a massive case of irritable bowel syndrome.

'I have an idea for a series of stories,' he continued, staring out at the dense thicket of concrete and grime. 'Eurotales...' His head bent upward and his eyes seemed to catch the glint of the sun between two batches of gloom-laden clouds. 'Euro-mysteries!'

He turned back around and I could still see the light in his eyes. 'Each story would be set in a different European location. They would all compare the old Europe with the new. Small stories that help give us a bigger picture. But something with a twist. What do you think? Are you the man for the job, Dumont?'

I was the man for the job, OK. But everything isn't always what it seems on paper. It's true my mother was German if you go by language and place of birth. Hitler, on the other hand, was more interested in race and blood.

My grandfather was Jewish. A gentle man, or so I've heard - unfortunately, we never met. My mother didn't speak much about him after the war. He was a musician and an artisan - a violin maker of some repute. In fact, I understand the cultured commandants at Auschwitz had him play sonatas for them in the soft, moonlit evenings of autumn as his brethren burned.

As for my father, he was a Frenchman who fled France in disgust after the Vichy government was formed. He became part of the motley Free French Forces based in London during the war.

I suppose, Lord Fontleroy had tapped into something I myself had been pondering - albeit from a different point of view. What is the Europe that's emerging? And was the end of the war a permanent dividing line between the old Europe and the new?

In a strange way, I thought, perhaps I was a good choice after all, having been a sort of midnight's child. But it was, eerily, like feeding a questionnaire into a computer and coming up with a perfect date between an orange and a fig.

I looked out of the window and saw the plane's shadow drifting through the clouds below. Between the banks of clouds the waters chopped, a murky blue like frothy ink from an injured squid.

As the plane descended, the ordered fields of Holland came into view. So different, I thought, than the England we had left behind and yet so much the same. Here was a sort of ordered chaos. People, factories, agriculture, towns all busily sharing the most minuteness of space. Not an ounce of precious land was going to waste.

Below, a tractor was tilling the fen-like soil, tracing the path of the plane. It followed us up to the landing strip. As I looked down, I thought I saw the driver wave.

Chapter 2

THE TRAIN FROM Schiphol Airport to CS Amsterdam is clean and fast. It leaves from directly under the terminal every ten minutes, whisking you past layers of suburban housing which, like rings of a tree, grow older as you near the centre.

Like the rest of Holland, there is something both determinedly functional and anarchistic about this train. The service is spot on. But you can purchase a ticket or not, it's entirely up to you. Sometimes a conductor comes to check, but this time when a rather jolly woman came around punching tickets, the two ragged youths in the seat opposite me took their tattered sacks and made a bee-line for the loo. She probably saw them - everyone else in the carriage did - but she went on her merry way, whistling up a tune.

There is a point, however, as you near Central Station where the train begins to parallel a small canal, a foretaste of the watery world to come. Then, as we enter the older brown brick suburbs, the conductor calls out over the intercom, in both Dutch and English, 'Amsterdam Central - final stop. Please take care to watch your wallets when you go out!'

The contrast between the modernity and the plastic, business-class tidiness of Schiphol and the squalor of the more aesthetically pleasing Central Station is apparent as soon as you disembark and begin walking down the dirty white tiled tunnel to the central ticket chamber. Several dozen lokets are open with long, restless queues fanning out like sensitised flagella. There are scattered clusters of pathetic-looking youngsters, very down and very out, eyes with pupils dilated like bleak, open pits. They mill around, searching for the innocent face connected to a hand that might be willing to toss them one last coin so they can finally have enough for yet another fix.

I bought some cigarettes at the kiosk, marvelling again how the Dutch manage to squeeze twenty-five into a pack at half the price that England gives for twenty. A young man with a Rostafarian hairdo that was so tangled and dirty it could have been used as a broom to sweep out the station, eyed me blearily as I pocketed my change.

I saw him edge toward me as I tore the cellophane from the pack and pulled out a smoke. I should have moved on and waited to light up, but it was already too late.

"Hey, man, can I have some change?" he said in perfect English.

I pulled out a guilder and flipped it into his nervous, outstretched hand as I started to move toward the door.

He followed me. "Hey, man, I need more. Just a few more guilders. Just a few more guilders, man. Come on. Just a few more."

"I don't have any more change," I said, lengthening my stride.

He knew I was lying. "Come on, man. Just a few more guilders. I really need it. I really, really need it. You got to give it to me man..."

It wasn't a threat. It was more of a miserable plea that emanated from a need so deep it throbbed like an ulcerous sore.

I stopped with a sigh and reached into my pocket, took out what change I had and emptied it into his shaking hand.

Then he left. He didn't thank me. Not that I wanted any thanks. In fact, I was grateful he didn't. It was a simple business transaction, that's all. He got his money. And I got him to leave me alone. It was a very Dutch solution.

Chapter 3

YOU STEP OUTSIDE Central Station into a sea of bikes, an ocean of bikes - black, basic and battered. They all look the same - worn, weather-beaten, built like two-wheeled tanks salvaged from a muddy canal, sublimely functional and practically inde- structible. They are ridden by businessman and hippie alike. Mothers use them to deliver their kids, bakers their bread, glaziers their glass. The old, the young, the rich, the poor - they're all alike when it comes to their big, black, dent-ridden, death-defying Amsterdam bike.

'To understand the karma of the Amsterdam bicycle,' Heinke once told me, 'you have to know a very significant moment in our past. During the war the German army confiscated Dutch bikes to use as their own. To Amsterdamers that was like stealing their babies. They said, 'You can take my drink, my bread, but not my bike!' And then, after the war,

Queen Beatrix made the stupid mistake of marrying a former German officer and during the procession people lined the streets not shouting 'God save the Queen!' as you might have done in England, but 'Give us back our bloody bicycles!'

I was thinking of Heinke and our strange, convoluted past as I boarded the No. 2 Tram at the plein outside the station. I knew Amsterdam from childhood memories, stories my mother told me and those carefree days of youth when I lived here as a student. But I never really began to understand the city, its heart and essence, or, as Heinke would have said, 'its curious cabala,' until I got to know him better as an adult rather than a distant and somewhat awkward childhood friend.

I remembered standing at the very spot I boarded the tram and Heinke giving me the benefit of his special and very peculiar insights (whether I wanted them or not).

'Here, the platform where we're standing, the Stationsplein, like the station itself, is a little island built on the mighty River IJ,' he said. 'It's like the stage of an enormous amphitheatre, with the semi-circular rings of dyks defining the area for the spectators. Except it's just the opposite because the performance is not here but there. In fact, this little island, the entry-point for our glorious production, is actually more of a launching pad.'

Then he pointed his long, thin, delicate finger in the direction of the wonderland that lay before us. 'Damrak,' he said, with a trace of disgust, 'the main artery into the lungs of the town. I used to hate that street, that magnificent avenue, given over to the demons of fast food and slow death - bits of factory cow and plastic chicken and genetically altered tomato covered cardboard they call pizza. But then I came to realise that Damrak is the main street of the Universal City, that international ghetto of this global age which could be anywhere - America, Africa, Russia, Japan. It serves as a decompression chamber, a comforting respite for tourists and businessmen who want to feel secure by seeing something they can comprehend and understand and not fear, like a McDonald's hamburger sign. They feel happy and satisfied to spend their money in places like these which are no threat to them - no linguistic, aesthetic or cultural demands are made. So give them this, a peek at the Red Light District, a couple of museum queues to stand in, a quick tour of the Diamond industry, collect the taxes and send them home. That way Amsterdam has more money for social welfare programs and these sort of people don't intrude on me at the Literary Café or some quiet spot in the Jordaan where I wouldn't want them to go.'

The No. 2 Tram doesn't go down Damstraat. It makes a little dog-legged loop, selecting the less garish Kalverstraat Niewendijk artery to wind through town, squeezing thinly past three-abreast bicycles and thick herds of pedestrians over bridges that narrow to the point of nothingness. It is a wild ride as no one - not the tram, nor the bikes, nor the pedestrians - deign to give way even when collision is imminent. 'There is' said Heinke, explaining the peculiar Amsterdam physics which prevents serious collisions, 'a special magnetism here. Everything has the same polarity and therefore an invisible shield. Like a drug-induced force field, it protects everyone.' By then, I knew from experience not to ask him what the hell he meant.

I looked at my watch as the tram reached Leidseplein. It was mid-afternoon, a little after three o'clock. Out the window, a small crowd had gathered to see the fire eaters who might have been on the plaza outside the Pompidou Centre in Paris or Leicester Square in London or the Barcelona Ramblas. The circus acts that toured the European cities were strikingly similar, distinguished only by the unstated question - how far will he go now? Will the fire eater finally erupt into flames? Will the sword swallower be disembowelled at last?

'Look how few cars there are here,' Heinke once said proudly, as we passed this very spot several years back, 'In medieval days Leidseplein was where everybody left their horse and cart. Even then Amsterdam had a transport policy that was sensible.'

He was so proud of his city, was Heinke, though he wouldn't admit it. 'Patriotism of any form is the last resort of assholes,' he kept reminding me. 'Isn't that what the English say?'

But he was right about Amsterdam's reluctance to embrace the car. It's the only city I know where the meter maid is a cultural hero rather than an object of derision. People here actually applaud when an errant automobile is shackled like an invading monster, lifted and then towed somewhere to the outskirts to pollute some other's air rather than their own.

Hurtling over Singel, the last in the series of canals that defined Heinke's allegorical amphitheatre, the No. 2 Tram arches its way along the narrow Hobbemastraat which cuts diagonally into the museum quarter. Suddenly the bustle of the central city recedes. The buzz of the candy-coloured strobes and the pulsating beat of the shopping district is replaced by quiet, tree-lined avenues.

Along the avenues leading up to Museumplein mothers are picking up their children from several of the nurseries that dot the road. The sun has just come out after having spent a while swallowed by the clouds. A woman smiles. At the corners, where the road widens, people sit outdoors under the awnings of the numerous cafés and brassieres.

The tram stops at Museumplein, by a little plot of pebbly land given over to a collection of kiosks that sit like a small encampment of gypsy traders. The proprietors are standing by their rusty box-like structures. A fey young man - foreign, but not clear from where - is tending his arts curio shop. An older Turkish-looking man has placed an Ola flag into its holder above his stall hoping to attract customers for his ice cream and canned drinks. Across the street people are queued up at the diamond cutting factory for a free guided tour.

Looking out, I can see myself and Heinke sitting on the bench facing the encampment, behind which the new Van Gogh Museum, half completed, is beginning to take the shape of a nuclear power station. We are smoking hand rolled cigarettes and Heinke is beginning to blather on about art and the artist. It is a tune I have heard many times before and that day I had done a good job of filtering it out. But now, curiously, I can hear the words again:

'The Rijksmuseum is the kind of museum I detest,' he said. 'It's like a mausoleum or a graveyard- lilies gilded by the State. But if you really want to know what Amsterdam's about, then you should go to a new room recently set up that commemorates the VOC - the Dutch East India Company.'

Sometimes Heinke could be insufferable, I remembered. One didn't as much converse with him as listen. And between flashes of brilliant insight, he could be incredibly patronising.

But he was also kind and generous. And there was our special link. His parents had put my mother up at the start of the war, just before she was sent off to England. Now his daughter, Marijke, had asked for my help because Heinke was languishing in prison.

Chapter 4

KIKO WAS BEHIND the desk when I arrived. She smiled sweet-ly. 'Oh, Mr Sacha,' she said, making a slight bowing motion of the head. 'It's so nice to have you with us again!'

It was a small hotel nestled nearby the Concertgebouw and run by a musical Japanese family who plastered the walls of the downstairs dining room with photos of their favourite soloists who had performed at the concert hall just down the road. The rooms were small, cosy and rather louche, with miss-matched furniture and balconies - overlooking a communal courtyard - that sagged precariously when you walked out onto them.   But it was very quiet, friendly and, by now, I had been coming there for years so felt reluctant to change. Besides, the idea of staying in a Japanese hotel in Amsterdam and eating miso soup for breakfast somehow appealed to me.

Kiko had given me a note along with my key which I read while I freshened up. It was from Marijke. 'I'll come to the bar at the Film Museum after work. Meet you around 7?'

I took off my shirt and trousers and tossed them over a nearby chair. Perfect, I thought. Time enough for a little nap.

Vondelpark where the Film Museum is located was just a short walk from the hotel. It is a wonderful patch of green fields and serpentine lakes which extends all the way from Singel to Amstelveenseweg - over a mile in length.

In the late afternoon, the paths and lanes which cheerfully circle through the park are filled with skaters, cyclists, joggers and young, barefoot people totting guitars. There is a pleasant feeling of shared abandon. Ducks, birds, dogs and people have all managed a moment of biological truce, a moment of peace in sunny tranquillity.

Or so it seems until the sun is swallowed up by darkening clouds and you hear the distant rumble of thunder.

Some years ago I chanced upon a statue set back on a grassy mound. It was a figure cast in iron, an image of someone in agony, the strips of metal, like bare lesions, pulling the sinews of the face so the features were distorted into a heart-rending expression. Even so, there's a strange sense of dignity about the piece which pulled me to it. And something else. Surrounding the piece were bouquets of flowers, still fragrant and fresh. And on the statue itself, along the outstretched arms, were candles and sticks of incense.

A middle-aged woman with a child had come up to the statue the same time as myself. With a sense of wonder she leaned down to inspect the flowers, reading some of the inscriptions which had by now blurred in the dampness, like heart-felt messages smudged by tears.

'Can you make out the writing?' I had asked her in English.

'A ceremony,' she replied, looking at me in confusion. 'But for what? All the messages are very unclear...' Then, glancing over at her child who was playing in the mud, she sighed, 'It's a mystery.'

The statue or why children are attracted to mud? I remember thinking that as I brushed some of the flowers away with the toe of my foot to uncover an inscription. My Dutch was limited, but I could make out the sense of anguish and the plea that this may never happen again - without being specific about what 'this' was.

It was, of course, Heinke who told me. We were drinking a beer at the Literary Café and I had said, 'In Vondelpark there is a statue, a very curious statue of a woman, maybe a man...'

That's as far as I had got before he looked at me strangely and said, 'Were there flowers?'

'Yes,' I said. 'They were fresh.'

We were sitting on a small, wooden indoor balcony, by a huge pair of foggy windows overlooking the canal which bisected Kloveniersburgwal on the edge of the Red Light District. Heinke was gazing through the windows. I followed his line of sight, across the canal, where three young drunks were standing with their zips undone, pissing onto a houseboat.

'The Dutch can be pigs,' he said, taking another swill of beer and looking away in disgust.

'So can the English,' I replied, thinking he was referring to the scene of blatant urination.

'Not all Dutch,' he said. 'I don't care where people piss...'

'As long as you're not underneath,' I suggested.

'I meant the statue,' he said. 'It was built to commemorate a murder. A young man, Surinamese, doing nothing, caught out by a group of toughs, beaten, mercilessly, clubbed until his skull caved in. People saw. No one came to help...' He took another drink of beer. Then, putting down his glass, he said in a softer, more contemplative tone, as if still trying to come to terms with the mindless savagery, 'Just because he was black.'

That scene came back to me as I wandered up to the Film Museum. Housed in a large white, colonnaded building - a type the Dutch call 'neo classical' - it could easily pass for a country hotel. In front, to the side, an outdoor café overlooks the lake. Through the leafy trees beyond one can see a little patch of blood-red poppies, a striking contrast to the very deep, almost visceral, green. Above, the trees give way to clouds and, every so often, traces of pale blue sky.

Inside, on the ground floor of the Film Museum, is where you go to order drinks. After working hours, around six to seven in the evening, the place is mobbed - no matter what day it is. To order a drink, especially for an Englishman without a degree in assertiveness training, takes a bit of perseverance as everyone crushes up against the counter waving guilders at the hassled bartender. After a while you learn that standing there waiting your turn is useless and you either join the fray or slink out with your thirsty tail between your leg.

When I finally caught the attention of the barman by thrusting a five guilder note into his face with all the force I could muster, I ordered a Grolsch and watched in disgust as he dipped the glass into sudsy disinfectant and filled it with beer before wiping it dry or even letting it drain. By then I had waited so long to be served and was so thirsty that I took it anyway without registering a complaint (which, because of the frenzied quest for alcohol surrounding me like sharks after blood, would have been a futile gesture anyway).

I took the drink outdoors, hoping for some calm. As it had begun to rain, I grabbed a table underneath a giant Chestnut tree that served as a canopy. A group of young men on skates stumbled over to the table next to mine. A cell phone began ringing. I looked in the direction of a tall man on a bicycle who had pulled a phone from his pocket and now was talking into it as he pedalled past.

A young woman came over to ask for a light. I took out my lighter and offered it to her. She bent down and lit her cigarette while continuing a conversation with someone I couldn't see behind her.

The rain was starting up again. No one seemed to care. I put my hand over my beer to stop it from being diluted with rain water and thought to myself that there is no calm in Amsterdam between the hours of six and eight.

Then, suddenly, everyone left. I looked at my watch. It was slightly after seven.

An older woman with two small dogs took refuge from the rain at the table where the skaters had been. She pulled out a letter from her handbag and began to read as the dogs wound their leads around her legs.

I was wondering about the woman with the dog - who she was, what was in the letter she was reading, what she fed her animals - when I heard a familiar voice.

'Hello, Sacha!'

I heard her voice before I saw her face. But I knew who it was.

I looked up at her pug nose, her bright blue eyes, freckled face and floppy red ringlets. 'Hello, Marijke,' I said.

Chapter 5

IT'S STRANGE HAVING known someone as a child and then seeing them again full grown. Layered memories, remembered more or less, develop the composition of a face into a montage of something recognisable. But the body is new - once awkward and gawky, it has become confidently poised. The grey fluff of the cygnet becomes the plumage of the swan.

So it was with Marijke. I had seen her on occasion through the years when I had visited Heinke, playing, I suppose, the role of 'uncle'. When she was young, I would bring her toffee and picture books. Later she requested clothes from a shop on Carnaby Street which no longer existed.

I used to wonder about her growing up on Heinke's houseboat without siblings to play with or a mother for support. But in Amsterdam you're never really alone. And Heinke's extended family was the community of artists.

She had propped her bike against the tree and had gone inside to fetch a beer. I had barely time to light a cigarette before she was back.

'You had better luck than me,' I said, gratefully taking the refill she offered. 'How did you manage to get served so fast?'

'I know the bartender,' she replied, pulling up a chair next to me. She sat down, put the glass to her lips and drank half a pint without stopping for air.

Marijke knew everyone. And those she didn't know, knew her.

'How's Heinke?' I asked.

She put down her glass and took out a cigarette from my pack on the table while using her free hand to fluff up her curls. Her lips formed themselves into sort of a pout. 'I don't know,' she said, lighting up her cigarette and then looking into my eyes.

It was a painful look, full of more emotions than could ever be said - at least at Vondelpark with a beer in your hand.

'He won't see me.'

'Why not?' I asked.

She made a little shrug with her delicate shoulders.

'Do you think he'll see me?'

'He won't see anyone.' She shook her head, stubbed out her cigarette which she had only puffed on once and immediately took another.

'Who's his lawyer?' I asked, taking out a tiny notebook and a pen from my shirt pocket.

'A man named Van Houten. His office is on Valerius Straat. Wait...' She reached over to fetch her bag which she had tossed onto the chair next to her. 'I have his card,' she said as she fumbled through the contents.

It took her a moment to sort through the bits and pieces of paper. Finding it, she handed me the card, saying, ' It's not far from where you're staying, I think.'

I took it and copied down the relevant information.

'Why don't you stay on the houseboat?' she said as I handed it back to her.

'It's better this way,' I said. 'Kiko keeps track of my messages and the newspaper foots the tab.'

A young couple came up to the table. The man was apple-cheeked, very tall, very thin, wearing a leather coat that fell down to his ankles. The woman was half his size. She had huge earrings and spiky hair.

They had a brief conversation with Marijke in Dutch, then, as she introduced me, the conversation shifted seemlessly to English. They spoke a bit about the upcoming Ozu festival and made arrangements to see Tokyo Story. Then the apple-cheeked lad leaned down, kissed Marijke on the lips and sauntered off again.

'I saw Tokyo Story a number of years ago with your father,' I told her after they left. 'I'm surprised young people would be attracted to that film.'

'Why?' she asked.

'Because even though it's about a seismic change that had taken place in Japanese society after the war, it's so slow and subtle that you could fall asleep if you were sitting in a comfortable chair.'

She leaned down on her elbows and looked at me the way her father did when he felt I had said something incredibly stupid. 'I guess it's not social history that attracts me to his films,' she replied. 'It's his imagery and the way he was able to capture it. He can fill the screen with meaning just through light and shadow and what he chooses to place within a frame.'

Heinke could have said that himself. In fact he probably had.

'What can you tell me about your father?' I asked.

The sun was beginning to set. Across the lake, the blood-red poppies had turned purple.

'What do you mean?'

'I mean what do you know about what happened last week.'

Her gaze drifted across the lake and upwards, into the darkening sky.

'If you don't want to talk about it now...'

She rubbed her nose with the back of her hand. Then she looked at me and shrugged. 'It's what I told you over the phone. Van Houten called. He said my father had been arrested. He said Heinke was OK but was in a very distressed state and, for the moment, didn't want to see anyone.'

'What did he say had happened?'

'There had been a shooting. In the Red Light District. A woman had been killed. Heinke had been found in her room.'

Across the lake, the trees had turned to silhouettes. The park was mostly empty now. The cyclists had gone home for dinner. In their place, flurries of dried leaves skated down the paths.

'That's all you know?'

She stared at me blankly. 'That's all anyone knows until Heinke decides to talk.'

'And the woman?'

'The woman?'

'The woman who was killed.'

She took another cigarette from the pack on the table and fondled it, brushing the tips of her fingers lightly over the paper before sticking it in her mouth. Her hand was trembling slightly as she reached for a match.

'A whore,' she said, striking the match and lighting up. She inhaled deeply, lifted her head and let the smoke out slowly, watching it spiral up into the encroaching darkness. 'One of those prostitutes who sell their bodies in the window to any man who comes along.'

'What do you know about her?' I asked again.

She shook her head, nervously fumbling the cigarette. It fell onto the table. She picked it up again and stuck it back in her mouth.

I could see the tears welling in her eyes. She looked at me, entreatingly. 'My father didn't need to go to those kind of women, did he? There were plenty of women around. He had his pick...'

She was right, I thought. Nothing about it made sense. Sure, Heinke knew some prostitutes. Everyone in the Amsterdam art scene did. They were as much a part of Amsterdam life as green pea soup and smelly canals.

But, like everything else in this fascinating city one had to balance the real with the mythological. The Red Light District had become a sort of Sexual Disneyland. It was open, colourful, relatively safe and an amusing place for tourists to hang out. And once you had got over the initial curiosity of semi-clothed women sitting behind shop windows selling themselves like robotic mannequins from a bankrupt lingerie store, you realised that the whole thing was about as erotic as a petting zoo for truant adults.

I took her hand and gave it an avuncular pat. 'Listen, Marijke,' I said. 'I've known Heinke a good part of my life. He's a kind and gentle man who wouldn't kill a fly even if it landed on his brush just before he was about to put the final daub of paint on his Mona Lisa.'

She made a brave attempt to smile and nodded her head.

But, to tell the truth, even though I knew him for many years, I certainly didn't know Heinke. In fact, the more I thought about it, the more I was convinced that I really didn't know him at all.

Chapter 6

CAFÉ DE JAREN is one of those special places that could only have been constructed by slipping some mad architect a few million guilders, giving him the guts of a grand old three storey bank and telling him to get on with it - the only stipulation being that there should be no interior walls and a maximum of wood and glass. The result is a magnificent use of space and light accentuated by a fantastic staircase to the upper mezzanine that could have been the prop for a Hollywood film. The fact that it's built into a little bay of the Amstel at the mouth of the canal that leads up to Nieuwmarkt - giving it a particularly prominent watery vista - means that the few million guilders were well spent and the café would have been a success even if the food was horrid.

However the food is good - a very nice plus in a world of mostly minuses - and the ambience cosily non-pretentious which is quite a surprise when you think of what the same thing would have turned out to be in London. But this, of course, is Amsterdam where life is nothing but a series of surprises.

Marijke, who was on her bike, got there before me even though de Jaren was just a quick tram ride from Vondelpark. But everything is quicker by bike in Amsterdam - the hierarchy of transportation modes being, in descending order, bike, tram, foot, car.

By the time I arrived - it was sometime after eight - the place was bustling as it was every night about then. Marijke was standing outside chatting with a group of students from the nearby theatre school who were in the process of carting some garish props either to the little theatre next door or away from it.

'I've been advising them on set design,' Marijke told me as we entered the extraordinary room, filled to capacity with animated people.

It was a different sort of set design that intrigued me as we came in. I put my hand on her shoulder and pointed toward the dining area. 'Listen,' I said.

She looked at me curiously. 'What?'

'It should be louder. In a room this size, with this many people, the sound should be deafening.'

'So?'

I was never sure with Marijke whether we were on the same wave length. Mostly, I was fairly convinced we weren't.

We found a table on the mezzanine. Marijke found it, I should say. Several people had been waiting, but I think she explained I had a gamy leg or was about to catch a plane - something like that. Anyway, she managed to commandeer it without being either exceedingly rude or overtly obnoxious, a skill I put down to her twenty-five year course in urban survival. In this city you could be poor but still feel like you owned the place. Especially if you were her age.

A waitress came by. She was young and slim - about Marijke's build - poised and relaxed. They chatted for a minute like old friends and then the waitress handed us a menu and left.

'Do you know everybody here?' I asked.

'No, of course not,' she said. Then, looking around, she said, 'Quite a few, perhaps.'

She's not a orphan, I thought. She's got a bloody big family - pretty much the entire city I'd guess!

'I'd like to visit the houseboat,' I said.

'Tonight?' She was looking at the menu, not at me.

'After we eat. Do you have the key?'

'He usually left it open.' She was still looking at the menu. 'If not, I know how to get in.' Then, suddenly standing up she said, 'I'll have the soup and salad. Be back in a minute.'

'Where are you going?' I asked.

'Water closet,' she replied, heading for the stairs.

Wonderful term, I thought. So direct and yet so euphemistic.

I looked over the rail into the main room below. There was an easy flow down there, from the bar - an outlandish piece of art deco - to the casual space in the centre where you could take your drink and peruse the daily papers, to the tables scattered around the periphery where people were eating.

She had stopped at the centre space and was chatting with a bald-headed man dressed in black who had been drinking coffee and reading a magazine. The top of the man's head was so shiny that it reflected the light like an organic prism.

Even from this distance I could tell their brief conversation was somewhat intense. It broke off abruptly. She walked away - I suppose to the toilets further downstairs.

As she left the bald-headed man looked up. His hand held his face - the thumb on his chin, the tip of his index finger methodically tapping the bridge of his nose as if he was seriously considering something. It took a moment before I realised that the something he was considering was me.

The waitress returned. She smiled in a friendly manner. 'Are you English?' she asked.

'How did you guess?' I said, thinking maybe there was something about me that stuck out like a GB sticker on a British car.

'I heard you talking...'

'But everyone speaks English here - most of them better than me.'

She laughed. 'But when Dutch people speak English it's with an American accent. Haven't you noticed? It's because of the movies I think. Do you want to order now or did you want to wait for your friend?'

I ordered and then took out my notebook and wrote down some of my thoughts. Then Marijke returned. She didn't look happy.

'Something wrong?' I asked.

'My father's in jail for killing a whore,' she said.

'I mean beyond that.'

'I have a sore bunion,' she said, sarcastically.

It took no time for the food to come and for Marijke to gobble it down. When she finished, she wiped her lips, looked at me in a challenging manner and said, 'Did you want to go to the houseboat or not?'

I was still piddling with my lasagne, fascinated by the change in colours as I stuck in my fork - uncovering the green pasta from the creamy white sauce while releasing a trickle of red from a submerged tomato. I found her tone annoying.

'I'm the man you called for help,' I reminded her, pointing my fork in her direction.

'So let's go!' she said, pushing her chair away from the table and standing up.

Her restless energy was giving me a stomach ache. I looked down at the food. It no longer seemed quite so appetising.

'I'll meet you downstairs,' she said, grabbing her bag and her jacket.

'Fine,' I replied. 'I need to make a pit stop anyway.'

'A pit stop?' She crinkled her nose at me. She had a delicious appreciation of any word or twist of phrase that was new.

'The term comes from motor racing,' I explained. 'When an overheated car stops by the side of the track...'

'Oh, you mean the loo...'

She loved that word which I had taught her last time I had come. And I loved the way she said it - with an extenuated 'ooooo'.

I signalled to the waitress to bring over the bill. By the time she brought it, Marijke had already disappeared.

Throwing some guilders on the table, I made my way downstairs to the lower level where the toilets resided and entered the chamber which, on a busy night, could have certainly kept several of the canals well awash. There was a neat line of cubicles as far as the eye could see on one side of the tiled room. And on the other was sinks and mirrored glass.

The vast room was empty except for the smell of deodorant, me and a rather loud snorting sound emanating from one of the cubicles.

I did my business and was washing up when, in the mirror, I saw the door to one of the cubicles open up behind me. The bald-headed man dressed in black came out, brushing some white powdery stuff from his nostrils, bits of which fell onto his black outfit like flakes of dandruff.

He came up to the sink next to me and turned on the water. His face, which I had remembered being greyish white had now turned more pink, like half-done pork of the kind one is taught never to eat for fear of trichinosis.

It was my reflection he was staring at with his vastly dilated pupils. So it was more my image than myself that received the brunt of his guttural Dutch.

'Try it again in English,' I suggested.

This time he looked at me in the flesh. It was an animal look which, in the jungle, would have made you reach for a weapon.

'Just watch your step!' he growled. Then, looking back in the mirror, he splashed some water on his face.

I dried my hands and left him there rubbing his nostrils.

Chapter 7

WE HAD BEEN walking for about twenty minutes through Spui and along Huidenstraat, then crossing the Singel canal and Herengracht and Keizersgracht until we finally came to Prinsengracht where we turned up. Marijke was trundling her bicycle like a reluctant horse, glancing at me every so often with a disdainful look as if to reprimand me for not having one of my own and thus forcing her to engage in a grossly unnatural act - namely, walking her bicycle rather than riding it.

I finally broke the silence by asking her about the bald-headed man I met in the Jaren toilets.

'He's trouble you don't want to know,' she replied.

'He seems to be trouble you do know,' I said.

She shook her head. The cold moist air made her hair limp so it no longer bounced like the coils of a tightly wound spring. 'I just know him from around.'

'Does he know your father?'

'Everyone knows my father,' she said.

The trees which lined the canal were glimmering in the damp light from the street lamps. A splash of inky green reflected in the murky water churning through the blackness of the night. Colours in the dark, Heinke once said, were the essence of mystery. The mystery being that you saw them at all, since you shouldn't see colour at night. It was, he said, the power of sepia.

Heinke's boat was moored by a little organic restaurant which had constructed a wonderfully fragrant garden in the tiny space by the side of the canal complete with benches and tables were you could sit and pretend you were in the countryside instead of being in the middle of one of the most densely populated cities in the world.

He had lived there forever. At least forever as an adult. As a child he had lived someplace else. But the break between childhood had never been complete. Like most good artists, the

30

child coexisted with the man bathing the awkward world of adulthood with its innocence and allowing a vision that was unhampered by the full force of arbitrary social demands. Which is only to say that he lived there as a child as well.

I remembered visiting him as a student. He had bought the leaky old tub for a few hundred guilders and was forever fixing it up with stuff he scavenged from building sites around town. The first time I had gone across that rickety plank which connected you from the relative firmness of shore to his smelly, water-logged hulk which leaked and seeped with every bit of odious stuff you could imagine being dredged from the Prinsengracht canal, I thought my time was up. Not only didn't I swim (I still don't), but I also had a dreadful allergic condition which was triggered by mildew and moulds.

But Heinke had created another world aboard this soggy relic of past commercial glory when canal boats were the link between the innards of this city and the bounty from the sea which gave it birth. From the chaotic morass he had created a magical space. And in the face of magic, expectation was transmuted, like alchemy, from lead into gold.

It also could have been the dope - hash, while still illegal, was always in abundance. I didn't smoke much myself. My head, as they said in those days, was someplace else. But you couldn't stay in that small contained space for long without getting high from breathing the air.

In fact, I don't think it was the hash so much as the oils. Heinke made a point of grinding his own pigments and mixing them together with a multitude of solvents that hung in the air like a chemical stew stirred with the moustache of Salvador Dali. There was always a multitude of canvasses on easels or leaning up against the walls, drying (though nothing really dried in there).

These smells remain in my olfactory memory. I couldn't recreate them. But they define the sense of place and time much better than visual imagery can.

As Marijke leaned her bike against a tree, I sat down on one of the wooden benches and took out a cigarette. She came and sat down next to me. I lit up a cigarette and handed it to her. Then I took out another one and lit it for myself.

'What do you remember about my mother?' she asked me, brushing back her hair and bathing herself in essence of tobacco.

I didn't recall her ever asking anything about her mother before. It was as if Pauline, for her, had never existed.

'She was very beautiful,' I said. 'Not in the ordinary sense. But very striking. You always knew when she was in the room...'

I looked over at Marijke and realised I could easily have been talking about her.

'Your father loved her very much,' I said.

She smiled with one side of her mouth while the other shaped itself into a frown. 'And you? Did you love her?'

I wondered what made her ask that. It wasn't so much the question but the way she asked it that got under my skin.

'Yes, I loved her,' I admitted. 'Everyone loved Pauline. She was a very loveable woman. But she had eyes only for Heinke.'

'What a curious English expression! "Eyes for!" Do you have ears or nose for someone too?'

I sort of chuckled. What I mean is that I didn't feel like chuckling but it came out anyhow. I flicked away my half finished cigarette and got up from the bench.

'What I like most about you, Marijke, is that I never know what the hell you're going to say next.'

'How fucking patronising!' she said in a rather amused tone.

'I rest my case,' I replied, looking over at Heinke's canal boat sitting darkly in the water. It was always a place of beauty and mystery, I thought. Wondrous things had been created there. Marvellous adventures launched. And now it just seemed forbidding. And cold.

Pulling up my jacket to stem the chill, I made my way to the rickety plank, and tested its stability with my foot as I had always done before putting myself at further risk by climbing onto the rotting wood.

Marijke, however, squeezed herself in front and leapt aboard like a two-legged gazelle. Then, staring back at me with a mocking expression she called out, 'Come on slow-poke!'

'Slow-poke' was a term I had taught her last time we'd met. She used it all the time now and when she did her eyes would light up and she would grin. (Sometimes I felt that my sole purpose in life was introducing her to curious, outdated expressions which she hadn't picked up from old TV films.)

By the time I had mounted the great black hulk with two front portholes trimmed in white, like the eyes of a very confused whale wondering how it got itself tethered in such ridiculous spot, Marijke had already dumped some water into the flower box and was now fiddling with the cabin door which led down into its guts.

'I told you it wouldn't be locked,' she said. 'It really doesn't need a lock. It only opens up to people it knows.' She made a couple a twists and well placed shoves. 'See?'

The door swung open.

She dropped herself down into the dark hole below. I bent over and peered inside. Seeing nothing but black, I called out, 'Marijke!'

I heard nothing in response. My voice seemed to echo in a great belch of mildewed air. Then I heard her shout.

'Shit.'

'What's wrong?'

'The lights aren't working. The mains must be out. He probably didn't pay his bill!'

Money, bills - they were, or had been, nothing to him. He didn't bother himself with finances of any sort. What came, came. What didn't, didn't. Fortunately, he had a string of people to look after him. Marijke being one.

There was a soft glow of candle-light now emanating from the innards. I carefully lowered myself down the steeply built stairs. She was lighting several other candles with the flame of the first, placing them in holders that were scattered around the cabin. This wasn't the first time the lights had gone out. It had happened many times before as the mounds of waxy droppings on tables and desk, on bookcase and chair, could prove, if any proof was needed. (Proof, however, was a strange thing on Heinke's magical boat. Proof implies logical patterns and here it was awfully difficult to differentiate circumstance from art. Was a waxy build-up part of a project where wax would be a component or did it imply alternative lighting? Or, as probably was the case, did alternative lighting produce the basis for waxy art?)

Anyway, the soft glow of alternative lighting illuminated the hold in a way that disoriented the senses, casting shadows obliquely on the walls which, due to the gentle sway from liquid foundation below, had a motion all their own.

I sat down in a well-used chair that had stuffing protruding from everywhere and felt a strange emptiness due to Heinke's absence. It was the first time I had ever come aboard when he wasn't there and without his energy, like a glowing hearth or a geyser or even a Mt. Vesuvius, the place just wasn't the same. Even the paint smelled stale.

'Why did you want to come here?' she asked. Her features, bathed in candle-light, seemed more mature. It was as if this special light cut through a layer of skin, a mask, exposing the face of a woman deep in sorrow.

'Did he keep a diary?' I asked.

'Who? My father?'

'An appointment book - anything like that?'

'No.' She shook her head. Ripples of light in darkening shades made her seem like a silhouette. The chiaroscuro effect, Heinke would have said.

Then, reconsidering. 'Maybe. Yes.'

She got up and went toward the rear of the hold, opening the door to a little enclosure and going inside.

I heard her disembodied voice. 'He used to say that all his best thinking was done on the shitter.'

She reappeared, carrying a roll of loo paper which she held up, triumphantly, allowing it to unwind, in fan-like sections, onto the floor. 'Viola! The appointment book!'

I had to laugh.

Then, suddenly, her face darkened.

'What's wrong?' I asked.

She was looking upward, toward the door. 'Someone's there,' she said.

I turned. The glow of the candle was still in my eyes. It took a moment for them to adjust. And then I saw him. I saw his face, his intricately braided hair, his sinewed body, arched thin, leaning menacingly from above.

Her voice sounded behind me. It was steady and firm, hiding any trace of anxiety in its precise and determined articulation of syllables. 'What do you want?' she said in Dutch.

He didn't reply. His eyes staring down like searchlights. His face ghostly tense.

'Are you a friend of Heinke's?' I asked, looking up at him sternly. 'Heinke isn't here. He won't be back tonight or tomorrow, in fact. This is his daughter, she's staying here. There's been some trouble. She's not in the mood for guests...'

There was something about him. I couldn't put my finger on it at first. But then I remembered the young black vagrant with dirty hair who had hit me up for change that morning. It wasn't him, but there was something vaguely similar.

Then he disappeared. It was just like throwing light on a shadow. He evaporated, leaving nothing behind. No scent. No sound. Not even his footsteps were heard.

Chapter 8

MARIJKE HAD OFFERED to give me a lift on her bike, but I felt like walking. I wanted to think and I think when I walk. I am what you might call a peripatetic thinker. I agree with Aristotle that movement stimulates the mind and that nature abhors a vacuum. Besides, Amsterdam is a walker's city. It has all the requisites - no cumbersome hills, an absence of heavily motorised roads, few straight lines, many narrow passages that lead nowhere in particular, lots of open windows to peer into, canals with pedestrian bridges and innumerable places to stop if you're thirsty or just want to sit a while and smoke.

It's also a city that never sleeps. It might rest. There are times when it is even rather quiet. But it never sleeps. Something is always happening. You always feel the pulse.

I walked down Prinsengracht as it arched along toward Liedestraat, back toward my hotel. Not far from Heinke's boat and the organic café, on the other side of the canal, was the house of Anne Frank. I stopped for a moment and stood over by the rail along the canal, lit up a smoke and stared over at the simple brick structure on the other side, so quiet and anonymous.

'There are two places in Amsterdam where ordinary people come like pilgrims to a sacred shrine,' Heinke once said. 'The Van Gogh museum and Anne Frank's house. And it's interesting, you know. There's a strange similarity between them. Have you ever thought about it?'

Heinke could find impossible connections between a goat and a shoe if given half a chance. But this one intrigued me. What did he see in common between a 19th century artist who cut off his ear and a young woman hidden from the Nazis who happened to write a journal?

'Think about it,' he said. 'Van Gogh was an artist who never received recognition in his time, who finally went insane and died having sold only two or three canvasses. Anne Frank was a pubescent girl who spent several years in a secret room before being discovered and carted off to a Nazi concentration camp. But how many others were there - failed artists who went mad and young women annihilated by the madness of war?'

This was one of Heinke's many rhetorical questions that had neither an answer nor required one. It was just a semantic lead-in to the mysteries of his convoluted logic where ideas were always ground up and regurgitated in another form - like making a piece of cylindrical dough into a pretzel.

'Many, I suppose, but what's the point?' I asked.

I remember him looking at me deeply with his magnificent penetrating eyes and sighing. Then gazing across at the other side - we were standing at the same place I was standing now - and gesturing at the long queue of tourists waiting patiently to gain entry to that non-descript house, he said, 'The similarity is that they've both become part of the popular culture the same way as rock stars. They both had good agents - in one case a brother, in the other a father - who took the stories and beat the drums and created the myths which the burghers of Amsterdam were quick to exploit.'

I remember shaking my head, both in wonder and disbelief at his uncharacteristic cynicism. 'Van Gogh was a marvellous artist,' I said. 'What he did with colour, no one ever did before.'

'How do you know?' he asked, looking at me very seriously. 'How do you know how many Van Goghs came before? How do you know how many great paintings are lost or destroyed?'

'It doesn't matter. His still exist. So maybe we do homage to them, the lost artists, through one who was found.'

'What a bunch of horse shit,' he replied. And then looking back at the tourists, he said, 'I'll bet that every single one of them has been to the Van Gogh museum, too. It's on the circuit. And they'll go home and tell their friends and feel very proud of themselves that they've gained a little culture by seeing an original painting hung up on a wall instead of viewing a picture in a book. But if you pulled any of them out of the crowd and sat them down in a room and showed them fifty paintings, without offering them the critical authority saying which of those paintings were 'good' and asked them to choose the one they liked and then showed them the one that was worth a hundred million guilders, how would they react? Because there is no relationship between quality and value. And the only way that relationship is sold is by forcing it down people's throats by setting up false standards and authorities to enforce those standards. It's a trick to make you believe an innately worthless object is economically valuable.'

'What does all that have to do with Anne Frank?' I asked, getting a little fed up with his circuitous rhetoric which was beginning to smack of a tired artist and grapes that were turning sour.

'Are you a complete idiot?' he replied, taking out his pipe and stuffing it with some foul smelling tobacco. When he got like that, he was impossible. Heinke really didn't believe in conversations in a civilised form. You either agreed with him or not. If you didn't, you were a fool.

As I stood there, now, looking across at the empty street and the empty house, I recalled the conversation with Heinke that day and wondered again about his crazy response. I could certainly understand how those two icons - and icons they were - Anne Frank and Van Gogh, had special meaning to him. Van Gogh, naturally, as the failed artist who made good in a world he never lived to see nor could have possibly understood. And Anne Frank...

It was the story of Anne Frank that linked us together. For it was the story of my mother - or could have been. And it was the story of his parents. In that way we were brothers, united by historical circumstance.

I never went inside Anne Frank's house. I couldn't stomach it. Neither had he, or so he said. When I was young, I was obsessed by the story knowing that in a very real sense it touched my own life.

My mother had told me that Otto Frank, Anne's father, knew her father - my grandfather. They had lived very near one another in the southern district of Amsterdam before the invasion. If it wasn't for a fortuitous connection in the world of symphonic music, my mother wouldn't have got the visa which allowed her to escape the tragedy which, as Heinke said, happened to thousands of other Amsterdam girls.

So, like many other refugees, my mother suffered from a cancerous guilt. Why did she survive? If there were only fifty visas available, it became a deadly lottery. The document you had in your hand meant another girl had not. It meant you lived and she died.

Anne Frank was one of those who lost. My mother won. She survived, married and had a child. But she never forgot. Anne Frank lived on inside her. And inside me. And, strangely, inside Heinke.

'Why not pay homage to a girl who died in the Holocaust?' I asked that day when Heinke and I stood there gazing across the Prinsengracht canal at the house. 'Those tourists come from everywhere. At least they think about it.'

'That's the point,' he responded. 'They don't think. They react like they do to a Hollywood film. That house is another theme park for people who want to experience horror safely and then go on with their addled lives. If they thought about it, they'd make some connections...'

'Like what?' I asked.

'Like with the Surinamese,' he said. And then, pointing to the infinite queue that stretched along the pavement as far as we could see, he asked 'How many of those people actually give a shit?'

I thought about that conversation walking back along Leidsestraat to Leidseplein, still bustling in the lateness of the night, and then across Singel, following the path of the No. 2 tram.

And I thought about what Heinke had said again as I passed the new Van Gogh museum rising ominously like a giant bunker in the wreckage of Museumplein.

'The critics who despised Van Gogh when he was alive aren't any different from the critics who glorify him now. They are the very same people. You can't separate the artist from the story. Without the story, a Van Gogh is just some paint on canvas. Without giving his work some extraordinary monetary value, he's just a mad artist to be mocked. But no one mocks a painting or a painter worth millions. Except he's dead, which is perhaps the ultimate irony. For in practical, economic terms, his madness now becomes part of the value and because he's dead it no longer intrudes on the myth. A mad artist alive is a nuisance. A mad artist dead is worth millions to some very sane businessmen.'

Walking down the quiet tree-lined avenue by Vondelpark, I began to realise that these thoughts had emerged once more because they had been playing around in my subconscious - because whenever Heinke spoke about anyone or anything, he was really speaking about himself.

'An artist doesn't choose at random. The act of selection is, itself, art - which gives meaning to chaos,' he had said.

I turned down a small street in the direction of the Concert House and then through a small labyrinth of lanes that led to the hotel.

The chilly mist, reflected in the moonlight and the soft glow from the overhead lamps, gave the air an electric tingle, like a vibrator's buzz, which sparked my battery even though it was late at night.

Standing outside the small hotel, finishing my cigarette and watching the curls of smoke disappear into the darkness, I became aware of the syncopated rhythms that, at first, I thought were just in my head actually were emanating from inside the building.

I took out the key which Kiko had given me in case I came back late. Opening the front door, I went inside to the reception vestibule. To the left was an opening which led to the breakfast room and a small lounge. The music, a cool and very mellow sound, like the best of 1950's Chicago jazz, was coming from in there.

And then I saw Joop.

Lean almost to the point of being emaciated, wearing a black Van Dyke and a welcoming smile, he held out his hand. 'Hey, man! It's good to see you!'

Joop was a jazz musician who had come back broke from Hungary where he had played for a number a years with one of the top Eastern European combos, touring the remnants of the old Russian empire. Now he worked as night clerk for various small hotels, picking up gigs here and there in the shrinking Amsterdam jazz scene.

We had got to know each other over a bottle one day a year or so ago, when I had come back late, like now, to the music of Ahmad Jamal and Joop, fending off complaints from some of the guests who said they couldn't sleep with all that racket, outraged, shouting, 'Hey, man, that's not noise! That's Ahmad Jamal!' And I came in and said, 'I love that piece. Where the hell did you find the record?' That one instant Joop and I became mates. Later he took me to the flea market by Waterlooplein and introduced me to a black man who sold me five Ahmad Jamal discs for thirty guilders and for that alone, Joop will always be my friend.

The grin on Joop's face didn't disappear. 'Got a surprise for you, man!' And ushering me into the lounge he pointed to a large blob reclining like a tranquillised grizzly bear on the settee.

Chapter 9

HUGO WAS BIG, brazen and fat, even for a cop. But there was a gentle side to him which only appeared after the brazenness wore out.

'I thought we were meeting tomorrow,' I said after enduring one of his bear-hug greetings.

We were up in my room. Hugo was pouring two glasses full of brandy from a bottle he had expropriated from Joop.

'I was passing by to leave you a note,' he said, handing me one of the glasses. 'Then your friend downstairs offered me a drink. That was two hours ago...' He grinned and downed half his glass in one enormous gulp.

'Were you able to get copies of the documents?' I asked, hoping to get business out of the way before he was too drunk to remember why he had come.

I knew Hugo from London where he had been sent about ten years back to investigate an enormous diamond theft that involved a group operating out of Amsterdam, London, Johannesburg and New York. I had been assigned to interview him as I was the only one on the paper with a limited knowledge of Dutch and some idiot editor didn't realise that any Netherlands cop sent abroad was bound to speak English better than most Englishmen.

But I showed him the sights of Soho and a pub where he could get a decent glass of gin, for which he was forever grateful. I got a good story out of it and we kept in touch over the years, doing little favours for one another as often happens with journalists and cops. Except I wasn't an ordinary journalist and he wasn't an ordinary policeman.

'There's not much to see.' He shrugged his great hairy shoulders. 'Your friend isn't being very co-operative. It seems he doesn't like to talk.'

It would be interesting, I thought, perversely, to be in a room with Heinke not talking.

'I've only heard what happened from his daughter,' I said. 'What does it say in the report?'

'Daughters are not a very good source if you want to find out about their fathers,' he replied, taking some neatly folded pieces of paper from his jacket pocket. 'Do you read Dutch?' he asked.

'Some. You better read it to me,' I suggested.

He perused the sheets of paper and then rubbed his big, bulbous nose. 'It happened in the Red Light District - in one of those little fucky-fucky rooms there. During the festival. Very noisy that night. No one claims to have heard the shot. But someone called the police. Your friend was found in the room. He was on the bed with the body of a woman...'

'What sort of woman?' I asked.

He licked the tip of his finger and used it to flick through the several pages. 'Café au lait complexion. Probably mixed race. Born in Surinam. Age 45...'

'Isn't that pretty old to be on the game?'

'You've been through those streets,' he said. 'It's a full service out there. Whatever you want - old, young, black, white. You want tattoos? Green hair? Chains dangling from a navel? Forty-five isn't that old. I've seen them 55 or 60. I don't know, some of these guys maybe want to fuck their mothers.'

'What's her name?'

'The whore?' He scanned the page quickly. 'Lulu,' he chuckled. 'That's a good one. Her real name was Rachel Desonsa.'

'Where did she live?' I asked, taking out my little notebook.

'In the Bijlmermeer,' he said. 'You want the address?'

I copied it down. 'Have there been any ballistics tests?' I asked.

Hugo had got up from the chair and walked over to the French windows which opened out onto the balcony. 'Nice room,' he said, brushing his meaty hand over the frayed upholstery of the elderly settee stationed by the window, 'but they could do with some new furnishings.' He opened the doors and stepped out onto the balcony to sniff the air. Then turning around toward me, he asked, 'Why do you stay here?'

'I like having miso soup for breakfast,' I said. 'About the gun...'

'That's one of the curious things,' he said, coming back into the room, closing the doors behind him. 'There wasn't any gun.'

'No gun?' I thought perhaps I had lost something in the translation.

He shrugged his heavy shoulders again and made a little puffing sound. 'No gun. At least no gun was found.'

'But she was shot?'

'Yes.'

'It wasn't a very large room was it?'

'Large enough for a bed and a wash basin. You've never been in one?'

'So where does that leave Heinke?'

'In prison,' said Hugo pouring himself another drink. He stopped as the bottle was nearly dry and looked at me questioningly. I shook my head and he let the last drops trickle into his glass.

'They've charged him with murder without a witness or a weapon?' I asked incredulously.

'He was found in bed with a dead whore. What would they do in England?'

There was no doubt in my mind what they would have done with him in England, but that wasn't the point. This, after all, was Amsterdam.

Hugo finished his drink and looked at his watch. 'It's late,' he sighed. 'I must go.'

'Thanks for the information,' I said. 'Can we meet tomorrow?'

'It will have to be a late dinner,' he said, slipping into his great purple coat which he had thrown casually over the chair. 'I'm working a convention this week...'

'Businessmen?' I asked, trying to imagine the big, ungainly Hugo in a room full of silk suits and chanelle.

He chuckled. 'An international meeting of drug enforcement officers.'

'Not a good time to be running cocaine in Amsterdam, I guess.'

'I don't know,' he replied. 'Maybe it is. How about the place we went last time?'

'The Waag? In Nieuwmarkt?'

'Nice atmosphere,' he said, going over to the door and opening it up. 'Good place to talk. Around nine?'

He stuck out his hirsute paw. I took it and gave it a shake. 'Right,' I said. 'I'll meet you there around nine o'clock.'

Chapter 10

I WAS ON my second bowl of miso soup of the morning when Kiko came over to my table, interrupting a conversation I was having with a young French woman from Brittany who had come to Amsterdam for a short course in Feng Shui. She told me I had a phone call.

I took the call in the lounge. It was Marijke.

'I've arranged for you to meet with Van Houten this morning,' she said.

'Heinke's attorney?' I asked, looking back in the direction of the breakfast room. The French woman had finished her meal and was leaving the alcove. She tossed me a Gallic smile and I replied with a little English nod.

'Yes. His office isn't far from your hotel. He has about fifteen minutes this morning before he goes to court. Can you make it?'

'When?'

'In about half an hour. OK?'

'Who did you say I was?' I asked her. 'Friend? Family?'

'I said you were a friend and a journalist.'

'Did he sound pleased or upset?'

'I couldn't tell. Can you meet me later? I want to show you some things I found.'

'Where are you?'

'I'm at home. But I'll be in the Spui. There's a new squat I'm helping with. We could meet over by Athenaeum around noon. OK?'

Van Houten's office was only a five minute walk from the hotel, on Valerius Straat quite near the park. The morning was fresh. The sun had broken through the perennial Amsterdam clouds and the neighbourhood was coming alive as I walked along the tree-lined avenue observing the bustle - stoops being swept, mail delivered, children dropped off, windows cleaned, store front displays organised - and wondering whether I had ever seen the English so good natured and eager to get on with life this early in the morning.

Just next to an Antik shop selling African masks, Oriental buddhas, old crockery and coloured beads was a polished brass plaque which read: 'Martin Van Houten, Advokaten.' I tried ringing the bell and then, deciding it was broken, pushed at the door which easily opened and made my way in.

I walked up a narrow flight of stairs to a brief corridor which led to a little ante-room. Through the opening I saw a middle aged woman standing on an unsteady chair watering a pot of geraniums, red as her hair, which rested precariously on an upper shelf between musty sets of law books. She was so busy at her work she didn't hear me come in.

I looked at her standing on her tip-toes, wobbling back and forth on the chair so that her stockings were slipping down her legs. To get her attention, I cleared my throat. 'Goedemorgen,' I said.

She turned around in surprise, shifting her balance abruptly. The chair teetered. She grabbed onto a shelf to steady herself, bringing down a shower of books in an enormous crash.

Her eyes opened in amazement, as if unable to comprehend what had just happened. Then, looking dejectedly at the mess below, her body seemed to sag like a wilted flower, her hand drooped and the water pot she was holding emptied its contents onto the scattered books below.

In a flash, the door to the inner office flew open. A tall man with a great mass of curly hair poked his head out. He looked at the woman who appeared very forlorn. He looked down at the mess on the floor. And then he looked at me.

'Mr Dumont?' he said.

I nodded.

He opened the door to his office wider to let me through. 'Won't you come in?'

I looked over at the woman who was still staring down with disbelief at the books scattered on the floor, holding the watering can limply in her hand.

'Come in!' he insisted, making a gesture like a policeman directing traffic away from the site of a terrible accident.

I went inside as ordered. He closed the door and motioned in the direction of a chair facing his desk. I went over to the chair and sat down. He settled himself behind his desk. 'She's new,' he said, in way of explanation.

It was a large office with a pair of enormous windows overlooking the avenue. The walls were covered with works of art, mostly modern and extraordinarily colourful. A few pieces of not bad sculpture were placed, haphazardly, around. A couch against the rear wall was set behind a long glass coffee table over which was strewn several days worth of newspapers and some slick and artsy magazines.

Van Houten was wearing a crisp white shirt set off by purple braces. He looked at his watch and then back at me with a pained expression. 'Marijke telephoned me yesterday and asked if I could see you. I told her I only had about fifteen minutes this morning. So...' His voice lingered in the air like a lobbed tennis ball. 'How can I help?'

'Heinke is an old friend...' I began.

'So I understand,' he cut in. 'But, really, at this moment there's not much I can do.'

'Can I speak with him?' I asked.

Van Houten shook his head. 'He doesn't want to speak with anyone. Not now anyway.'

'Why?'

'You tell me,' Van Houten said.

'How would you describe his mental state?'

Van Houten thought a moment. Then he said, 'Calm and determined.'

'He hasn't confessed to the murder, has he?'

'How do you expect me to answer that? I am his lawyer and you are a journalist.'

'I'm his friend,' I said.

Suddenly there was a sound from the ante-room like something else smashed. Then a muffled groan. Then quiet again. Van Houten closed his eyes and took a deep breath.

'How well do you know him?' I said.

'Who?' he asked, opening his eyes and staring at me as if I was from another planet.

'Heinke. Your client.'

'Not well. I was his father's attorney.'

I tried to estimate his age. From his face I would have said he was forty, perhaps forty-five.

'Not that long,' he said, as if reading my mind. 'I helped him settle his estate.'

I didn't know Heinke's father very well. I had seen him occasionally as a child and not very often as an adult. He had died about five or six years ago.

'Are any of those paintings done by Heinke's dad?' I asked, looking over at the canvases adhered to the walls. 'He painted under the name of Vanderzee, I think.'

'That one,' he said, pointing to a big yellow abstraction of a dog with huge green eyes and pointy ears set off against an orange background. The style was playful, almost childlike.

'Do you know about the COBRA school?' asked Van Houten.

'Not much,' I replied, recalling a few mentions by Heinke as well as having seen the posters on his wall.

'It was a post-war group of surrealists and expressionists who had been part of the resistance in the occupied northern countries. The name is derived from the initials for Copenhagen, Brussels and Amsterdam,' he said. 'Their work is gaining popularity again. In fact there's been a new museum built to display their paintings...'

'That one south of the city - in Amstelveen?'

'Yes. Have you been?'

'No,' I shook my head, remembering that was one of the places Heinke had demanded I visit last time I had seen him.

'You should go,' he said, glancing at his watch again and then standing up. 'It would make a far better story than the trouble with Heinke minor.'

It was hard making sense of his off-handed manner. Maybe he was in a rush or maybe he didn't like talking to journalists.

'Thanks for your time,' I said, getting up from my chair. 'Who would you suggest I speak with at the COBRA gallery if I go there?'

He took a pen and scribbled down a name on a piece of note paper. Then, handing it to me, he said, 'Kirstin Koepel, she's director of publicity.'

Chapter 11

THERE'S A RULE of thumb that if a lawyer suggests you go see someone, there's usually a quid in it for them somewhere.

There's also another rule that says if someone is anxious to speak with you, they probably work in publicity.

It was still early in the day when I left Van Houten's office. I had some time to spare before meeting Marijke, so I decided to ring the woman at COBRA.

'You'd like to do a story? Of course, I'd be happy to show you around our museum,' she said. 'Are you travelling by car? No? Well take the No. 5 Tram. It's only about a twenty minute ride from where you are.'

I caught the No. 5 in front of the Stedelijk museum right by my favourite herring stand. In fact, even though it was a bit early, I couldn't resist stopping by for a snack. The herring there is absolutely gorgeous! Fresh and succulent, with a nice silvery sheen and meat just the right shade of red, it's sliced into bite - sized pieces and served up with gherkins and onions on a little paper plate. Besides, it's just as easy to keep an eye out for approaching trams from the kiosk as from the platform in the middle of the road where you'll only get wet and be envious of the others who were smart enough to wait in a warm, dry place with a dish full of fish.

It's a pleasant ride out to Amstelveen on the No. 5 Tram which passes through little neighbourhoods you wouldn't otherwise see - quiet places with lots of green, public housing blocks neatly constructed to take advantage of light and space.

This is Nieuw Zuid, the New South which Berlage and his friends in the emerging labour party used as their model for progressive architecture in the first decades of the 20th century. The idea that form and structure of living space, good functional design, had a major influence on social welfare and the betterment of the working classes was first put into practice here.

A little to the east, around Beethovenstraat, is where my grandfather lived when he first came to Amsterdam in the early 1930's. The Frank family lived close by at Merwedeplein. Back then the area was thick with writers and artists, refugees from Germany and Austria, bringing with them the richness of fin de siecle Vienna and Berlin.

Hardly anything of that period survives here now. It was erased as if someone had deleted a virtual reality program. My mother took me there once, to where the old house had been, and after that she never returned. She couldn't understand how such a vibrant culture had been so totally eradicated. Her idea of history then shifted dramatically. For if this culture, so intensely rooted, which existed within her lifetime had vanished without a trace, what did that say about others where there was no one left to tell about it anymore? As for the idea of 'permanence', forget it. Nothing was permanent for her - neither buildings, nor societies, nor people, nor even love.

But the No.5 Tram runs to the west of these bitter memories. Which is just as well. Instead, it dodges through a more optimistic view of urban worlds. Until it reaches Amstelveen, a newly sterilised shopping centre utopia, where the tram tracks end and everyone disembarks.

It's not exactly clear what you're supposed to do when you see the tiny sign posted on a pillar next to the tram stop which has an arrow followed by the word, 'Museum.' The fact is that walking in the stated direction means you're swallowed up by one of those agonising malls and all its plastic corporate charm, ground up in some quasi burger cum donut world where every tooth is whiter than white in a vast consumer fantasy that finally shits you out - but where?

I found myself at the anal end in an oozing swamp bordered by piles of toxic building materials. Asking directions, even in Dutch (for finally I had reached the limit of the English-speaking world), merited looks of bemusement. 'A museum? Here?'

Yet I was only a stone's throw from the edifice, blocked from view by all the frantic construction, the scaffolding, the half-finished walls, the cranes and bulldozers, rushing to complete this monstrous whatever which had taken on a life of its own - like a suburban godzilla.

To reach it I had to walk a half mile out of my way, circumventing the vast circus of misconstruction to get someplace that was actually just on the other side of a barbed-wire fence. And quite a journey it was. Mired down in the bog, my shoes sopping wet. Only to be told, later, that if I had gone out the mall by another exit I would have landed dryly in front of the COBRA.

In a zen-like calm it juts up against Mammon. Turn toward the East there's greenery and lakes. But instead of a pagoda, a fortress wall greets you. Can this be it? Heinke had extolled the virtues of this place, the marvellous ambience, he said. And to me, it stands there reminiscent of a great, enormous red brick blockhouse where horses, cows and other large domestics go to ruminate.

But like the new British Library, it's inside you must go to appreciate the brilliance. Similar to a trick box, the outside is a container which tells you nothing about what's in.

It only took a moment after I entered to know exactly what Heinke meant by a living museum which becomes part of the process of viewing rather than providing barren walls to hang dead pictures. There was creative thought that went into this design where space and light and form and texture were balanced and promoted through a kind of subliminal architecture. I made a mental note to ask the French woman at the hotel whether this is what Feng Shui was all about.

The woman at the ticket counter seemed surprised and somewhat befuddled when I asked her to call Kirstin Koepel. Looking at me suspiciously, she reached for the phone, mumbled something into the receiver, looked up at me, asked for my name and then, whispering it back into the telephone, finally smiled as if all was OK and she hadn't done something she shouldn't.

I was told to wait in the adjoining café which was reached, like most museums struggling for financial support, by trudging through the gift shop and bookstore. I stopped for a moment to page through some oversized artbooks about the COBRA movement which were on display. What struck me, besides the vibrancy of colour and the boldness of form was the child-like playfulness which seemed to stamp their work. It was, in many ways, very contemporary, very modern.

'Most people are drawn here by Constance and Karl Appel but, really, we're much more than that...'

There was a lovely scent of lavender. I looked up from the book and saw a very slim, petite blonde with a pleasant face. She smiled and my immediate thought was that if appearance is publicity then she certainly fit the bill.

'Kirstin Koepel,' she said, giving me her well-manicured hand which I shook very gently lest it fall off. 'May I show you around?'

She led me into the central room. In the middle was a translucent cylindrical enclosure containing a sculpture garden built on a sea of pebbles. Around the periphery, display panels came out obliquely. Bathed in light, the room took on a glow that transcended the morning gloom. The paintings seemed to come alive on the walls without glare or reflection.

'Mr. Quist, the architect, spent a long time studying the directions of the sun at various times of day at different seasons. The display walls are angled in such a way as to prevent direct exposure. You wouldn't find so much glass in most museums...'

I looked around. The galleries were large and ran freely one into another, but the wonderful feeling of space and openness was truly exploited by the great walls of glass which established a continuity between inside and out.

She led me up an open staircase to the gallery above. 'This is our permanent collection,' she said. 'What most people come to see. Our Jorns, Dotremonts, Noirets, Appels, Constants and Cornelles. But really, we're much more than that. Down below we have some marvellous exhibitions of new artists - many from Eastern Europe who are rarely displayed but whose work is in the COBRA tradition.'

'Do you have any Vanderzees?' I asked.

She looked at me curiously. 'Why do you ask?'

'I know his son, Heinke,' I explained. Then, studying her expression, I said, 'You seemed surprised that I asked about him.'

She shrugged. 'He's one of the lesser known COBRA artists but several people have been coming in to enquire about him lately.' She pointed to a canvas, very much in the style of the abstract dog I had seen earlier in Van Houten's office. 'We have several but most of his work is in private collections.'

It didn't take long to walk through the rest of the galleries. Heinke was right. Like him, I found the art on display original and refreshing, quite different from the stuff they embalm in the dark, sterile rooms that typify many other museums.

We ended by going back to the little café for a coffee and a chat. She presented me with a publicity packet and said, in a most charming manner, 'I hope you send us a copy of what you write. We keep everything on file, you know.'

'It's a wonderful museum, but tell me something,' I said, motioning in the direction of the labrynthian mall, 'Why have they hidden it back here? How can anyone find this place?'

'Space in Amsterdam is not so easy,' she said, making an apologetic face. 'And here, one side at least looks out onto water and green fields.'

I considered the emptiness of the galleries - even though it was mid-morning there was only several people viewing the exhibits - and thought of the endless queues at the Rijksmuseum and the Stedelijk. 'But no one's here,' I said.

Smiling sadly, she replied, 'And that's why we need you.'

Chapter 12

ON THE WAY back to the city, I looked through the packet of literature Kirstin had given me and began to make sense of the movement Heinke found so compelling.

It was born from war, from the humiliation and isolation of occupation. From the depths of destruction, young artists wanting to build the world anew, breaking with the past, the horrors, the oppression. Going back to the source of human creativity - folk art, children's drawings, the strange, surreal world of the insane. What they had lost was their innocence. Innocence is what they longed to regain.

Yet they wanted so desperately to communicate their rush of ideas, making up for all the terrible time ripped from their lives.

Words weren't enough. But neither was the brush. So words and brush were intermeshed. They painted as poets. They painted their words. They painted their dreams. They painted their manifestos. And yet there was more. There was the energy and joy of youth. Of being young. Of having survived the dark years. The holocausts. And more, as Constant wrote, '...there still remains to do for all those who consider art as a weapon of the spirit, as a tool for the construction, the transformation of the world, and the artist as a worker who subordinates all his possibilities, all his activities to the common task, and who does not seek to be great but useful...'

That was in '48. By '51 the COBRA artists had moved on. And in '62 Christian Dotremont, looking back at those years, had painted on canvas, 'COBRA? It's like going on a train journey. You fall asleep, you wake up, you don't know whether you've just passed Copenhagen, Brussels or Amsterdam.'

Three short years and COBRA was gone. It didn't die. It wasn't dead. It had transformed.

Heinke had a photo on the wall underneath the COBRA banner. It was a group of artists, men and women. One of the women was holding a little child whose fist was clenched as he sucked his thumb. The photo was dark, so the faces stood out rather than the figures. What I remember is tousled hair, berets, dangling cigarettes and one balding man at the side playing a recorder. None of the faces were really smiling - no self-satisfied grins - but a strong sense communality, of people united in something other than just being there. It was the photo of a movement. And, I remember thinking, in that instant the photographer who took it had captured a bit of eternity even though in a few years the people in that photograph would have dispersed and that movement, as a movement, would have ceased to exist.

One face had been circled with a red, felt-tipped pen. It was the face of a man, square-jawed, wearing black horn-rimmed glasses, close-cropped hair, protruding ears, a little older, a little more serious-looking than the rest. I had asked Heinke who it was and he had told me it was the artist Vanderzee, his dad.

Chapter 13

ATHENAEUM BOOKSHOP OPENS out onto the crazy world of the Spui which seems to compress in its location all the strange and wonderful peculiarities that make Amsterdam so special. Vast, cockeyed, ill-defined - half square, half circus - there is always something going on. It's so much part of the life of the city and so central that it's hard to believe only a hundred years back the Spui (which literally means 'sluice') was just another bit of water which flowed into the Amstel.

In the sixties and seventies it was Provo territory as the chic cafés and restaurants which looked out onto the cobblestoned arena made perfect viewing for the spectacles, repeated night after night, of agitation and propaganda directed toward the well-dressed burghers dining by candlelight who, in turn, applauded the very performers who took delight in mocking them.

Further down on Spuistraat pitched battles would be held by insurgent squatters trying to barricade themselves into one of the vacant buildings along the road. I used to watch them from the safety of my window - the police were not such paragons of restraint back then - and often, I recall, my eyes would wander two flights up across the street where a young woman would be watering her flower pots, every once in a while spilling some liquid onto the heads of the cops. Whenever she made a direct hit and a watered-down policeman looked up with daggers in his eyes, she would put her hand over her mouth in a gesture of abject innocence and then, two seconds later, do it again to the next one.

That young woman, who I came to adore, was named Pauline. Her mother was French and her father a Pole. She was training to be a concert pianist. I made the mistake of introducing her to Heinke, who at the time was directing, by torchlight, the painting of a vast mural which was taking shape, inch by inch, on the side of an occupied building at three o'clock every morning. They fell in love and had a kid whose name was Marijke. Two years later Pauline was dead after a long and horribly drawn-out battle with cancer. Heinke was never the same again. Neither was I.

So there was something vaguely resonant about meeting Marijke in the epicentre of my youthful stomping grounds. For Athenaeum had from its earliest days been a meeting place and sanctuary for disaffected artists and intellectuals. Back then, more so than now, it carried with it a sweet and lingering sense of anarchy on the dumpy display tables and miss-ordered shelves. If you felt like pulling out a fag, sitting down on the floor and reading a book, so be it. No one minded. No one cared. In fact, someone probably would join you. I can still taste the tobacco on my lips from sloppy roll-ups and smell the delectable odour of ink from virgin books, their esoteric pages still uncut.

Marijke was already there when I arrived. I saw her through the plate-glass window engrossed in a glossy magazine. I stood there for a moment studying her image filtered through the smoky silicon. It was remarkable, I thought. It was so clearly her presence. And yet not.

She was dressed in a black knee-length slicker and a silk scarf. The top half was chic. Then I noticed she was wearing pink trainers and purple socks.

It was almost as if she could feel my presence studying her. She glanced up from her magazine and for a moment threw me a forbidding look until she saw who I was and then, giving me a little wave, she plopped the magazine back into the rack and came out.

'Hi!' she said, planting a little kiss on my cheek. She slipped her arm around my waist and I gave her a hug.

'How are you?' I asked. Her face looked drawn and her eyes a bit puffy, like someone who hadn't slept.

'OK.' She shrugged.

Behind her was the Lieverdje, one of those amusing city statues that pop up in unlikely places - this one being the image of a street urchin, which half of her reminded me of.

'Where shall we go?' I asked. 'The Hoppe?' I glanced over at the brown café across the square.

She shook her head. 'I prefer De Zwart,' she replied, pointing to the one next door.

In fact, I preferred De Zwart as well but always felt inclined to suggest the Hoppe because it's such an institution and so very 'brown' with centuries of smoke encrusted on its walls. De Zwart was brown as well, but maybe not so proud of it.

'I'm going to try again to see Heinke today,' she said, as we walked.

I gave her hand a little squeeze. 'Good,' I said, encouragingly.

She turned her head to look at me and I could see the hurt in her eyes. 'Why do you think he's being this way?'

We had reached the café and found a table under the awning. 'You know your father better than I do,' I replied, pulling out the chair for her to sit in.

She almost smiled at the gesture she considered quaintly British. Then, catching herself, she frowned. 'I don't know him at all!' she said, sitting down. 'Why is he doing this?'

'He has his reasons,' I said. 'You have to trust him.'

It was as if she was trying to make sense of my words, which I had only half meant anyway. She narrowed her eyes and said nothing until the waiter came. I ordered a beer and a liverwurst sandwich. She ordered cheese.

'You wanted to show me something,' I reminded her, after the waiter went away.

She reached into her sack and pulled out a photo which she handed to me. I studied it for a moment. 'Where did you find it?' I asked.

'It was in a box of stuff I was looking through - I found it underneath his bed,' she said.

'When?'

'This morning. I couldn't sleep. I went back. I thought I could find something that would give me just a little clue...'

I turned the photo over. Nothing was written on the back.

'Do you recognise him?' she asked.

I nodded. It was a different expression, almost serene. Very different from the look in the wild eyes I had seen last night staring down at us from the entrance to Heinke's cabin.

'You're certain you've never seen him before last night?'

She shrugged, impatiently, and then catching sight of something in the square the expression on her face changed. 'I forgot to tell you. There's someone I asked to join us.'

I followed the direction of her gaze and saw a young man walking toward our table. He was so thin that even from a distance you could see the shape of his bones through his pale white skin. His hair was long, brown and kinky. He wore wire-rimmed glasses and a blue serge jacket that was too large for his frame.

Marijke made a little wave as he came up to us, and his face, which seemed to be naturally morose, lit up. I stood, shook his hand and thought from its softness that he had never lifted anything heavier than dog-eared book.

He leaned over and gave Marijke a shy peck on the cheek and then he sat down across from her, looking slightly uncomfortable.

'This is Simon Nassy,' said Marijke.

Nassy nodded his head and tried to smile politely.

'He works for the Jewish Historical Museum," she explained.

His face expressed the shock and surprise of someone who takes the precision of words very seriously. 'No,' he corrected. 'I don't work for the museum. I work for the university.'

'I thought you said you worked for the museum,' she said, tilting her head and giving him a curious look.

'No. I work for the university. Sometimes I do some work for the museum, but I don't work for the museum. I work for the university.'

She narrowed her eyes. 'So you do work for the museum.'

'No. I work for the university.'

Marijke sighed. And then, looking at me, she said, 'Nassy stopped by the boat while I was there this morning. It seems he was doing some research for my father.'

'I'm very sorry to hear about Heinke,' he said. 'I didn't know about his problems until...'

'Nassy and I had a little talk,' she interrupted. 'And I invited him along to meet you.'

'But I don't know how I can help,' said Nassy, turning up the palms of his lilly-white hands and looking extremely befuddled.

'What kind of research were you doing for Heinke?' I asked.

'He was interested in having me do a little genealogical study for him. He wanted to know about a family that had gone to one of the Dutch possessions in the Caribbean.'

'When was this?'

'In the 18th century.'

I shook my head. 'I mean when did he ask you to do the research.'

'A while ago,' said Nassy. 'A few months.' He looked at Marijke apologetically. 'He didn't have much money and I didn't have much time.'

Marijke shrugged.

Then, turning to me, he continued, 'I would have done it sooner, but he didn't seem to be in a hurry and I was buried in work. In fact...' He glanced at his watch and then looked back at me with a face that was truly wretched.

'No one's blaming you,' I said, starting to lose my patience. 'Who was the family he wanted you to trace?'

'A family of Sepharidic Jews who left Amsterdam for Surinam in 1710,' Nassy said.

'Did he say why?' I asked.

Nassy shook his head.

At that moment I felt Marijke's hand clutching mine. It was a cold, icy grip that channelled an electric anxiety straight into my skin. She didn't say a word. She didn't have to.

I followed her line of sight and saw a young man standing just beyond the tram tracks. Staring at us. His complexion was dark but he was too far away for me to clearly see his features.

'What is it?' Nassy asked, sensing something had happened which went far beyond his understanding. 'What's going on?'

Marijke, stood up, almost hypnotically. I stood up as well.

I followed her as she moved from the table. He was standing about thirty yards away, as still as the statue on the other side of the tracks, clearly visible even as people strolled past.

And then, suddenly, a tram. It rolled in from nowhere hiding him from view.

Bells clanged. The tram rolled on. I followed as Marijke pushed her way through the crowd to the other side of the tracks. Once more the view was clear, but the man had disappeared.

I looked over at Marijke, questioningly. She pointed to a figure darting around the corner, down the busy Nieuwezijds Voorburgwal, in the direction of the tram.

She dashed into the crowd. I followed. But it was hopeless. People were flowing down the boulevard in a multicoloured swarm which swallowed everything around it.

'It's no good,' I said, grabbing her hand.

She looked at me, frantically. 'Who is he? What does he want? Why does my father have his picture?'

Standing in the middle of the surging crowd, I took her in my arms and let her sob. I felt her tears soak through to my shoulder.

Chapter 14

BY THE TIME we returned to De Zwart, Nassy had left. Our table was empty. The waiter came by and gave us a curious look. As far as he was concerned, we had run off leaving Nassy with the tab.

'Don't worry,' said Marijke, as we walked back out into the square. 'I'll make it up to him.'

'I'm a bit concerned about leaving you on your own,' I said. There was a look about her which I hadn't seen before. Marijke was one of those people who always seemed to be on top of things even if she wasn't. The tiny lines which had appeared in her face reminded me of the first sign of cracks in a swollen dike.

'Don't worry about me,' she replied. 'I've got friends. Someone's spending the night.'

We stopped outside of Athenaeum books, by the statue.

'You think it was him?' she asked, as if suddenly unsure of herself. 'You saw him too...'

'I couldn't really see his face,' I said.

'I couldn't see his face either,' she admitted. 'But it must have been him. Why would he run away?'

'He didn't run away,' I reminded her. 'We lost sight of him. He left.'

'He saw us coming,' she insisted.

'Listen,' I said, 'I'd like to go down to Bijlmermeer...'

'Why?' She looked at me curiously.

'That's where the woman lived - the prostitute. But I need a translator...'

'I don't speak Creole, if that's what you mean.'

I shook my head. 'No. It's just that I'm not sure how many people down there speak English.'

'Probably more than you think. But I'll go with you if you want.' She looked down at her watch. 'I've got an appointment now, but I can meet you around three.'

'Where?' I asked.

'By the Metro entrance at Central Station.'

And then throwing me a kiss, off she ran.

Standing there in the middle of the Spui, I watched her go, her figure getting smaller and smaller until she merged completely into the noon-time crowd. And then she disappeared from view.

I stood a while, resting myself against the Lieverdje. I lit up a smoke and turned to look at the ridiculous statue. Only in Amsterdam, I thought, could someone plant a statue of a street kid in a square like this and get away with it.

'You want a smoke?' I asked, holding out my cigarette to the sculpture.

'Thanks,' said the kid, 'I was hoping you'd ask.' And he took a long and grateful puff.

Things like this happen in Amsterdam, but only if you've smoked enough pot. I hadn't and it didn't. Though, somehow with Marijke I always felt left with a contact high. It's just part of the magic of Toy Town, I suppose.

Chapter 15

JOHANNES WAS A friend from the old days - one of the group who hung around the boat. I hadn't known him well back then. He was younger than us and rather quiet. But I liked him. He was a serious and committed artist - and always there when you needed him. (As art and social reliability seem to be mutually exclusive by nature of the beastly muse, those two aspects rarely come together in one individual.)

As the years went by, Johannes moved from painting into film, a step which probably saved his artistic life. One by one, the old crew fell by the wayside. He and Heinke seemed to be the last whose youthful careers survived.

I decided to look him up, as I had a little time before meeting Marijke, and he was one of the names on Heinke's toilet paper list with 'Maritime Museum' written parenthetically and a telephone number beside it.

'What are you doing? Building model ships for toy navies?' I asked when I got hold of him there.

'It's a contract for a multi-media production. You know, what it would have been like to sail on an East Indiaman in the 18th century - that sort of thing. It's been fantastic! Sure, come over. I'll meet you in the café. You know where we are?'

Of course I knew where he was. It was one of our haunts. Heinke and I would spend hours there after walking along the old wharves, him stopping to make sketches of derelict buildings and dry-docked boats while I made notes on the odd characters who lived and toiled in those damp, abandoned spaces. And we would dream of what it would have been like a hundred, two hundred, three hundred years before when the harbours were gorged with schooners and sloops and lighters and the warehouses behind us were bursting with lush, exotic goods - colourful silks and soft black satins; tobaccos, rich and golden brown; delectable spices, piquant, tangy and fiery hot; and sweet, erotic oils which made you dream forbidden dreams, unlocking chambers in your mind you never knew existed. Whatever you wanted. Whatever you fancied. It was there. It was here. In Amsterdam - the storehouse of the heart, the belly and crotch of the world.

And then we would end up in the Maritime Museum at that great café warming ourselves with a dish of wonderful pea soup while gazing out the huge plate glass window which overlooks The Amsterdam, that extraordinary working replica of a three-masted schooner which plied the East Indian trade routes back when Holland vied with Britain in building an empire to rule the world.

Except, as Heinke never tired reminding me, unlike Britain, Holland never really wanted an empire to rule. They just wanted the products to stuff into their depots. For first and foremost they were traders and quite good they were at that. Where they ruled, they ruled reluctantly and so badly that if any nation every wanted to take lessons in how to muck another country up they could do no better than study the terrible example of the Dutch. So said Heinke. And who was I to disagree with him?

I caught the end of Johannes's show. Enough to see the value of his work. He and his team had created a miniature extravaganza on a woefully limited budget. But what came to mind after all the fun of drifting off to sea on an 18th century schooner (Did I say 'fun'? Shipping out in those days was about as much fun as sticking your head up the butt of a constipated lion while someone is feeding him laxatives at the other end) - what came to mind was that even back then Europe was hopelessly amorphous. The crew of an East Indian ship was about as 'Dutch' as the Netherlands army. Scots, Poles, Germans - they were all on the road in those days. And many of them ended up in Amsterdam, where Rachmanite inn-keepers were only too happy to provide them lodgings for credit bills which were then sold on to ship owners who collected by offering bonds of indenture - two years at sea, all expenses paid (if they survived and most of them didn't.) And those Poles, Scots, Germans and assorted others who survived, if they didn't spend the meagre nothing they retained after some many awful months before the mast on one huge, grand bender, whoring it up (the Red Light District existed even then) occasionally took their earnings and staked themselves in some trade, finally becoming an Amsterdamer. (One of the many unanswerable questions I asked Heinke was 'Who is a Dutchman?' And he, in his own inimitable way answered, 'Someone who lives in the Netherlands and speaks Dutch.' And then thinking a moment, he amended it by saying, 'He doesn't have to live in the Netherlands, I suppose.' And thinking a little more, he continued, 'Nor does he necessarily have to speak Dutch.')

Johannes was in the café rolling a fag when I came downstairs. The last time I had seen him, he had hair down to his navel. Now he was slightly bald. But his eyes still had a special twinkle. We shook hands.

'You want some soup?' I asked. 'They have great pea soup here.'

'I'll have a beer,' he said, lighting up. 'Maybe you should settle for one, too. I wanted pea soup for lunch but they ran out.'

I gave him a very disappointed look. 'No pea soup?'

He nodded his head. 'I'm afraid it's true. What did you think of the show?'

'I only caught the tail end, but it's good. Are you happy doing this?'

He shrugged. 'It's OK. It's interesting and it pays the bills. But I'd rather be doing things like Bill Viola. Do you know him?'

'Not that I recall.'

'You should. There's an exhibit on now at the Stedelijk. It's fantastic.'

'Painting?'

'No. Conceptual art. Deconstruction of television.'

'As far as I'm concerned it never should have been constructed in the first place,' I said. 'You want a beer?'

'I'll have a Mais.'

I brought back two beers from the self-service bar and as I poured mine from the bottle into a fluted glass, I told him about Heinke. He was stunned.

'I don't believe it,' he said, forcefully shaking his head (a difficult act in former days as his long hair would have wrapped around his neck causing near strangulation).

'When was the last time you saw him?'

'About a month ago.'

Heinke's toilet paper list must have been fairly old, I thought to myself.

'How's Marijke holding up?' he asked.

'Pretty well. She rang me last week. Asked if I could help. I've been trying to piece together his recent affairs since it seems he doesn't want to speak with anyone - at least not now. I thought perhaps you'd seen him more recently...'

Johannes rubbed the side of his face and looked out through the great plate glass window. 'I hadn't seen him for a while. Then he rang me about a month ago. We met - here in the café...'

'What did he want?'

'He was doing some historical research and he wanted my help. It had to do with the West Indies and I told him that we were mainly concerned with the East Indies here...'

'Didn't he say what he was researching?' I asked.

'Not directly. Something about one of the Dutch colonies in the Caribbean. The West and East were very different. The Dutch East India Company was based around the factory system - setting up two-way trade with established communities. In the West, especially in the Caribbean, which by the time we got there was basically depopulated, it depended on setting up permanent farming colonies...'

'Plantations.'

'Yes. Sugar, coffee, tobacco - that was like gold in the 18th century. I gave him the name of a friend who works for the Tropical museum who I thought might be able to assist him.'

'That day you saw Heinke, how did he strike you?'

'I hadn't seen him for a while,' Johannes replied, 'but he seemed to be very centred, very focused - like someone obsessed...'

'Obsessed with what?'

He looked down into his beer. Crease lines appeared in his forehead as he squinted his eyes. Then, dipping his fingers into the froth he pulled out something that looked like a fly. He held it up for me to inspect and said, 'Obsessed with whatever he was obsessed with.'

Chapter 16

I KNEW HEINKE to be a purposeful man whose mind worked in very mysterious ways. To make sense of what he had been up to, one needed to enter his skin - a task both impossible and for-bidding. It was like studying the complexity of an atom while realising that the mere act of observation makes it change.

Two ideas that Heinke preached, however, had to do with the power of patience and intuition. There was a structure to things, he said, which wasn't entirely obvious. In order to see it, one needed time and focus in a very impatient world. Which is why he said most people end up never seeing anything.

Perhaps I am one of the guilty ones, myself. Being educated in Britain meant being taught to view things in very straight lines and see things in terms of simple cause and effect. I was taught the mechanics of argument and debate in a structural form of right and wrong which left very little room for grey. And I learned to write in a style that answered quite specific questions like a locomotive going down a iron track with little time to clean the dirt from the windows and peer through the primeval mists into the phantasmagorical universe.

But I also came to realise that getting into the mind of an artist like Heinke could be like buying a one-way ticket to never-never land without ever reaching a station on the other side.

I thought about this as I made my way down along the water to the Metro station. And I thought of Marijke and wondered what she really made of all this. And how she coped. And what she wanted from me, anyway.

However - and I must emphasise this point in bold and underline it as well - it is very dangerous to think like this, walking through the confluence of roads, tram tracks, bicycle paths and waterways that separate the pedestrian from that great whizz-whizz, bang-bang, ding-ding, whoosh of a launching pad outside Central Station known as Stationsplein. This is because you might end up as a mangled speck of organic refuse after your body has been decimated by all the mechanical monsters whose mote you've carelessly stepped in.

Stationsplein is always a buzz, rain or shine, no matter what time you get there. It's an open-air extravaganza without a ringmaster or even rings. Everyone in Amsterdam passes through there sometime - at least twice - once to come and once to go. But most people use it more often as a central point to catch the trams, the metro or the train. Some use it everyday. Some never leave the bloody place. Which is why it's a terrible spot to meet anyone. Especially Marijke who is usually late.

I stood there in the drizzle. Waiting. Wondering why I had agreed to meet her there and reminding myself to make an appointment to get my head examined.

When...

Through the air, like one extended human blur out of the drizzly blue ending in a stupendous triple somersault, his tiny arms extended triumphantly, his mouth stretched into a wide toothy grin, he landed - plop! - right in front of me.

'Hi!' he chirped, staring up at me with large, twinkly eyes. His head came nearly up to my belt. 'Are you English?'

He wore the costume of an elf and that's exactly what he was.

There's nothing more annoying than someone who guesses your nationality without even hearing you speak. It's like matching a photofit file with a box full of stereotypes.

'Are you Dutch?' I asked, with a note of sarcasm. (The problem with sarcasm is that it loses something in translation between sender and receiver if both aren't speaking a language at a similar level - and he was three feet while I was closer to six.)

'It depends what you mean by "Dutch"', he responded. 'I was born in Zeeland but I've lived in Amsterdam ever since I ran away from the circus.'

'I'll make a deal with you,' I said. 'You don't tell me your life story and I won't tell you mine.'

'OK, Englishman.' Again he grinned, showing me his teeth stained with years of tobacco.

'How did you know I was an Englishman?' I asked, unable to restrain myself any longer.

'A lucky guess,' he said. 'You could have been French. But a Dutchman wouldn't have stood so long in the rain without an umbrella or a hat.' Then, reaching into his trouser pocket he pulled out a coin and showed it to me. 'Since you are an Englishman, perhaps you can help me out. Someone put this in my collection box. It's no good to me, but maybe you can use it...'

I took the coin and inspected it. It was a quid, all right, but I've never seen one so mangled before. It had been chewed so much you could almost see the teeth marks.

'I think the current rate of exchange is four guilders,' he said, holding out his little misshapen hand.

'Three more likely.' Then, glancing down at my watch, I said, 'But I'll tell you what, I'll give you ten.'

His eyes lit up. 'Guilders? For the coin?'

'Yes,' I said, taking a note from my wallet and handing it to him. 'You'll be around here for a while, won't you?'

'Sure! Where else in this city would someone give you ten guilders for a pound?'

'Then keep an eye out for a young woman - curly hair, slim, her name is Marijke - and tell her I'll call later...'

Chapter 17

BELOW THE FRIVOLITY of Stationsplein is a bleak, dark hole. There was an attempt to make this hole not so bleak and dark but, it was woefully unsuccessful.

Most urban transportation holes are modified by the glare of artificial lighting which causes great bolts of static electricity to zap through the air, further infuriating the already manic hordes of underground travellers. But in cities like Paris and London and other great metropoli of Europe, underground rail is still the best way to transit the city. It's a world unto itself, full of strange, urine drenched surprises. But life exists down there. And excitement. In Amsterdam, it is the Obverse Universe - the alternative side of the urban coin. The Metro is what Amsterdam could have been if no one gave a damn about it.

Perhaps this is because the Metro isn't for Amsterdamers or for tourists. It's for the Others - those unlucky masses who have been exiled to the suburbs. In London, people commute back home with a grateful sense of relief. In Amsterdam it's just the opposite.

But it's the Metro you take if you want to get to Bijlmermeer. Not that anyone really, truly wants to get to Bijlmermeer no matter what all the publicists for 'New Amsterdam' say about it.

The thick smell of ganja and multitude of black faces made me think I was on the train to Brixton, though the train to

Brixton was never like this. Two men with Rastafarian hairdos were using the back of their seat as bongo drums, beating out a pulsating rhythm as they sang, 'We are riding on the Bijlmermeer Express! Oh, yes! We are riding on the Bijlmermeer Express! Oh, yes!' And on and on and on.

Heinke once told me that most of the Rastas you see in Amsterdam are fake. In the early seventies, the West Indian blacks from Suriname and the Antilles who had come to live in Amsterdam became infected with the rhythms of Reggae that they never heard back home, even though they grew up only a stone's throw from Jamaica. Then they started aping the manner and the dress of Bob Marley and smoking ganja and soon you couldn't tell the difference between them and a British Rasta except for the accent and the fact that most of the Dutch Rastas didn't know a bloody thing about Haile Selassie.

Not that the entire train was black. It was about half and half. Which is what Bijlmermeer is about and you have to give the Dutch full marks for that. They didn't want to create a racial ghetto with all the negative implications. So they created a mixed-race ghetto instead.

The Bijlmer station is also the stop for Amsterdam's grand new football stadium. What that means on soccer nights is left to the imagination. But on ordinary days like the day I came here, the place was large, empty and bleak. Especially at four o'clock, before the rush of commuters coming back.

To get a true appreciation of the enormity of the 'New Amsterdam' one needs to go up from the station to the overpass where little knots of people are waiting for the various buses which will take them ever deeper into the forests of concrete which have been built, like giant hedge rows on the polder. From there, as far as the eye can see, are the modern-day relics of suburban sprawl trying to pretend it's something else.

Godard might have called this 'Betaville'. It's not as dreary as Amstelveen which is true suburbia and mostly lilly white. If anything, Bijlmermeer is even more frightening because it's being hyped as modernity.

Below, as you walk out through the station, you are swallowed up by a yellow brick mall flanked by stern, wall-like office buildings. Once inside, the mall becomes a commercial labyrinth - a village of commodities for newly arrived immigrants to feast their eyes on. Yes, there are flowers, but you have to buy them in a shop. Underfoot, the earth has turned to stone. There is no humour, not as in the city. No gentle anarchy. Everything seems planned, populated and positioned. Communal it might be, but it has a feel of communal pretence.

You walk and walk and finally you emerge out of the commercial enclosure and into the relentless cadres of living quarters built for the masses. They're not bad as living quarters go. Ostensibly clean and light, but oh so sterile. So regimented. One cries out for colour. But you only see it in the faces of the people. Lost. Rootless. Here. In Bijlmermeer.

I explored the area, looking vainly for the address Hugo had given me. Showing various people the slip of paper on which it was written resulted in blank stares and shrugs.

It was only when I trudged back out of the labrynthian mall that I noticed an office which, in translation, read, 'Information about Bijlmermeer'.

Inside, the room was filled with promotional literature and large display models and architectural visions of this city of the future. In miniature, made out of paper and glue, it didn't look half bad. But that's the problem with models, isn't it? You could make a model of a concentration camp that looked quite appealing, I guess.

What was clear, however, was that a lot of hubris was being pumped into this place with the idea that something great was there to be sold. The trouble, though, was I was the only one who had come to look.

The office was empty except for me and the young man behind the expansive information desk who looked both bored and nervous. He tried to smile as I approached. What came out was more of a twitch.

I told him I was searching for an address and, pulling out a great plan of the area, he seemed anxious to help. Until, that is, I showed him the slip of paper on which it was written.

Then his face darkened and looking at me, severely, he asked, 'Are you a reporter?'

I didn't deny it, though I wasn't sure what made him ask.

'It's unfortunate that you people don't want to see the positive aspect of what is being done here rather than dwelling on the past,' he said, folding up the map. 'Much time, energy and thought has gone into constructing this community. It is liveable, workable and has few of the racial and cultural antagonisms you find in other areas of this sort. In fact, it could be a model for Europe. And yet you persist in dredging up what happened over six years ago...'

I was slightly taken aback by the vehemence of his outburst. 'I'm sorry,' I said, apologetically, 'I think there's a misunderstanding. Actually, I just wanted to locate an apartment where someone lives...'

He looked at me suspiciously and then, as if finding it hard to believe it himself, he said, 'You mean you don't know?'

'Know what?'

He shook his head and pointed to my slip of paper. 'That address no longer exists. It was part of a housing block that was destroyed in the El Al plane crash.'

Chapter 18

THINGS STARTED CLICKING in my head as I made my way back from Bijlmermeer to my hotel. I remembered being in the newsroom when word came in of that terrible plane crash somewhere in the suburbs of Amsterdam. How many years ago was it? Six? Seven?

The photos that came down the wire told of sheer devastation. A gaping section, over ten stories high, ripped out as if some giant claw had reached down from the sky, severing off forty or fifty flats and strewing the debris over a barren wasteland. The skeletal remains, like the mark of a bombed-out city, lay in heaps, while in the background rose a toxic mist of hot, corrosive metals. The heat was so intense that even the concrete was glowing red.

But this event, so horrific, began to fade as the years passed, as other images prevailed in so many tragic places, with similar scenes of terror, suffering, pain and horror, till all that was left was a vague memory that, oh, yes, something dreadful had once happened in a suburb of Amsterdam. Remind me. What was it again?

Back in my hotel, I made a phone call to a contact on De Volkskrant, an Amsterdam newspaper.

'It's interesting you bring this up,' my contact said. 'I'd like to talk with you about it, but I'm on a deadline. Could you ring me back tomorrow?'

After the phone call, I lay down in bed and stared up at the ceiling, trying to put the pieces together. A Surinamese woman was found murdered six years after her apartment had been destroyed by an Israeli plane. She worked as a whore in the Red Light District. Last week she was murdered. Heinke, my friend, was found in her room the night she was killed. And he refuses to say a word.

I leaned over to retrieve my pack of cigarettes from the bedside table where I had emptied the contents of my pockets and lit up. I lay back down, inhaled the delicious nicotine and let the smoke drift upwards, watching the swirls fade softly into the stale hotel air.

What was Heinke researching? I wondered. Why was he so obsessed with the West Indies? What did it have to do with the woman from Suriname?

I sat back up in bed, reached for the phone and tried ringing Marijke. No success. Kiko was good about delivering messages. She always made sure they reached me one way or another - either in person or by slipping a note underneath the door. I had waited for Marijke over half an hour at the Metro stop. So why hadn't she tried to get in touch? She could be a little dingy at times, perhaps a bit impulsive, but she wasn't totally irresponsible.

I felt annoyed and ill at ease. But it wasn't the first time I'd been annoyed with her. Or her dad for that matter.

I took a final puff on my cigarette before stubbing it out. Then glancing at my watch, I realised it was almost time to leave for my appointment with Hugo. But there was still a few minutes for a shower and a shave before dinner, I thought.

Chapter 19

THE WAAG RISES up from Nieuwmarkt square like a baroque castle that somehow lost its way. How it ended up smack dab in the middle of the Red Light District reincarnated as a mixture of internet café and new wave restaurant is one of those curious time-travel adventures which makes history seem like a shaggy, pug-tailed dog with floppy ears and one lame leg.

Dating back to the late 15th century when it was part of the city's fortifications, it became a weigh house after Amsterdam expanded eastward, filling in part of the Kloveniersburgwal canal to form a marketplace. Later, the upper floor was given over to the Surgeon's Guild, the new central tower becoming an anatomical theatre (where Rembrandt painted The Anatomy Lesson of Dr Tulp).

In recent years it served as a fire house and city archives. For a while it housed the Jewish Historical museum, which seemed quite appropriate as the area just east had been the city's main Jewish quarter before the war. And, by the way, Louis Napoleon used it as a site for his public executions.

But on a sunny day, when the air is fresh and the sky is blue and the marketplace is in full flower and the Waag sets out rows and rows of tables, it's the place to be. And historical memory fades to insignificance as you savour some of the best food in

Amsterdam at the most favourable vantage point to relish the Nieuwmarkt scene

However, it wasn't a sunny day. It was a rainy, wind-swept evening when I arrived. Wiping away the moisture which was dripping from my forehead, I spent a moment adjusting to the waxy light that glowed, erratically, from an enormous candelabra (containing a multitude of real candles) suspended from the great ceiling above.

Unbuttoning my macintosh, I glanced around the busy room trying to navigate through the din of alcohol induced conviviality which, unlike England, bathed the place in a wash of bonhomie and good cheer. I spotted Hugo toward the back, engrossed in drink. He saw me the same time I saw him and waved one hairy paw, lifting his half-filled glass with his other and bellowing, 'Sacha, my friend! Over here!'

'Popular place,' I said, after making my way to his table and sitting down.

'Even more because of the rain,' he replied, motioning to the busy waitress who happened to glance our way. 'People will leave when it clears up.' Catching her eye, he pointed to his beer and stuck three fingers up.

'I don't know about you,' I said, 'but I can only drink one at a time.'

'I took the liberty of inviting the American,' he said, gesturing toward an elongated table which ran through the centre of the room and held a row of computer monitors. 'I hope you'll find it in your heart to forgive.'

I followed his line of sight to a tall young man, conservatively dressed in a blue suit and tie, connected to one of the monitors, flailing away at the keyboard in the manner of a kid at an electrical arcade.

The waitress brought the three beers quicker than the electrons which were zapping a few feet away. Hugo held one up and called out, 'Franky boy! Drinky time!'

The young man turned and seeing him full face I realised he wasn't so young at that. It must have been his Wheetabix type energy and crew cut hair that made him seem like a stretched out kid in big man's dress.

Frank pried himself loose from his electronic Siren and ambled over to us, grinning broadly as Hugo made his introduction, holding out his hand with an overly-friendly 'hiya!' and gripping mine in a vice-like hold that threatened to crush every metacarpal bone that upstairs Rembrandt had once sketched.

'Hey, you know they let you connect for free?' he said, poking his thumb back toward the row of flickering screens. 'I was trying to access CNN to see what happened to the Yanks. Christ, nobody here follows baseball, do they?' His face wore a punctuated expression which I took to mean that he found that fact inconceivable.

'Frank works for the American Drugs Enforcement Agency,' Hugo explained. 'I've been giving him a little tour of our Red Light District.'

'Some really nice looking broads out there,' he said, appreciatively. 'And some really ugly ones.' He considered his words for a moment and than asked, rather sincerely I thought, 'Shit, how do they compete in the marketplace?'

'To each his own,' said Hugo.

Frank was still thinking. 'Maybe they charge less. Or maybe if you had a lot to drink, the ugly ones start looking beautiful and hey if you get a discount who cares?' He held up his beer, laughed and then gulped half of it down. Then, suddenly, his face grew serious and looking at me, curiously, he said, 'But who the fuck goes in there? I mean, right in the open. You've got to knock on the door and negotiate in full view...'

'Perhaps that's part of the delight of an open relationship,' I suggested.

'But think of the photo opportunities,' he said. 'Whoa!' He shook his head. 'Imagine if our newspapers got hold of something like that! Really, who the hell goes in there?' he asked, turning to Hugo.

'I suppose people who don't mind getting their picture taken,' Hugo shrugged.

'But who wouldn't mind? What if your employer got hold of it? Or your wife?'

'Would your wife mind, Sacha?' Hugo asked me, taking out a cigarette and lighting up - an act his American friend seemed to find objectionable as he moved his chair closer in my direction.

'I'm not married,' I reminded him.

'You're a journalist,' said Frank. 'Anyway, that's what Hugo told me. So why would you care? You could always say you were doing research!' He winked and gave me a boyish grin.

'So, Franky, you like Amsterdam, then?' asked Hugo, blowing some smoke in his direction.

Taking a scented handkerchief from his jacket pocket, Frank used it to cover his nose and said, 'No, actually I think its a shit-hole...' And then, noticing that the waitress who had come to clear up the empty glasses was glaring at him, he said, 'Sorry, Ma'am, but it's a fact. I mean there are some good things about this city - like it's pretty enough and most people do speak English. But the canals smell like sewers and whoever's in charge here has the morals of a drain pipe. I mean people smoke wherever they want and whatever they want. And they urinate right out in the open. I might be wrong, but I can't believe that's what two thousand years of civilisation is all about. Do you?'

'No,' she said, 'I guess it's more about bombing the people of a poor defenceless nation.' And saying that she moved off to another table.

'What the hell do you think she meant by that?' asked Frank, truly outraged. 'She couldn't have meant Iraq, could she?'

'Maybe she meant Sudan or Afghanistan,' I suggested.

Frank shook his head. 'I don't know what it is with you Europeans. If it wasn't for us, you guys would all be marching in goose step and chanting "Heil, Hitler!"'

'Don't take it personally,' said Hugo, stubbing out his cigarette and lighting up another. 'I, for one, grew up on cowboy movies. I love John Wayne!' And shaping his fingers into a gun, he started firing at various tables - 'Bam! Bam, Bam! Bam!'

'Come on, guys, you've had your fun,' said Frank. Then, looking down at his watch, he said, 'Hugo, I've got to run. See you, tomorrow, huh?'

'Sure as shootin',' said Hugo, in a perfect Texas accent.

Then the American, tall and lanky, looking now like a youngish Jimmy Stewart, stuck out his hand, 'Sacha. Been nice meeting you.'

The memory of his bone-crushing grip was a bit too recent so I winked and gave a little wave instead. And I lit up a cigarette, which, to that sort of American was like garlic is to Vampires, I suspected.

He gave a little shrug as if to say 'who'd want to shake your hand anyhow'. Then, putting on his topcoat which he had draped over his chair, he made for the exit.

Except, as he was making his way out, the waitress rushed over to him and, handing him a little box, smiled and said, 'Memories of your trip to Amsterdam.'

Frank looked at the box, then looked at her, nodded his head, pocketed the little box and walked out.

'What was in the box?' asked Hugo, in Dutch as the happy waitress walked past.

'We have a clogged toilet,' she explained. 'I thought it was better giving it to him than tossing it in the canal.'

Chapter 20

'WHO THE HELL is he again?' I asked Hugo, starting my fourth beer of the night.

'I told you. He works for the American Drug Enforcement Agency,' Hugo replied.

'They couldn't all be like that,' I said.

'Then you should meet his boss,' said Hugo. 'He makes Franky boy look like a Provo. One of our guys tried to take him to a coffee shop just to see what it's really like and the good gentleman nearly had a fit. The fact that these places are safer than most American bars or English pubs made no difference to him. It's simply a moral issue - cannabis is bad, full stop. That's all there is to it. You can't even make the argument that half the world smokes it anyway, that it's less toxic than alcohol, that most people who smoke don't go on to harder stuff and that if you're going to have a policy of tolerance - which most of Europe does because if they didn't they'd have to lock up half their children - then you might as well be open about it and tax it as well. You can't legislate something out of existence that's been around for so many thousands of years.'

'You're a policeman, Hugo' I reminded him.

'Right,' he replied. 'But just because I'm a cop doesn't mean I have to be stupid.' Then, gesturing to the waitress, he asked, rather rhetorically, 'You want another beer?'

'Let's eat,' I suggested.

Over dinner of fresh trout and new potatoes, I told Hugo about my curious experience in Bijlmermeer.

'Most likely after she moved, she didn't change her official address. Which means that wherever she moved to wasn't under her name,' he suggested.

'Isn't there any way we can find out where she really lived?' I asked.

Hugo shrugged and shovelled another forkful of food into his bottomless pit. Then taking a serviette and wiping his lips, he said, 'I'll look into it.'

'Also, see if you can find out anything about Heinke's lawyer.'

'What's his name?' asked Hugo.

'Van Houten. He has an office on Valerius Straat.'

Coffee appeared, as if by magic. 'I thought you needed it,' the waitress said. Before drinking, I gave it a little sniff. It seemed OK.

'What do you think the connection is?' I asked Hugo.

'Between what and what? A herring and a gherkin? A walrus and a frog?'

'Between my friend, Heinke, and the Surinamese lady with no traceable address.'

'He's your friend,' Hugo reminded me.

'Just based on the information you have,' I said.

'Beyond sex?' He dumped three sugars into the tiny demitasse cup and gave it a stir. 'Drugs, I suspect.'

'I suspect not,' I said.

'Why?'

'Heinke wasn't that sort. He might have tried things, but he wasn't a dealer.'

'How do you know?'

'Because it wasn't part of his frame of reference.'

'That, as our American friend might say, is a bunch of crap.'

'Why?'

'Because,' said Hugo, finishing his coffee with a slurp and looking quite satisfied, 'you never know anyone that well.'

'Then why do you say it's drugs?' I asked, feeling a sense of annoyance.

'You asked me to guess and that's what I'm guessing. Most prostitutes are on the horse. How the hell do you think they get through a night of twenty slimy drunks? And then there's the question of Suriname...'

'What do you mean?' I asked.

'Well, if you listen to Frank, you'd think that tiny place was flooding Europe with cocaine. They've come up with some incredible statistics that says something like 70% of all the cocaine in Europe is shipped out from there.'

'They produce it?'

'No. The cocaine itself is from Columbia, Bolivia, Peru. It's trans-shipped from Suriname into some Dutch port. According to Frank, that is...'

'What do you think?'

'That the Americans have a bug up their bottom. According to our people the European borders are just one big sieve. Most of the stuff now is transported from places like Afghanistan through Eastern Europe right into Germany and France. But it suits their purposes to focus in on Amsterdam...'

'Why is that?' I asked.

Hugo gestured to the waitress for her to bring the tab. Then looking back at me, he gave a tired smile. And lifting his eyebrows, he said, 'I think, my friend, it's the threat of a good example.'

Chapter 21

THE RAIN HAD eased off outside and people had begun to emerge from the various cafés and restaurants of Nieuwmarkt where they had taken refuge.

'The murder took place somewhere around here, didn't it?' I said to Hugo.

'Yes. On Gordijnensteeg. It's right around the corner,' he said.

The bright lights of the shops were muted by the damp air, toning down the garish colours that shouted brashly in a manner that cheap thrills tend to advertise themselves. Except this was more an out-front, comic book kind of area. It was, I thought, what Andy Warhol might have done if someone gave him the keys to the city and a brush and told him to design a street full of sex shops. It wasn't the sleaziness of London's King's Cross. Even in the rain the place gloried in itself.

Gordijnensteeg was a little alley off Monnikenstraat. Near the junction of the two streets we passed a small café with little tables and shady looking characters, lean and glassy-eyed, mopping up their greasy food with rancid chips.

'The woman who runs this place is Surinamese,' said Hugo. 'We can talk with her, but she'll tell us nothing.'

'Why not?' I asked.

'It's full of pushers. If she talks to us, she loses her trade.' Then, motioning me forward, he said, 'Come on.'

It was a short little street with only four or five houses and a wide esplanade. A vacant wall had a mural - a surreal sketch of mountains by a lava-like sea. Midway down, between two more substantial houses was a one story shack, brown, with a single red neon light running across the front. The shack had two display windows, the shades of which were drawn.

'That's the place,' said Hugo, pointing to the shack. 'She had the window on the right.'

'And the window on the left?' I asked.

'It was vacant that night,' he said.

The place was tiny. Not much more than twelve feet across. Half of that would make six. And maybe it was ten feet deep giving each section a total space of sixty square feet, front and back. And since the front display where the woman sat was at least four feet deep, that left only thirty-six square feet for the back - just enough, I guessed for a wash basin and a narrow bed.

'The average time is twenty minutes in and out,' said Hugo. 'The price is about fifty or sixty guilders. But the rents are high. So the women need to pull at least five or six tricks just to pay for the room. You can make a lot of money but you have to do a lot of fucking for it.'

Suddenly the whole thing seemed sleazier than Warhol.

'Her shades were shut a lot more than twenty minutes that night. Didn't anyone notice?' I asked.

Hugo shrugged. 'They're not prisoners. They're free to go out.'

'And no one heard a thing? Not even a gunshot?'

'Listen,' said Hugo. 'What do you hear?'

There was a lot of clatter as a bunch of drunken thugs walked past. One was beating on his chest with a beer bottle making himself into a human drum. Another was dragging a lethal-looking stick against the wall. A third was chanting something in a mindless staccato that sounded like a jackhammer digging up the road.

'That night was especially noisy. There was a festival. And fans from several German football teams were in town. Whenever that happens an alert goes out. Any girl who's clever takes her vacation then.'

'It sounds to me,' I said, 'like they're working in fairly hazardous conditions.'

'Most of these girls are very good at taking care of themselves,' Hugo replied. His face reflected the red pulsating lights. 'They've got some protection. They've even got a union. They can refuse a trick. It's not that easy to barge your way in.'

'But nobody knows what happens once the shades are drawn,' I said.

'That's also true in life,' Hugo replied.

'And no one saw anything,' I shook my head. 'That's quite hard to believe.'

'People might have seen something. But getting them to speak - that's another thing again.' He gestured in the direction of a small group of men huddled over by the mural. They were middle aged, foreign by appearance and one or two of them kept nervously looking over their shoulder. 'Turks,' Hugo said. 'Playing a little shell game. I wouldn't be surprised if they were there that night. But you think they'd say anything?'

'Why don't you try asking?' I suggested.

Shrugging his thick shoulders, Hugo started to walk over to the group who were crouching over some money that seemed to be quickly changing hands. As soon as they saw him coming, they began to disperse. But Hugo quickened his step and caught one by the nape of the neck before he had time to escape.

Throwing him roughly against the wall, Hugo began shouting at the man in Dutch. The man cringed. Hugo shouted louder and then punched him in the gut. Then the man started rattling on, as if explaining something very complex. Hugo listened for a while and then threw up his hands, pushed the man again hard against the wall and than turned and walked back toward where I was standing as the Turk ran off.

I had never seen Hugo in action before. If this was a simple questioning of a possible witness, I didn't want to see him at work again.

'No luck,' said Hugo, as he came closer. 'He claims they just came in from Rotterdam. Likely story. Who knows, maybe its true. But you can't trust a word these people say.'

Perhaps he saw the look in my eye. Anyway, he felt obliged to explain. 'If you work on the street, you have to be tough, Sacha. If you interview a man for a newspaper, maybe you get the story wrong. So what? But when lives are at stake, you have to be tough.'

'Whose life is at stake?' I asked him.

Hugo looked at me sternly. 'Mine,' he said. 'You make enemies fast in this line of work. If you show them any fear at all, you're dead!'

Chapter 22

I WALKED BACK to Nieuwmarkt after parting with Hugo. Sitting down on a bench, overlooking the square, I lit up a cigarette and thought.

I'd known Hugo for a number of years. I even once worked on a case with him in London. He always impressed me as boisterous and loud, aggressive perhaps, but ultimately gentle. What happened here on the street presented me with a Hugo I didn't know at all.

And then I thought, maybe Hugo was right. What do I really know about Heinke? What do we really know about anyone?

But there was a difference. Hugo was a cop. Maybe after so many years the job rubbed off on him. Maybe in his mind a certain amount of violence was justified. Maybe it came with the territory. Or, maybe, he truly was frightened and reacted as frightened people often do by lashing out.

Maybe toy town wasn't toy town after all.

I looked out onto the vast open square. I inhaled deeply, tasting the tobacco on my lips. There was a lovely sensual feeling sitting here. I've sat here often, in evening and in daylight, in all type of weather. There's a charm about the place, an essential humanity that I devour - something nurturing and warm bringing with it a sense of life being lived to its fullest.

I remember back to other days. Like sitting outside the Belmondo. A beer in hand. Watching the two elderly women across the way tending their flower stall. The day is frosty and they clap their mittened hands together to keep warm. Then I see the waitress from the Belmondo bring an unsolicited tray of coffee to the flower stall. The coffee comes as a welcome surprise. And they kiss the young woman, thankfully, on the cheek before she scampers back to her many customers.

Now as I sit here at night, overlooking the empty square, I see something different. The sky has finally cleared. The clouds have dispersed. The moon is bright.

I recall a story my mother once told me. For Nieuwmarkt square, it seems, was used during the war as the collection point for Jews who were being summoned for deportation. And now, through the curls of smoke drifting upward from my cigarette, I see them standing there. My grandfather, old and grey, is among them. He looks up, sees me and nods his head.

I sat there for a moment, absorbed in this image. And then, dropping my cigarette and grinding it out underneath the heal of my shoe, I got up and left.

Chapter 23

IT WAS ABOUT eleven at night as I walked up Zeedijk, which wound its way from Nieuwmarkt toward Central Station.

Some years before it would have been almost impossible to have walked down this street at this time of night without having been hassled by a steady barrage of small-time dealers trying to sell you some 'brown' or 'white'.

'It was the Chinese who brought in the opium trade,' Heinke once told me. 'Right after the war. They also brought in the first decent food, so we have a lot to thank them for.'

Did he really say that? For the life of me, I couldn't remember what were his actual words or what was just going through my head. Certainly he knew a lot about the history of the bohemian scene. Of which, for better or worse, dope was an integral part.

He told me, for instance, about 'Big Bet' who had a place on Zeedijk in the 1930's that became one of the first gay and lesbian bars - though she only allowed 'same sex' dancing on the Queen's birthday. She ran it till her death in '67, when she was laid out in state on one of her pool tables.

He also told me the story of 'Zwarte Joop' who started his career by showing porno movies in a dingy back room and ended by controlling a sex and gambling empire, with his own security force of toughs who maintained 'order' when things got rough. In those days, anyone who was black and out on the street after two o'clock, was automatically considered to be a drug dealer and was thrown into the canal.

But on Zeedijk, it was the Chinese who were the power behind the scene. At least according to Heinke. And even in the early 70's you could still see those hard, sleek-suited men from Singapore, golden tooth-pick in mouth, posing in front of Zeedijk doors.

By then they had found some eager runners in the mass of immigrants swarming into the Netherlands from the West Indies, giving the Zeedijk a feel of Caribbean street life. There were so many kids on the make back then it was easy enough to spread the risk by hiring separate people - one to make the sale, one to hold the supply, one to safeguard the money and several whose only job was to stand as lookouts.

And he pointed out the heroin cafés, the small family businesses where the working life of a seller was six months maximum and lookouts warned of potential trouble by pounding a stick on the outside drainpipe.

Heinke knew it all like a dance routine. Who was the seller, the holder, the supplier, the lookout. He took great pleasure in showing me what was what in the mechanics of dealing. It was something like an ornithologist explaining an intricate mating ritual. At least I thought so at the time.

Now the Zeedijk has changed. Certainly it's nothing like what it was. Sure you see some blacks on the hustle, eyeing the passers-by and every so often going up to a potential customer and whispering words that most of them fail to comprehend. But the days of 'Big Bet' and 'Zwarte Joop' and 'Singapore Sam' are pretty well over.

I stopped by a small Chinese restaurant with a brace of roasted ducks hanging by their neck in the window and looked across the street. A massive building site was separated from the road by a chain-link fence about eighty feet in length. How many of the old building were torn down? I wondered. What was replacing them? Not heroin cafés, that was certain.

If this were any other city, this street, so central, so close to the thriving hub, would have been sanitised long ago. Its quaintness would have been preserved in an aspic facade. That Amsterdam took so long to dig out its guts and plaster over its seamier side was quite astonishing.

Yet Heinke always said that as long as the seamy side existed, rents would be relatively cheap and artists would find work space. Try finding work space in central London or Paris, he said. That was why the artists, writers and bohemians always followed the whores, the small-time dealers, the transvestites, the urban down and outs. It was simply a matter of economics with the added advantage that areas like that had characters who were more colourful than someone dressed in a three piece suit and whose ear was attached to a cellular phone. (I did point out to him that most small-time dealers had cellular phones these days and he berated me for not following the essence of his remark.)

Now Zeedijk itself had turned into a construction zone with great yellow diggers parked safely behind a high metal fence (used constructively on the other side as a place to chain bicycles). All that was left for the artists were a few barren walls exposed by the demolition on which someone had painted a herd of long neck giraffe grazing through the remains of their curious forest.

I continued walking up Zeedijk, following the narrow twists and turns, until it emerged into Prins Hendrikkade, the boulevard that ran along the River IJ as it formed into the Oosterdok, across from Central Station.

Chapter 24

STATIONSPLEIN WAS BUSTLING with people queuing up to take the last trams back. I was headed for the No. 2 tram, which was loading on the far platform on the west side of the square, when I heard a shout.

'Hey, Englishman!'

I turned to see my little friend from early that afternoon. Even at this time of evening he seemed brimming with energy and cheer.

'I looked for your woman but I didn't see her,' he said.

Then I remembered - Marijke. What had happened to her? I wondered.

'Are you always here?' I asked him.

'Sometimes I'm always here,' he replied. 'Other time I'm not. Maybe I'll go to Utrecht tomorrow.'

'Why Utrecht?' I asked.

'It's not such a bad place,' he replied. 'I have friends...' He did a little back flip and spread his arms wide open. 'From the circus!' he grinned. 'Do you have a cigarette?'

I took out my pack, held out one for him and took one for myself. Then I reached for my lighter and bent down to light him up.

He inhaled, gratefully, and then, looking pleasantly satisfied, said, 'I don't like it when someone says they will meet you someplace and then they don't show up.' He made a face. 'It leaves me feeling bad inside. Like the emptiness in your stomach before you've had a meal. And then even a meal doesn't satisfy the emptiness.'

I nodded. 'Well, this wasn't a very important meeting.' Though, saying that, it did make me recall that I was annoyed with her.

'Have you tried calling her on the telephone? Maybe she's in trouble.'

'Marijke's never in trouble,' I assured him. 'She causes trouble for other people.'

He winked. 'Women, huh?' He winked again.

'Not exactly. She's a daughter of a friend.'

'Every woman is someone's daughter,' he said.

It occurred to me that I had never really thought of Marijke as a woman before. She might have looked like a woman, but to me she was always a girl.

'There are telephones in the station but it's quieter if you go in there,' he said, pointing to the white wood structure behind us, which I knew to be the tourist information service. 'I have an extra guilder if you need one,' he said, sticking his small, misshapen hand into his trousers and pulling out some change.

Maybe I should call her again, at that, I thought to myself. 'Thanks, but I've got a phone card,' I said, actually quite touched by his generosity.

The Tourist Information building was still open though the information section was closed. I walked inside and then downstairs where I knew there were toilets and a phone.

Taking out my appointment book, I paged through the telephone index and found Marijke's number. I dialled and waited, not really expecting her to be home.

But someone answered on the other end. It was a man.

'Marijke?' I said.

The line went dead.

I dialled again. This time no one answered the ringing phone.

Could I have dialled the wrong number? I wondered. I didn't think so.

I hung up and dialled a third time. Again the phone continued to ring without anyone lifting the receiver on the other end.

Putting the receiver back on the hook, I stood there for a minute, considering what I should do next. I was tired. I wanted to go back to the hotel and get some rest. But there was something strange going on which made me concerned. There was no alternative than to go over to her flat and that thought made me even more annoyed with her.

I glanced over at the entrance to the toilets just a few feet away. The table was empty where the attendant usually sat. It was an open invitation for a free piss, an offer too good to ignore.

I went inside and relieved myself. As I was completing my little task, I heard someone open up the door and come up behind me. I finished, zipped up my trousers and turned to see one of the ugliest looking men I could ever recall - and that is after having been in some pretty dire urinals throughout the world. His face was just one horrible network of scars, which in itself was just pathetic. The ugliness seemed to seep through his skin from the bottom of his smelly boots to the top of his shaven head, on which was tattooed a giant knife with the following words, in English, engraved on its blade: 'WHO YOU LOOKIN' AT MOTHERFUCKER?'

He didn't appear as if he wanted to use the toilet.

'Excuse me,' I said, trying to get past.

Then I noticed. There was a real knife he was holding in his hand. Bigger than the tattoo and sharper as well.

It was one of those nightmarish situations you dream about and then wake up, not wanting to go back to bed.

The knife was the focus of my attention, not the man. It seemed to become larger as I stared at it. I could see little specks of blood adhered to the handle. At least I thought so then.

One hand was clenched around the knife. The other, I noticed was held out, in the supplicating manner of a beggar.

I took out my wallet and extracted a ten guilder note and put it in the hand caked with calluses and dirt. The hand remained outstretched. I looked up into the terrible face and saw from his eyes that it wasn't enough. I took out another ten but that satisfied him less. There was nothing to do but hand the whole thing over to him.

Then, without breaking his stare, he pocketed my wallet, thrust his knife into his belt, buttoned his jacket, turned, and left.

I closed my eyes, took a deep breath and slowly let the putrid air out of my lungs. Then I went to the sink, turned on the tap and splashed cold water over my face. I continued doing that until the cold of the water overcame the hurt in my head.

Outside I saw the short fellow hustling a tourist. When he noticed me he stopped what he was doing, came over and said, quite perceptively, I thought, 'You look like you didn't have a very good conversation with your friend's daughter.'

I told him what had happened and, nodding in an understanding way, he said, 'From your description it sounds like Schlakker...'

'Well there can't be too many crazies going around Amsterdam with a knife tattooed into their skull that's engraved with such a lovely little motto,' I said.

'You were right to give him your wallet,' said my friend. 'Otherwise he would have slit your throat.' And he made a motion with his finger across his neck which ended with his eyes fluttering and his tongue hanging, limply, from his mouth.

'Sounds like a nice guy,' I muttered.

'He's not,' said my friend. 'Did you lose a lot of money? I can lend you ten guilders if you need it.'

He looked so sincere, I had to smile. 'I lost a little money, but, fortunately I keep all my credit cards and ID in a separate holder. Thanks. I'll be all right.'

'Are you going to call the police?' he asked.

'Would it do any good?' I replied.

'No.' He shook his head.

'Well, thanks for your help,' I said. 'I guess I'll be off...'

'Where are you going?' he asked.

'There's a friend I want to check on.'

'The girl?'

I nodded.

'Have a nice time,' he said. And he threw me a lascivious wink.

I began walking away. When I got to the corner of the boulevard, where the trams either turn right or continue on straight, I looked back. He was still standing there, watching me go.

I turned right and walked along Prins Hendrikkade for a few yards and then stopped. I stood there a minute and then turned back toward Stationsplein.

He wasn't where I had left him. He had moved further back past the entrance to the metro stop and was now walking across the tracks toward the east end of the station.

I followed him at a distance, keeping well out of sight. Then I saw the ape, crouching in the shadows by the far side of the station wall. The little man walked up to him. Schlakker - if that really was his name - took out my wallet and began counting out the notes, giving the little man some and keeping the rest for himself.

Having completed the transaction, they walked off into the darkness together. I waited a moment and then went over to where they had been standing and retrieved the empty wallet that knife-man had ditched.

Chapter 25

MARIJKE HAD A room on the fringe of the Red Light District directly above a sex shop. The area was loud and didn't go to sleep until well after two in the morning. But since Marijke kept odd hours and the rent was cheap and the room was spacious, the noise and the strange assortment of people attracted to the area seemed to cancel each other out.

When I arrived the place was still buzzing. Tourists out for a midnight stroll and others drawn by the bright lights like fluttering moths, passed by, glancing into the shop windows as if they were on the High Street back home considering the new range of seasonal fashions. Except here, instead of cardigans and drapes, it was giant, blow-up penises, rubber vaginas and vibrating dildos.

A middle-aged couple, bundled up in their padded jackets, were gazing into the window of the sex shop. He was wearing a worker's cap tilted just slightly, exposing a fringe of white hair and she, a beret pulled over her ears. Both were tightly clutching their purses even though they were securely strapped around their bellies. They peered inside the window hypnotically, without a smile, without a grin. And I would have given more than a penny to have known what strange fantasies were going through their brains. Although, thinking back on it again, maybe not.

The door to the upstairs rooms was around the corner. Fortunately, the outside door which usually was locked, had been left slightly ajar. Fortunately for me. Possibly unfortunately for the people who lived above judging from some of the unsavoury types who came out from underneath their rocks this time of night. As I ascended the stairs, I made a mental note to tell Marijke to take the matter up with her landlord.

There were two doors on the second floor landing and I always forgot which one was hers as there were neither names nor numbers. I put my ear to the first door and hearing nothing I went to the second one and leant up against it. Through that door I could hear the faint strains of a Chopin sonata. Probably not her room, I thought. But at least someone was there. So I knocked.

The door opened. A young man looked at me curiously. From his appearance and what I could see of the room through the opening, I guessed he was a student.

'I'm sorry,' I apologised. 'I thought this was Marijke's door.'

'No,' he said, brushing his sandy hair from his eyes, 'she lives over there.' And he pointed to the door I had skipped.

'But...' he continued, as I started to move off, 'she isn't there.'

I turned back toward him. 'How do you know?' I asked.

Looking at me, suspiciously, he said, 'Who are you?'

I explained who I was and assured him I was a friend of her father's - nothing more. That seemed to satisfy him and he explained.

'I saw her leave. About a half hour ago. There was a commotion in the hall. I opened my door and I saw her with another man. They were arguing about something. She was very mad...' He looked at me, sympathetically, and muttered, 'Women...' And then his face grew very sad.

Shit, I thought to myself, the poor kid was probably in love with her. Marijke had the habit of leaving a trail of fragile, young hearts wherever she went.

'What were they arguing about?' I asked.

'I couldn't tell.'

'You wouldn't have any idea when she might come back?'

'No time soon, I expect,' he said.

'Why do you say that?' I asked.

'Because she was holding a suitcase.' His face looked quite unhappy again.

'And she didn't say anything to you about going away?'

He shook his head. 'I don't think she ever sees me.'

The young man probably meant 'saw me' and misused the tense. But what came out had a bit more resonance.

I thanked him and started to walk away and then I turned around. He was still standing in his doorway.

'The man she left with,' I said. 'What did he look like?'

'Not very pretty,' he said. 'Somewhat older.'

'Anything else?' Maybe it was his lack of English, but for a supposed student he wasn't being very descriptive.

'His head didn't have any hair...'

'He was bald?' I said.

'Yes, his head was very shiny. And he was dressed in black. All black.' He squinted his eyes. 'Like Mephistopheles,' he said.

Chapter 26

SOMETIMES YOU'RE so deep in thought that your body goes on automatic and when you finally realise you're someplace, it isn't where you thought you were. In fact, I had been walking for half an hour, trying to make sense of a certain young woman's life, before I saw that I was standing next to her father's houseboat.

I sat down on the garden bench, where I had sat with Marijke the night before, lit up a smoke and watched the ripples of water in the Princegracht canal reflecting the pale moonlight.

It was strangely comforting sitting there looking at the boat. It was as if this wooden hulk, salvaged from junk, with all its leaks, with all its smells, provided the one note of consistency in a world of maddening artists and their troublesome daughters.

But there was more. It reminded me of youthful promise, of glorious adventure, of romance - of all the things someone my age begins to forget as the first pangs of arthritis begin to set in. And sitting there, I could once more taste the hesitant flavour of excitement on my lips. It tasted sweet as honey fresh from the honeycomb right before the bees had noticed you.

And then I saw him. Sitting there like a masthead chiselled into the prow. Staring out in the direction of the endless sea. His body silhouetted by the moon. He was so focused, so rigid, that it was hard to perceive him as a flesh and blood human.

I flicked my cigarette away and stood up. 'Hello!' I called out.

He turned, like an animal turns when a blaring light confronts them on the highway. He stared at me, hypnotically, with eyes as wild as the sea itself.

'Stay there,' I called to him. 'I'm coming up.'

But as I headed for the wobbly gangway, he suddenly darted toward the rear of the boat.

Holding up my hand, as a gesture of restraint, I shouted, 'Wait, I just want to talk.'

His eyes were set on me as I made my hesitant way up the rickety plank. But as soon as my foot touched the deck, he leapt over the side, like a great, black cat, sailing gracefully into the air, alighting on shore and then, without a sound, loping off into the night.

I watched him go, filled with wonder. Whoever he was, whatever he wanted, the beauty of his motion overcame the frustration of having him, once more, slip away.

Now there I was aboard Heinke's boat. Alone. I had never been there by myself before. I felt strangely drawn to go inside and I worked the cabin door open, as I had watched Marijke do some hours before.

Peering below, I saw one candle was lit and was still burning. I called out, though I was certain no one was home. My voice echoed back through the flickering shadows.

I made my way down the steep ladder and quickly scanned the place for any sign of human presence. Besides the burning candle, there was other evidence that someone had been here since my last visit - most probably the quick black cat. Surrounding the table was a curious display - chicken bones, feathers, bits and pieces of what I guessed were entrails placed in a circle as if some animist ceremony had been performed.

Whatever it was, it had already begun to stink. And I went to the galley where I found some supplies, came back and cleaned it up.

Then, feeling a bit queasy, I searched the cupboard for something to drink. Finding a bottle of Cuban rum, I uncorked the top and gave it a sniff (as you could never tell what Heinke put in his bottles, no matter what the label said).

It seemed all right. I found a glass, rinsed it out and poured myself a very substantial tipple. Going over to the easy chair - the one with the stuffing popping out - I sat down, lit up a cigarette, and slowly transferred the substance from the glass down the hatch that led the amber essence directly to my stomach. It was like lighting a fire in an unseen hearth. It felt cosy and warm. Soon visions of sweet nothing appeared in my head.

'This is very good Cuban rum,' I said to myself. And I wondered if Castro had a snifter full before he put the lights out.

Then everything made sense. Which is to say, nothing made sense but didn't need to. Sitting there in a comfy chair, drinking rum in this curious sanctuary, where magic and art coexisted, I felt at ease, at peace with myself and with the world outside the rotting hull of this leaky boat which, the more I drank, was a boat no longer but a bubble floating in the endless universe.

After a while I became aware that my eyes had focused on the table before me and, slowly, a strange vision began welling up inside my head. I began seeing images of the young black man with wild eyes doing a contorted dance. He was holding on to a squawking chicken. And as he danced, he began to twist the chicken's neck.

Suddenly, the chicken's head was ripped clean off and from its neck gushed a torrent of blood, splattering the cabin walls and covering the pictures, paintings, everything in a sticky, hot, red treacle.

It had taken me so much by surprise, this terrible image, that I sat there stunned for a moment. Then, rubbing my eyes, I got up from the chair.

The room had begun to spin. Feeling quite dizzy, I started to make my way over to the bunk which was about ten feet from where I was sitting.

As I stumbled across the room, I tripped up against something on the floor that was sticking out from underneath Heinke's bed. It was a metal box filled with pictures and memorabilia. I emptied the box and lay the contents out on the mattress. The pictures seemed to come alive. Images from the past. From forgotten times. I got into the bunk and fell asleep with them.

Chapter 27

MY WATCH ALARM went off screeching frantically in my head. The noise was deafening as the watch was still attached to my wrist and I had been sleeping with my hand underneath my ear.

I got up from Heinke's bed still feeling quite disoriented from the night before, went to the loo, rinsed myself off and then came back dying for a cup of coffee but now reluctant to drink anything here that hadn't first been factory shrink-wrapped. Fortunately, Heinke's boat was near one of the best open air markets in Amsterdam and on Saturdays (checking my watch I confirmed that this was, indeed, Saturday) Elisabet was sure to be there.

The Boerenmarkt - the farmer's market which specialised in organic foods - was set up on the square around Noorderkerk at the top of Prinsengracht each Saturday and had the feel of a community festival. Residents of the area came and mingled as much to gossip and chat as to buy the tasty treats and exotic herbal remedies on sale there. Crusty breads still piping hot from the oven, cold pressed oils, fresh cheeses of every description, marinated olives spooned out of vats, and crates upon crates of giant vegetables, dripping with dew and flaked with clumps of certified organic soil.

Along with the produce, in the open spaces between stalls, were roving troubadours - mostly refugees from the former Yugoslavia, the tragedy of their divided land giving an added piquant flavour to their songs. The strange combination of concertina and guitar somehow blended in nicely with the scent of fresh herbs and the shouting of vendors.

It was a celebration of life in the crisp open air. A convivial circus of music and food and frolicking children and tail-wagging dogs. All that was missing was a good cup of java.

But you could have even that.

Surrounding the market was a ring of cafés. And as long as there wasn't a torrent of rain or sheets of hail, you could sit and watch the show, eat a fresh baked croissant and dally over a double espresso.

Which is exactly what I did.

Grabbing an empty table at the first café I found, I drank one dark brew and then another and, suddenly realising that it was, indeed, a sunny day and now feeling flush with twin shots of caffeine rushing through my system, I went off to find Elisabet.

Elisabet worked one of the stalls at the north end of the market where the non-food dealers set up and where you could spend what remained of your shopping money on records and clothes and curious trinkets from places as far away as Tibet on one side of the globe and Peru on the other. She, herself, dealt with the Peruvian side and upward on the map, through Colombia and Central America to the Yucatan Peninsula in Mexico.

I first knew her back in my student days when she was a budding anthropologist and I was still searching for my destiny. We had a glorious summer's romance on a Grecian Isle and then, as our studies forced us down separate paths, we drifted apart like two sparrows flying effortlessly together suddenly finding themselves taken up by different currents of air and then soaring in opposite directions into the clouds.

We'd see each other occasionally when I came back to Amsterdam. She knew Heinke, too, and sometimes we'd meet on the boat. Sometimes we'd even take up where we'd left off those many years before. And, curiously, it always seemed very natural and right. Which is more a testament to her than me as she always found it easier to say 'goodbye' without a modicum of guilt.

Walking through the market to where she usually set up her stall, I began to wonder whether she was there. This was the time of year she usually flew off to South America on one of her extended buying trips. It was still early in the month, but sometimes she went early just to hang out and meet friends.

I was beginning to feel definite pangs of disappointment, when, through the crowd, I saw her stall, unmistakably trademarked by the brilliantly coloured Guatemalan tapestries which hung on a clothesline, making the stall into an exotic tent.

Then I saw her. She was standing near the gap in the fabric which served as a door showing a customer one of the fine copies she had of an ancient Mayan codex and, as I came closer, I could hear her telling him the intricacies of the various glyphs which together constructed an amazing window into another concept of history and time.

I stood there for a minute, watching her. She was wearing a Peruvian skirt and a thick wool jumper. A colourful cap was pulled down over her ears exposing just an inch of light brown hair. Her clothes made her seem a bit bulky, even though, underneath there was a figure kept trim by years of hard, physical labour. But it was her bright, open face that first attracted me to her. And, I thought to myself, even today after all these years, her eyes still glistened.

It took a while before she noticed me. And then a wonderful smile spread over her like a beam of sunlight and, excusing herself, she put down the codex and came over to where I stood.

'Sacha!' she exclaimed. I felt myself enveloped in her woolly embrace. Then, looking up at me, she said, 'When did you come? How long have you been standing here?'

'Just a few seconds,' I assured her. 'I was enjoying watching you. You're still enthusiastic about your work after all these years.'

'It's my life,' she said. 'I love it.' She hugged me again. 'It's so good to see you!' Then, looking back at her stall, she said, 'Give me a minute. I'll just finish with this customer and then get Annika to watch the shop.' She reached into the purse that she wore around her neck, pulled out a key and placed it in my hand which she, then, gently squeezed. 'I'll meet you at the flat in about twenty minutes.'

Chapter 28

ELISABET'S FLAT WAS just a five minute walk from the market, in the centre of the Jordaan, one of my favourite sections of Amsterdam.

The Jordaan is quite a diverse area immediately west of Prinsengracht which started off as garden markets just opposite the original canal belt, and therefore outside the realm of the 17th century planning authorities. Which meant that as the area expanded, if a street or alley decided to follow the erratic twists and turns of a drainage ditch no one was really going to mind. So, of course, for the wealthier citizens ensconced in their comfortable town-houses to the east, it became the perfect place in which to exile the smelly stuff - the tanneries, breweries, refineries and the unkempt people who went with them.

The Jordaan, therefore, was not the place to go if you didn't fancy slop buckets full of excrement being dumped into empty carts, often splattering onto the road just as you were coming. But, back in those days (which weren't so very long ago), the middle classes didn't venture into the Jordaan without good reason. Very early on, the Jordaan community established rigid loyalties that answered any attempts to defy them with a hail of dug-up paving stones.

That was then. After World War II, as new housing estates lured the workers even further west and south, a different community started moving in, doing up the rather seedy houses in a process of gentrification that, at the same time, was happening back home in places like Camden.

Except here it was different. The working classes didn't totally desert the area. They weren't forced, as in England, through economics and cultural isolation to seek refuge in some public housing architect's nightmare vision of what urban monstrosity could best punish semi-skilled labourers for the crime of being skint.

In the Jordaan, a good many workers stay put. And the new moneyed immigrants learnt how to co-exist. So the area came to have that lovely sense of richness and diversity which only happens when some attempt is made to breach the class divisions.

And, strolling through the quiet streets and alleys that led to Elisabet's place, I marvelled at all the small cafés, the artisan studios, the tiny galleries and closet-sized bookshops that had sprung up even since the last time I had been here. It had both a homey feel and a cosmopolitan charm that drew me to it and made me think, yet again, how easy it would be for me to live here.

Elisabet's flat was located on a little alley that ran between Bloemstraat and Westerstraat. It was a simple four storey building painted a pleasant shade of blue with large, lattice work windows looking out onto the cobblestone lane.

Next door was a building that had been taken over by an art collective. There was a small storefront gallery that never seemed to be open and had in its display window a miniature herd of plastic cows.

In fact most of the windows on the street were curtainless with curious displays of various forms of still-life, such as projections of giant shadow clocks and furniture dressed up as wild animals.

Compared with her neighbour's, Elisabet's display was much more mundane. Through the lattice work, on the far wall of her sitting room, you could see two colourful prints of Aztec design. Also, you could see the room was neat and tidy in an artsy sort of way. There was nothing fancy or ostentatious. Just minimal furnishings tastefully displayed. (That was the room on display, of course. The others were a little more messy.)

'Windows,' she once told me when I noted the cultural disparity between London and Amsterdam, 'are meant to be openings to the world. Not only inside looking out, but outside looking in.' And then, gazing at me curiously, she asked, 'don't you want to know how other's live?'

'In England it's considered in bad taste, but that doesn't mean we don't want to know.' Then I reminded her it was the room on display that was seen, the others weren't on show. So people didn't really see the way she lived at all.

'It isn't that we never close the shades,' she said. 'I mean you don't really want to see people's dirty underwear. But it's so much nicer this way. Don't you think so?'

'Takes some getting used to,' I replied, watching a couple stroll past, nod their head and wave at us.

The entrance to the house was surrounded by a wrought iron fence and between the fence and the wall was a whole menagerie of plants in clay pots and wooden barrels.

I carefully made my way past the daintiest of flowers and used the key she had given me to open the door.

Inside there was a wonderful fresh smell, unlike the dankness of Heinke's boat, like someone had been baking bread. I made my way into the kitchen, which looked out onto yet another garden, and noted that my olfactory senses had not steered me wrong as several new loaves stood cooling on the counter.

I took a knife and sliced a thick piece of bread, covering it with a layer of honey I found in a plastic container that was shaped like Winnie-the-Pooh (there are more similarities in modern Dutch and English iconry than differences) and thought back to the time I had first learned the Dutch word for the sweet stuff from bees.

I had gone to a small basement café on the other side of the city. It was one of those intriguing places that you pass several times, promising yourself that one day you'll go in. And finally I had. It was just a simple arrangement of tables. Neither the food - mainly a variety of exotic sandwiches - nor the decor had lured me to the café. Instead, it was the window that was placed at street level so that when you sat at the table underneath you got a very curious view of the world - just an endless array of people's feet walking past. I think it reminded me of a Hitchcock film I had once seen.

Anyway, I glanced through the menu and my eye struck an item that sounded good. It was a sandwich made from a ciabatta roll with feta cheese, basil and something called honing. I understood the words for all the ingredients except honing, so I asked the waitress across the counter and she made a fluttering motion with her hands and finished with a squeezing, pouring one, saying 'You know, honing...' So I ordered it. And it was the most disgusting thing I have ever tasted in my entire life. There is nothing to compare in pure odiousness to feta, basil and honey on ciabatta - all heated up in one slithering mass of soury sweetness.

But this sandwich that I made with Elisabet's fresh bread and the stuff that came out of Winnie-the Pooh was excellent. I ate several slices and, satisfying myself, I realised that what I really wanted was a little lie down as I was still groggy from last night's rum - if that's really what it was.

I made my way to the loft and that wonderful, inviting bed with the down mattress and the fluffy, fresh duvet that made you feel like you were being lulled into some safe and fragrant slumberland. I hadn't closed my eyes when I heard her voice.

'I was hoping I'd find you in here,' she said in a delighted tone. I turned and saw she was undoing her clothes. 'You won't believe this. But just before you came, right before the codex sale, I was having an erotic dream. And guess who played the leading man?'

She crawled under the covers and pressed her body close to me and she whispered in my ear, 'Care for a cuddle?'

The glow from her smile seemed to envelop her entire body. I stroked her cheek. 'You have a beautiful face,' I said.

'I don't think a man has ever said that to me before,' she replied, giving me a kiss.

'No?'

'Not in bed. They might have said I have beautiful tits...' And she laughed.

'That too,' I said.

Chapter 29

'YOU SEEM PREOCCUPIED,' she said, looking over at me with eyes full of concern.

We were sitting in that great bed of hers which took up almost the entirety of the loft, built into the far side of the front room half way up the wall (and above the prying eyes of window watchers). It was a wonderful space. Secluded, cosy, warm. Once we had stayed the entire day taking turns going up and down the ladder only to bring provisions (and seeing to other bodily functions which couldn't be dealt with there).

Remains of olives, cheese and homemade bread were the only clues to an orgiastic feast after a sweet hour of making love. Now we were sitting upright against the bolster, each smoking a cheroot she had brought back from Mexico and drinking some hot, steamy coffee from a small finca in Costa Rica.

I took the opportunity to tell her about Heinke, Marijke and why I had come. She considered my words carefully and then shook her head.

'I saw him only several weeks ago,' she said. 'No one told me. I had no idea...'

'Had you seen him often?' I asked.

'Just occasionally over the years. Mainly when you were in town.' She looked at me and smiled. Then her eyes grew distant. 'But thinking back, you know, he seemed different somehow. I put it down to mood, but it wasn't the same Heinke...'

'What did you talk about?'

'He had come to see me about some research he was doing. About Suriname...' She let out a little laugh. 'That took us full circle.'

'What do you mean?' I asked.

'Well, that's how I met him, you know. At one of those student convocations back in the late 60's - '68, '69, '70. We were always talking about Suriname back then. Don't you remember?'

'That was a little before my time,' I said. 'I came in '71. Then everyone was talking about Vietnam and Indonesia.'

I could see she had transported herself back to those days. I could tell it from her eyes. They looked so distant. Then she came back: 'It was war games, remember? The world was on fire and we all wanted to be soldiers in the fight for what we thought was justice. For Suriname, Vietnam, Indonesia...' She ticked them off on her fingers. 'And how many others? But we knew so little about their history and culture. At least that was true for me and I suspect it was true for most of us.'

'That was a long time ago,' I said. 'What was it Heinke wanted to know and why did he want to know it now?'

She shrugged. 'Maybe he was just trying to catch up with himself. He had a very inquisitive mind and when he wanted to find out about something he was obsessive. It took me years of living in South America before I began to understand, myself.'

'Understand what?' I asked.

She used her finger to stir the remnants of her coffee and then looked down into the dregs. 'The nature of exploitation. What we had really done to that place. I mean, we were the snakes in the garden of Eden.'

'You might be getting a trifle romantic about your Aztecs, Maya and Incas,' I said. 'As I recall they had their brutal side as well.'

'But they respected the land and they respected each other. Yes, they could be cruel. Nature can be cruel. But the Maya in particular had a culture that was both humane and intelligent. And what did we civilised Europeans do when we came into contact with them? We murdered as many of them as we could lay our hands on. We very nearly wiped them out!'

I could see we were getting onto ticklish ground. So I tried to back track. 'What was it exactly that Heinke wanted to know? Not about the Maya, was it?'

She had taken a deep breath in an attempt to calm herself and was slowly letting it out. Then she said, 'I'm not exactly sure. I told him what I knew about the early history of Surniame. How, after the English, French, Spanish and Portuguese had divided up the Americas, the Netherlands were left with some small islands in the Caribbean and a bit of land at the tip of South America next to French Guyana (which the French used as their most horrible prison known as 'Devil's Island'). The place was so rough and inhospitable they called it 'The Wild Coast.' Apart from the shore line and a strip of land that bordered the river, Suriname was impenetrable jungle. No one lived there except a few, isolated Indian tribes who, like the Amazonians, were lost in the dense and sweltering forests.

'But by the 18th century, Europe had looted and pillaged the Americas for so long there was little left of value - except the land, itself. And then they started raping even that by creating the most evil farming enterprise ever known - the terrible plantations. Because Europe was now hooked on this,' she said, raising her coffee cup. Then she lifted the sugar bowl. 'And this.' She pointed back to the coffee. 'Black gold.' And then to the sugar. 'White gold.'

'Surely Heinke knew about that,' I said.

She shrugged. 'Maybe he needed reminding. Maybe we all need reminding of what the plantation system did to us. How it corrupted each and every one of us. How no one was exempt...'

'Why no one?' I asked. To tell the truth, I loved her outrage and her passion. But I got a bit fed up with her sweeping generalities that dumped everything into the same bread basket. Maybe it was my Englishness. Or maybe it came from my years of arguing with sloppy reporters.

'Because it unleashed the most horrible evil every known - the evil of mass slavery. And that, indeed, corrupted everyone...'

'But slavery has a long and ancient history,' I reminded her.

She shook her head. 'Not like that, Sacha. Not on that scale. And it was the sheer enormity of horror that made it so corrupting. Never before had millions and millions of people been torn from their homes, men torn from their wives, children torn from their mothers. They were treated like animals. No, worse. Much worse. They were herded onto ships in a way that farmers would never do to their livestock. Because it was cheaper to throw their bodies off the side than to properly feed them!'

Tears started welling from her eyes. I took her hand and gave it a gentle squeeze. Who else but her, I wondered, could actually weep - cry real tears - for injustices perpetrated centuries ago?

And in a softer, quieter voice she said, 'Sacha, listen to me. How much different was it? Really, how much different was it? When we blame the bureaucrats, the train schedulers, the engineers, the pipefitters - as well we should - for participating in the Holocaust. How much different was it? How can we not blame the financeers, the accountants, the ship builders and all the sailors who worked in that evil trade?'

'It was different,' I said. 'But I see what you're getting at.'

She wiped her eyes. 'I'm sorry,' she said. 'I don't know what got into me. Maybe it's what you said about Heinke. And that poor daughter of his.'

'But I still don't understand,' I said. 'I still don't understand what information he wanted. What was he looking for?'

'To tell the truth, I'm not sure what he wanted myself. It was as if he needed to absorb himself in details about that miserable country. He knew I'd been to Paramaribo - Suriname's city. And I spent a while in the bush. That's all there is. Just Paramaribo and the bush. Not even a decent beach for the tourists, if tourists ever come, that is.'

'So nothing specific. Nothing you can think of at all?'

She squinted her eyes as if that helped her recall her meeting. 'Well, he did want to know about a ship...'

'A slaver?'

'No. A small cargo ship that sailed between Suriname and Amsterdam in the 18th century. I put him in touch with a friend, a young man who works for the university...'

I felt myself cringe. 'Nassy?' I asked.

'Yes. A very sweet young man. Do you know him?'

'I met him briefly.' Then, reluctantly getting out of the toasty warm bed, I said to her, 'Would you do me a favour?'

'Of course,' she replied. 'What is it?'

'I'd like you to come someplace with me,' I said.

Chapter 30

I TOOK HER back to Heinke's boat. 'I haven't been here for ages,' she said as we climbed aboard. And then she stopped and scanned the deck as if looking for something. 'It's so different. But it's so much the same. Nothing has changed, but everything has.'

'We've changed,' I said.

She bent down and felt a piece of mouldering wood. And then looking at me, she said, 'It's rotting, isn't it?'

'It was always rotting,' I reminded her.

She let out a sigh and said, 'It was wonderful for a while. All those endless nights locked in communal fantasy. What a world we had created! So many things explored, so many passions unlocked. Dancing with the unknown. Flirting with taboos. Questioning the unquestionable. Everyone needs a time in their life when they can do that...'

'And then?'

She smiled. Rather sadly, I thought. 'And then I had to leave. For all those things that had been freeing, suddenly became suffocating. I had to leave to find myself...'

'You weren't the only one,' I said. 'Everyone left.'

She nodded. 'Including Marijke. I always wondered about her growing up in such an environment as that...'

'She seemed happy enough,' I said.

'Oh, yes. She was marvellous. The problem is she had to grow up as an adult in a boat full of children!'

Maybe she was right at that, I thought. Perhaps Marijke needed time to be a child, now that she was an adult. But I worried about her, none the less.

I opened the door to the cabin and climbed down into the hold. Elisabet followed.

'It's so empty,' she said, looking around as I lit the candles. 'I've never been here when it was empty before.'

'It's full of spirits. Full of ghosts,' I said. And then I told her about the young black man with wild eyes and the ceremonial offerings at the table.

'Was he Surinamese?' she asked.

'I don't know,' I said. 'Perhaps. How can you tell?'

'You can't, unless you heard the dialect. But chances are he was because the vast majority of blacks in Amsterdam do come from Suriname.'

'And if he was?'

She went over to the table and rubbed her finger across it. 'You cleaned it up,' she said.

'Well, it was pretty rank,' I told her. 'I didn't want to leave it there.'

She thought for a moment. Then she said, 'It reminds me of some of the animist ceremonies I saw in the bush. A hodge podge of different rites and rituals like a multi-cultural stew of magic and witchcraft. Do you know anything about the Surinamese Bush Blacks?' she asked.

I shook my head. 'Should I?'

'Yes. They're a fascinating study, especially for anthropologists. And, really, it has to do with the special history of Suriname. You see, the early plantations were very labour intensive, they needed thousands of slaves to tend the crops. But not many whites wanted to go to Suriname because who would want to willingly go to a place like Devil's Island unless you were desperate. So the ratio of blacks to whites was around three hundred or four hundred to one.'

She sketched out a little map with her finger in the dust that was left on the table. 'The plantations were all along the banks of the river, heading south toward the Amazon. The clearings went back maybe a half kilometre or so and then everything turned into jungle - a jungle so inhospitable that few white men could survive...'

Then she looked at me and smiled. 'But that wasn't true for many of the blacks. It just reminded them of home. So, from the very first, a good number of the new slaves just took off for the jungle...'

'When are we talking about?' I asked.

'From the very beginning,' she replied. From the late 17th century onwards tribes of black Africans were living independently in the jungles of Suriname. But the interesting thing, you see, is that these tribes were made up of Africans from all over Africa because the slavers made a point of splitting up not only families but communities so that individual slaves would be isolated culturally and linguistically...'

'So the slaves who ran away and formed themselves into tribes didn't even speak the same language?'

I could see the Anthropologist in her bursting out in the kind of wide-eyed enthusiasm that young academics might have when everything is fresh and new for them but quickly pales after the years of tedium, reading and writing reams of rhetorical and dreadfully boring pap. Pap or not, somehow it never grew old for her.

'That's the point, you see. They had to create a common dialect from all the various languages of the people who formed these new tribes. And they had to form a common culture. Bits and pieces of this and that. And later, as more and more blacks left the plantations to join them, they incorporated the languages of the plantations - Dutch, English, French, German - and even Ladino!'

'Ladino?'

'Yes. You know that Jewish dialect that's a mixture of Spanish and Hebrew.'

'Fascinating,' I said, mulling the thought over in my head.

'Yes, isn't it? But quite a problem for the settlers who were trying to run the plantations. These tribes - there were twelve or thirteen of them, all unique, all different - waged a constant guerrilla war against the plantations that lasted over two hundred years!'

I looked down at the table where the bones and entrails had been positioned and where Elisabet had drawn her primitive map and said, 'So you think he's a Bush Black?'

'Not necessarily,' she said. 'There are some Surinamese here who can trace their origin back to the bush, but I think we're dealing with a youngster who's on a romantic journey with the past...'

'How so?' I asked, curious as to what she really meant.

She shrugged. 'I don't know. It's just that a few of the leaders of those tribes have become cultural heroes to some of the young blacks from Suriname. They see them as great guerrilla fighters. Heroes in the struggle for liberation. Like some of us used to look at Che Guevara.'

'Except for them the link is more direct,' I said.

Then, looking at me, with her head slightly tilted - rather sweetly, I thought - she asked, 'Is that why you brought me here? To show me the table?'

I glanced up at the COBRA poster on the wall. And then, below it, at the blow-up of the group picture. Elisabet was there in the middle row, wide-eyed and innocent.

'Do you remember when that photo was taken?' I asked

She went over to where it was tacked to the wall and inspected it. 'So many years ago,' she said. 'In the days when I wanted to be an artist.'

Turning back to me, she said, 'It was based on an old group photo of the COBRA artists. We all adopted similar poses. We loved COBRA. It was our link to the past, our spirit of liberation. It came out of the resistance, you know...'

'Yes.' I nodded my head.

'It fed into my love of tribal cultures and societies. They were searching for innocence. They thought they found it there and in the imagery of children. But it's a very simple view, isn't it?'

I studied the poster and then the photo and thought to myself how hard it is to recreate the past. 'It was more understandable in the wake of the war,' I said. 'They came of age in a world of terror and destruction. For them there was no childhood. So, perhaps, it came out in their art...'

'And we were their children,' she said. 'We played at art for a while and then drifted off.'

'All except Heinke,' I reminded her.

'Ah, but he was born into it more than us. He had a pedigree.'

'More like a cross, I suspect.'

'What do you mean?' she asked.

'I don't know. I was thinking about being born into something. It can be a burden.' I shrugged.

'He had no choice,' she said. 'He was what he was.' And then she gave me a horrified look. 'Oh! I'm talking about him as if he were dead!'

And, suddenly, I realised. Maybe I was as well.

Chapter 31

WE HAD LUNCH at a restaurant on Tuindwarsstraat, back in the Jordaan not far from her house. It was a place I'd been to before and was very 'New Amsterdam', very 'Jordaan' - friendly, comfortable, relaxed, no pretence, good food. The walls were tiled white, which could have been a disaster, except they were covered with giant-sized posters and outrageous paintings which made the white tiles more camp than toilet. There was also an enormous clay urn which dominated the entryway with a humorous frieze that turned a ridiculous piece of design into a light-hearted joke. What's more, it was a 'vegetarian' restaurant that served meat - though certified organic (whatever the hell that meant).

We ordered some hot bread, olives, pistou soup and pasta with a sauce made from pastachio nuts. And a carafe of wine.

I poured her a glass and filled mine and then proposed a toast: 'To meeting up again,' I said.

She smiled and clinked my glass.

'And to Heinke...'

'To Heinke,' she repeated, lifting her glass again. 'I hope he's all right.' And then her smile faded. 'He's not a murderer...'

'Most murderers aren't murderers,' I said. 'Not cold blooded murders, anyway. But sometimes people find themselves in extraordinarily horrible situations and do extraordinarily terrible things.'

'Extraordinarily terrible, perhaps,' she said. 'But not taking another person's life. Not Heinke.'

I ate some olives and buttered some bread with a garlicky concoction, ate that, and then said, 'You know that photo on the wall. The group picture...'

She was nibbling on some olives, too. But with less gusto. 'Yes?'

'I was curious about the young woman with the dark complexion. The one at the bottom row, sitting at Heinke's feet.'

I could almost feel her thinking as she tried to transport herself back to that moment, so long ago, when some unseen photographer snapped the shutter of his camera, forever fixing in time an image which now hung on Heinke's wall.

She rubbed the cool rim of her wine glass against her lower lip, as if the sensation would help her remember, and then she said, 'It was strange, you know. She wasn't really part of the group. Just a friend of Heinke's who happened to be there. And she was invited in...'

'Into the picture?'

'Yes. That's the way were, of course. A group. A non-group. We didn't believe in groups but we were one, none the less. An amorphous group without a centre. At least that's what we said. But the centre was Heinke, really. Without him the group didn't exist.'

'Did you know her at all?' I asked.

She shook her head. 'I think I had been away for a while. I just popped in to say hello, so they put me in the picture, too.' And then she laughed. 'We all looked so serious, didn't we? Like we were a real movement...'

'Like you were COBRA II.'

She laughed again. 'Yes. COBRA II. Except COBRA lasted for about two years and we lasted for fifteen minutes!'

'Do you think she was Surinamese - the dark woman in the photo?'

'Yes, she was Surinamese. I'll tell you what I remember. I asked about her once, because she looked very interesting and, really, we didn't have many Surinamese friends. And someone, I can't remember who, told me that she had gone back...'

'Back to Suriname?'

'Yes. I remember being quite surprised because we all knew how difficult things were there and how much people from Suriname wanted to come to Holland.'

'So why do you think she went back?'

'I don't know. Except - don't you remember how it was back then?'

'I wasn't here yet,' I reminded her.

'Yes, of course.' She slid her finger over the moist rim of her glass and it made a strange humming sound. Then, looking into my eyes, she said, 'Some of the bright ones, at the University, they wanted to go back. Revolution was in the air. There was Cuba, Chile, Bolivia. There was Chedi Jagan in British Guyana. In Nicaragua there were the Sandanistas...'

I nodded. 'Did many go back?'

'Not many. A few.'

'What happened?' I asked. 'I don't recall...'

'There was a revolution of sorts. More like a coup. It had a short Spring and then it fell apart. And the country became even more bankrupt than before.'

'And no one heard from her again?'

'Well, I didn't anyway. But you know how it was. You said so yourself. Next year there was Vietnam. And Indonesia...'

'You don't remember her name?'

'Is it important?'

I shrugged. 'She's a Surinamese linked to him. That's all.'

'A very long time ago,' she said, reaching into her purse and pulling out a packet of cheroots.

'I don't have much to go on,' I said.

She offered me one of her cheroots. I shook my head. To tell the truth, I couldn't stand them. I lit up one of my cigarettes instead.

'I really wish I was here to help you - to help him,' she said, glancing down at the table.

'When do you leave?' I asked.

She looked up at me, surprised. 'Sacha! Didn't I say?'

'No, I don't think you did.'

Reaching out and taking my hand, she said, 'I'm leaving tomorrow...'

Chapter 32

I HAD KNOWN she was going - eventually - but I hadn't known she was leaving so soon. Perhaps my disappointment showed on my face. A bit of melancholy seeped through her veneer as well but it was quickly exchanged for an upbeat smile. 'We still have some time,' she said.

I glanced down at my watch. 'Don't you have to pack?'

'It's just a short trip this time. Just a few weeks. All I need is a toothbrush and a few changes of clothes. I keep a small wardrobe there, you know...' She tilted her head, slightly, in a charming way and laughed. 'Don't look so glum!'

'I wouldn't mind spending the rest of the day in bed with you,' I told her, 'but I've got so much to do...'

'Maybe I can help. What have you planned?' she asked.

'Planned?' I raised my eyebrows. 'The word isn't in my vocabulary, I'm afraid.'

'Yes,' she sighed. 'We have been through this before, haven't we?' And then she smiled again. 'Do you have any idea?'

'Well, I had thought of tracing down the Rachel woman - finding out where she actually lived. But now I'm rather keen on getting back in touch with that chap Nassi who Heinke saw. I also want to contact Heinke's lawyer. And now there's Marijke. I really need to find out what's up with her...'

'That's quite a lot,' she said, looking slightly amazed. 'Where do you begin?'

I shrugged. 'I start by making some phone calls. Seeing who's in. It works like a big roulette wheel. An infinite number of possibilities narrow themselves down through the laws of chance. You just have to be flexible enough to take advantage of whatever opportunity presents itself. That's what it's all about I guess.'

'But what are you really working on?' she asked.

'A story,' I said. And then I added, 'I'm also trying to help a friend. The two may be incompatible, however.'

'What do you mean?' she looked at me curiously. 'I'm not sure I understand.'

'I might find out some things I really don't want to know,' I said, getting up. 'In which case I might not be helping him at all.'

The telephone was downstairs, outside the loo. I started the lottery by ringing Van Houten, Heinke's attorney. He wasn't available , but I could have guessed that. And the number Elisabet gave me for Nassi just seemed to ring and ring interminably. Fortunately, Hugo was attached to his mobile.

I hate mobile phones but I must admit they do have their uses. In the best of all worlds, we would have everyone's mobile number but we wouldn't have mobiles ourselves. And they would be outlawed on all forms of transportation, public and private, as well as in restaurants, cafés, pubs, cinemas and all places where more than one person congregates at any time. In fact, the only place where they could be used would be in sound proof kiosks conveniently located outside fast-food outlets and tobacco shops.

'I was able to find another address connected to your friend's dead whore,' said Hugo. I waited while he found his notation and then wrote it down as he spelt it out. 'It's on the Western Isles,' he said. And then, continuing, he said, 'By the way, there's someone I think you should meet...'

'Who's that?' I asked.

'An American reporter. I had a drink with him at the dope conference. He's very interested in the murder case. How about tonight?'

'I'm not sure about tonight,' I said, trying to disguise my annoyance. 'Maybe tomorrow. But thanks for the tip.'

Back at the table Elisabet was lingering over her demitasse and writing some notes to herself on a paper serviette. 'Any luck?' she asked, looking up.

I showed her the address Hugo had given me and she looked surprised. 'That's very close,' she said. 'Just on the other side of Westerdok. It's only a ten minute walk from here.'

'Good,' I said, taking out a credit card from my pocket in order to pay the bill. 'You want to come?'

'Sure. And you can put your card away. The bill's already paid,' she said.

Chapter 33

THE WESTERN ISLES sound quite romantic - like some exotic place with craggy cliffs and wind swept beaches. In fact, this being Amsterdam, the 'islands' are rather more like clumps of silt and heaven knows what else dredged out of the muddy waters. And great flattened mounds of excavated dirt is exactly what they were - in the beginning, some four hundred years before.

The reason for all the dredging back in the 17th century was that Amsterdam had become so extraordinarily wealthy with so many goods coming in from the far reaches of the earth, that it was quickly running out of warehouse space. From the primeval crud, therefore, more and more docklands were built along the River IJ for trading ships to offload their luxurious stuff. Here, too, rich merchants built depots with glorious gablestones, each one unique so that clients could establish their whereabouts in the days before Napoleon, with unpoetic imperial pedantry, came and numbered them.

But even good times peter out. And eventually the Western docklands lay moribund, a consequence - as the cargo routes had shifted - of being in the wrong place at the wrong time. The grand storehouses once stocked with treasures now sinking slowly back into the slimy mud.

We walked up Brouwersgracht - the old brewers canal - and continued north, crossing the busy Haarlemmer highway and then passing under the arched railway viaduct that led into the Western Isles.

The only way you know you're on an island is by reading the name on a map and knowing something of its history. Otherwise it's a peninsula. But crossing under the viaduct you sense you're on an island, none-the-less.

I couldn't imagine what it was like in former years when it was a busy harbour, for now it was a sea of tranquillity. Separated from the sprightly streets of the Jordaan, just a stone's throw away, the mood here was almost suburban. But it was a different sort of suburbia. It was like being in a park in the middle of the city. Surrounding you is hustle and bustle but inside it's peace and calm.

'Of course,' said Elisabet, 'most people are still at work and the children haven't come home from school yet, but it has a wonderful feel, doesn't it?'

From the few people I saw walking the twisty streets, going in and out of doors, carrying laundry or shopping or just out for an afternoon stroll, there was a rich diversity here - blacks, Asians, whites, all the colours of the human rainbow. And peering into windows - though still feeling awkward next to Elisabet who was truly an open and unapologetic voyeur - I could see that the diversity was economic as well.

'This is what public housing should be, could be, can be and, in this instance, is - though, unfortunately, it's far too rare,' she said, taking me down a street called 'Ketelmaker' which ran into a passage called 'Zeilmaker' giving some clue as to who lived there before.

The housing was light and airy. All the apartments had their own balconies which, on one side looked out onto the wide, watery inlet of the River IJ and on the other onto a tree lined esplanade.

'No cars,' I said, appreciatively.

'It makes a difference,' she replied, going over to a bench placed conveniently by the water's edge. She looked across the river to a small, working shipyard. Further down were some artisan studios. 'It seems so natural, that mix of people and work, as long as their housing is adequate. Architecture is so vitally important.'

'You'd never find this in England,' I said, looking around and admiring the pleasant surroundings. 'This space is much too valuable. They'd tear it down and build something for the rich.'

'Don't think it isn't a struggle,' she said. 'It happens here...'

'But this happens here, too,' I said.

'It only remains because of the mix,' she replied. 'If the middle-classes decided they didn't want to share this space with the poor then it would go..'

It all seemed so bloody civilised. 'It really works?' I asked. 'You get so cynical, you know, after so many fallen utopias.'

'This isn't utopia,' she said, looking at me sternly. 'It's real life, with all its problems and dangers. But it's life on a better scale. People can live together in a saner way as long as you don't force them into ghettos. It requires a certain amount of tolerance. The man playing Beethoven on his radio has to learn to tolerate the man playing Marley on his stereo next door. And the woman who's a cleaner has to live with the fact that the woman above her is a teacher and earns twice as much as her. But people are proud to live here. They come because this is what they want...'

As I listened to her, I wondered whether this, in miniature, was what urbanised Europe could become. It was almost as if she could read my thoughts because, in the next breath she added, 'Just up the road is a symbol of our failures. Do you know about the Silo?'

'Of course,' I said. 'But I haven't been there for a few years...'

Heinke had taken me there and when I first saw the place it was hard to believe. Sitting out on the edge of the peninsula was an enormous granary, some ten storeys high. The very size of the place took your breath away such were the gargantuan proportions. Empty for decades, it had been left to rot like a beached whale until some youngsters with a grand idea decided to take it over as the world's biggest squat. And it worked. People congregated in their hundreds: artists, writers, sculptors and ordinary people off the street joined together to transform that titanic structure into a showcase for some of the best self-organising anarchy can offer.

'They were kicked out,' she said.

'When?' I knew a fight was going on, but the last I heard the place had become a flourishing café and night-club run as a co-operative by the residents.

'Some time ago. There were pitched battles in the streets. Very severe. People were surprised at the ferocity. But they couldn't hold out.' She pointed north. 'It's not far. Just a five minute walk. I'd take you over to see except it breaks my heart.' She looked at me sadly. 'Europe's biggest squat is becoming Europe's biggest luxury housing project.'

'So even here corporate interests win when the prize is big enough,' I said.

'There have been victories and there have been losses. But at least there have been victories.' She glanced back at the pleasant surroundings and then looked at me and smiled. 'You know, models are important. People need to see possibilities even if the possibilities don't last. We live in an age when people have stopped believing. And that's very sad. But nothing is permanent. And why should it be? Life is too erratic for permanence. But that's no reason to stop believing that things are possible.'

'And the Silo?' I asked.

She shrugged. 'That the Silo happened at all is amazing. That it lasted as long as it did is even more amazing. People who were part of it had an experience that will remain with them for all their lives. And in that way the Silo exists and will always exist. Even if only in people's thoughts.'

Chapter 34

WE STROLLED THe twisted pathways along the small canals that cut through this hidden sanctuary like the darting of woodland streams through urban countryside. Past willow and oak, peeking though copses of conifer, here a playground and then, further on, a tiny boat yard built into a watery curve and then gardens, tomatoes ripening on vines, a lithographer's studio next to a printing shop and further on a warehouse, and then another housing block, a sculptor's workshop nearby a square with a café and a few small stores and then more gardens with enclosures for chickens and pigs and finally a little alleyway, set back from the street, with a row of elderly dwellings.

'Could I see that address again?' Elisabet asked.

I showed it to her.

'I think this is it,' she said, pointing to a ramshackle building with a missing front door. The outside was pealing strips of rustic brown. Inside was just a hole where the ground floor had once been. A flight of stairs came halfway down, stopping short in mid-air, joined to the doorway by a single plank of wood that led upward at a dizzying angle.

'You might check that address again,' she said, raising her eyebrows as if to say this couldn't really be the place.

'Maybe I copied it down wrong,' I said. 'But I had him repeat it to me twice.'

'Maybe he copied it down wrong,' she suggested.

On the far side of the alleyway an old woman was coming toward us, a cane in one hand, a lead in the other. The lead was attached to a dog, probably as old as her, slightly lame and, from the looks of it, slightly blind as it kept bumping into things as it followed its mistress down the road.

I looked at Elisabet. 'Do you think...' I began. But she knew what I wanted without me having to say it.

Going over to the old woman, she chatted to her in Dutch while kneeling down to pet the dog. They were a few yards away from where I was standing but I could see that Elisabet had easily charmed her into telling whatever it was she knew about the inhabitants of the road.

They spoke for a while. The woman, it seemed, was pleased to have someone to chat with. The dog was pleased to have someone to pet it. Neither was in a hurry to break off the conversation, I thought, as I glanced down at my watch.

Five minutes went by. Finally they said their goodbyes and Elisabet walked back to where I was standing. The old woman came by and nodded. The dog sniffed at my shoe. And they went on their way, down the road, the dog bumping into lamp posts, the old woman trying to steady herself with her cane.

'Very sweet person,' said Elisabet, as she watched them go, the lady and her dog. 'Her name is Hannah.'

'And the dog is called "Spot", I imagine.'

'She didn't say.'

'What were you doing?' I asked. 'Exchanging pancake recipes?'

She gave me a look. 'No. But I had to gain her trust, didn't I? She's lived here all her life, you know. Right here, on this very street!'

'What does she know about the house?' I asked, pointing to the dilapidated structure next to us.

'She said people were living there up until six months ago. Then the builders started work - tearing the place apart. And then they stopped.'

'Why?' I asked.

Elisabet shrugged. 'Maybe the contractors ran out of money. Who knows. She says it's been in this state ever since.'

'You'd think they'd board up the door at least,' I said, peering into the darkness of the building.

'She's phoned the authorities. They're looking into it, they said. But so far no one's come.'

'Did she say who lived here?'

'She said there were several Surinamese in the house.'

'Several?' I surveyed the facade. There must have been three or four flats there at one time.

'There was a mix of people. But everyone left. Except...'

'Except what?'

'Except she thinks that someone still lives here.'

'Well, it's an open invitation to drifters, isn't it?' I said.

'She thinks it's someone who lived here before. A very strange young man,' she said.

'Did she describe him?'

'Dark complexion, unkempt hair, easily frightened.'

I peered into the guts of the building again and then looked back at Elisabet and sighed. 'I suppose I'd better go up,' I said.

She looked at me as if I were crazy. 'Those stairs aren't safe,' she warned. 'And you haven't a torch.'

I took out my lighter and gave it a flick. 'Then this will have to do, I guess.'

Putting the toe of my shoe onto the plank, I tested its stability and then, realising that stability wasn't what it was all about, taking a deep breath I bounded across the plank, landing onto the free-hanging stairway.

It swayed a bit. Not too much, but just enough to get my heart beating. I looked back at Elisabet who was watching me from outside the door and shrugged.

Then, looking up into the darkness and holding the flickering light before me I ventured forward, carefully, running my hand along the side of the wall as there wasn't any rail.

Making my way up the stairs to the landing, a few steps from the top, I bent over, pushing down on the floor with the palm of my hand before putting my full weight onto the creaking wood. It seemed relatively safe so I continued on.

There were two doors on either side of the landing. The closest one was jammed shut. Feeling my way along the wall to the other side of the landing, I suddenly tripped over something, lost my balance for an instant and propelled whatever it was over the side of the open stairwell where it dropped through the darkness, falling with a crash into the construction site below.

I listened to the ugly echo and thought that my body might have made a sound like that if it careened over the edge.

'Sacha! Are you all right?' she shouted.

'I'm fine,' I called back. 'It was just something I stumbled over.'

'You should come down!' she warned. 'It's not safe up there!'

'I'll be down in a minute. There's just something I want to check,' I yelled to her.

I made my way to the second door, turned the knob and pushed. It swung open easily.

Hazy light filtered through some ragged curtains hanging from a single window. I looked around. It was a large room without furnishings. Just a bare wooden floor. But it was still lived in. I could tell that from the mat that was stuck against the corner of the wall with a pillow and a moth eaten blanket.

And something else.

As I walked over to inspect it, I heard some footsteps. I felt a sudden dryness in my throat as I quickly turned to see a flash of light in front of me.

'Sacha?'

'Elisabet?' I felt a sudden sense of relief.

'I thought I better come up to take you down before you hurt yourself,' she said, blowing out her lighter.

'Look at this,' I said, pointing to the mantelpiece.

On the stone ledge above the hearth was a ring of candles. And in the centre, propped up against a make-shift frame, was a photo of a woman.

'It looks like a little shrine,' said Elisabet.

I picked up the photo and inspected it. It was half a photo, actually, as the picture had been torn judging by the jagged line that severed her from whoever had been standing adjacent on her left. That there had been someone standing next to her was clear from the remnants of an arm which had been carelessly left when the photo was cut.

'Do you recognise her?' I asked, handing the picture to Elisabet.

She studied it for a moment. 'No. Should I?' she said, handing it back.

The woman was tan, middle-aged, with a round face and frizzy, unkempt hair. There was something about her eyes. They looked tired, weary. But there was something else. It was as if you could see the trace of a spark that had once been there and was now extinguished.

'Isn't there a resemblance to the young Surinamese woman in Heinke's COBRA II picture?'

She studied the photo again. 'Perhaps. It's really hard to say.'

Then it clicked. I reached into my pocket and pulled out my wallet - the one that almost had gone missing - and retrieved the picture that Marijke had given me. The one of the wild boy she had found in Heinke's boat. It, too, had a jagged edge. On the right.

I put the two halves on the mantelpiece and slowly moved them together. They fit. Perfectly.

'Bingo!' I said, taking the two halves and sticking them in my wallet.

'Wait,' she said. She took my wallet from my hand, extracted the half with the woman and propped it back up against the frame. There was a softness in her voice and a gentle look in her eyes as she said, 'That's where it belongs, Sacha, doesn't it?'

Chapter 35

I SPENT THE evening with Elisabet at her Jordaan flat. She cooked up a Spanish omelette made with tomatoes, garlic, green pepper, chillies, scallions, capers and hearts of artichoke. She fried the lot in a heavy iron pan foaming with butter and laced with a sweet liqueur from Curacao. I made a salad with the veggies she had picked up from the organic market. With a thick slice of her home-made bread and a glass of chilled Chardonnay, it couldn't have been better.

Except neither of us had much of an appetite. For food, that is.

We had a nibble and then spent an hour making love in her wonderful bed. Then we were hungry. But by now the food was cold and warmed over omelette isn't really what you want after the taste of the real thing still lingers on your pallet.

'Do you think we did it the wrong way round?' she asked, feeding me an olive.

'There is no wrong way round,' I assured her.

'I meant the food. Maybe we should have cooked up the meal afterward.'

'Who's to know?' I said. 'I don't think there's a rule book.'

But maybe there is. There's a rule book on so many things. Except in Amsterdam. In Amsterdam they threw the rule book away long ago.

And maybe there was another reason neither of us felt much like stuffing ourselves with food, I thought, as I watched her pack her suitcase.

'What time do you go?' I asked her.

'I'm taking the early flight,' she said. 'Ten o'clock.'

'Ten o'clock?'

She must have picked up a note of disappointment in my voice because she smiled and then, looking at her watch, she said, 'Don't worry. We still have twelve hours left.'

And then she brought out a bottle of Cognac and several brandy glasses, which she had warmed in the kitchen. And we drank until the bottle was empty, talking about old times and Heinke and the boat and the mysteries surrounding it. Of how we came together and parted and came together again and parted once more. And again. And again. And how each time we came back together, it was better than the time before.

And then I made the stupid mistake of saying, 'Why don't you stay?'

'Why don't you come?' she replied. 'I'm sure there's room on the flight.'

'I can't,' I said.

'Why not?'

'It's my work.'

'Ah, ha!' She laughed and pointed her finger at me.

Then she came over behind me, mussed up my hair and whispered in my ear, 'Isn't it better this way, Sacha? We only have fun. We never fight. If we were together all the time, think how much we'd fight!'

'What would we fight about?' I asked.

'Dirty socks. Who knows? I'm sure we'd find something.' She kissed my ear and then slid effortlessly into my lap. Then putting on a phoney pout, she looked into my eyes and said, 'Don't be so glum!'

'I'm not glum,' I said.

'Oh,' she replied. 'Maybe it's me then.'

I thought she was joking. But, suddenly, her expression changed and she turned her head away as she wiped a tear from her eye.

Stroking her hair, I realised that I, too, was feeling a deep sense of melancholy, though her sudden tears surprised me.

She brushed the moisture from her cheek and said, 'I can't help thinking about that house and that photograph. And that unhappy woman. And that strange young man. And...'

Her voice trailed off.

'And what?' I asked.

She closed her eyes as if to better focus on her words. 'And Heinke. How could it be?'

'There's nothing certain. We really don't know what happened yet,' I said.

'And that's why you can't leave,' she said. 'It's not your work.'

'In a strange way it is,' I said.

There was silence for a moment. And then she said, in a quiet voice, 'And that's why I can't stay. My work is also my life. My life is also my work...'

I was about to say that wasn't really what I meant when I noticed her eyes were closed again. She had fallen asleep on my lap.

Chapter 36

IN THE DAWN I accompanied her to the Central Station. I helped carry her luggage up to the platform where we waited for the Schiphol train.

It was one of those glorious Amsterdam mornings when the air is crisp and so very bright it hurts your eyes. We stood side by side gazing out the great glass arch that overlooks the River IJ, with the brilliant light flooding in, setting everything aglow - including her face which seemed to emulate the sun.

The train was coming in. We embraced and I was just about to speak when she put her finger over my lips and said, 'Don't say it, Sacha.' Then she whispered something in my ear.

I held her hand for a moment. There was a beautiful smile on her face as she grabbed her luggage and boarded the train. And then she disappeared.

The train pulled out from the station. I watched it go, slowly getting smaller and smaller until it disappeared as well.

I sat down, lit up a smoke and stared out at the river through the great glass wall. I felt a gnawing ache inside me.

It was different this time, I thought. There had always been something quite extraordinary about our relationship. We hardly ever communicated when we were apart. I'd feel her presence sometimes, but we rarely wrote. And then when we got back together it was as if we had never left.

Once or twice I had expressed my amazement about how easily it worked and she would say, 'Why question something good that happens? Take pleasure in it. Enjoy it. Don't be afraid of it, Sacha.'

Maybe it was my background - the stories of my parents, the stories of the war, of people lost and loyalties betrayed. Or maybe it was England and that strange undercurrent running like a deep, malevolent stream which says life is to be suffered, tolerated perhaps, but never enjoyed. And that pleasure, essentially, is a sin.

But even more, perhaps it was a hidden fear. Why didn't I tell her I was coming? I didn't even know, myself, until just before it happened. And then I was full of anticipation and terrified that she wouldn't be there.

I looked down at the glowing ember of tobacco I held in my hand magnified by the rays of the sun. She was right to say not to question it, I thought. Because once you start questioning fantasy it evaporates into thin air, just like the smoke from my cigarette.

She had offered me her key, saying I could stay in her place while she was gone. I refused. I loved her flat. But I couldn't stay there without her. It would be too confusing, I said. And she understood.

But still the emptiness persisted.

I looked down the track where her train had left. It was empty as well. I felt the cold steel of the rails inside me like the absence of life in barren earth.

And then I saw her. She was standing there, smiling her beautiful smile. And I heard her whisper again in my ear, just before she left, 'Please, find out about Heinke. It's so very important for all of us, Sacha...'

Chapter 37

STATIONSPLEIN WAS GLISTENING in the brilliant sun when I came outside. The bright light combined with the morning rush to give a stroboscopic effect, an eerie, other-worldly feel of staccato movement like an old film in black and white - at least until my eyes adjusted.

I saw the little man over by the entrance to the metro, chatting up a tourist. He didn't see me until it was too late. By then I was already standing next to him.

'Hello, Englishman,' he said, ignoring his latest prey and showing me his nicotine grin.

'Hello, yourself,' I said, pulling out my wallet and displaying it to him. 'Look what I found.'

He touched it with the tip of his stubby finger. 'Very nice. Is it leather?'

'It was leather and paper. Now it's just leather.' I said.

'Was there any identification in it?' he asked, innocently.

'Yes,' I said. 'Mine.'

'You mean you found your own wallet?' he said, pulling at his Van Dyke. 'How interesting.'

'What's even more interesting is how I found it. I came back a few minutes after it was stolen and saw your friend Schlakker over there,' I said, pointing to the end of the station. 'It seems he has a confederate.'

'Most of them do,' the little man agreed.

'Well, he and his confederate - a chap about your size - were splitting up the loot.'

'Now that's very curious,' he said. 'Because I saw Schlakker just after I saw you and convinced him to give you the money back. I said you were a friend and that I didn't like him treating my friends like that.'

'That's very good of you,' I said, holding out my hand.

Reaching into his pocket, he looked up at me and said, 'How much was it again?'

'Seventy-five pounds or thereabouts. Let's call it seventy, OK?'

'Right,' he said. 'Of course, I had to let him keep some for his troubles...'

'His troubles?'

'Of course. He was doing me a favour. He didn't have to return the money. It's the way he earns his living - his profession. You might not like his profession, but it's his profession none the less. He could have robbed someone else - someone who wasn't a friend. Then he would have kept everything. So, he was quite within his rights to keep something, don't you think?'

'Except it's my money,' I said, impatiently.

'No. It was your money. Now it's his money.'

'But he stole it from me,' I reminded him.

The little man shrugged. 'I told you. That's his profession.'

'OK,' I sighed. 'How much did he keep.'

'Fifty percent.'

'Half?'

The little man nodded. 'And I expect you'll want to give me a finder's commission.'

'A finder's commission?'

'Yes. That's usually fifty percent of what's left. So, let's see. You said there was about 70 pounds in your wallet. So Schlakker kept 35. And with the finder's fee deducted, I owe you 17.50. All right?'

I held out my hand again. 'I'll take it in guilders,' I said.

He dug deep into his pocket and then an unhappy expression came over his face. 'You know, I just realised. I only have Portuguese escudos on me. If you wait right here, I'll run into the station and change them for you...'

Grabbing him by his jacket, I said, 'Wait a minute. I think we can settle this without you going to the bank...'

He squirmed. His face took on an ugly look.

'I've got a deal for you,' I continued. 'You keep the money. Shlocker can also keep his share...'

The ugliness melted. He was his jolly self again. 'So what's the deal?' he said.

'I want some information,' I said.

'Possibly,' he nodded. 'But I can't betray my friends.'

'He might not be a friend. Anyway, all I want is a name,' I said. 'He's thirty-something, bald and always dresses in black...'

The little man shrugged. 'People are getting bald younger and younger. Have you noticed? I think it's something to do with their diet. And black - well that colour is very much in style...'

'Cut the crap!' I said, angrily. 'One thing more - he's got a mole or something on his hand. It looks like a long-tailed rat.'

The little man's face suddenly darkened. 'It's not a rat. The man you want to know about is called "The Ferret". And, Englishman, he's very, very dangerous. Next to him, Schlakker is a poodle.'

Chapter 38

I WENT BACK to the hotel and got there just as Kiko was serving the last of her guests their morning meal.

I went upstairs, showered and shaved and then came back down.

Kiko came into the breakfast room carting a steaming bowl. 'I saved some miso soup for you,' she said. 'You look like you need it.'

One of the reasons I liked staying there was that nobody ever questioned my whereabouts. If I was away for a day or two or even three, she knew I'd be back sometime. And there would always be a hot bowl of miso soup waiting for me.

'You have some messages,' she said, dropping two folded bits of paper next to the soup bowl.

One note read: 'There's an emergency. I need to go. Sorry I can't explain. You'll just have to trust me - Marijke.' The other one was from Hugo. It said, simply, 'Call me. When in blazes are you going to get a mobile?'

I looked at her. 'Did you take the calls personally?' I asked.

'The one from the young woman,' Kiko said.

'How did she seem?'

'Like she was in a great hurry. There was a lot of noise. I could hardly hear. She must have been at the station - someplace like that...'

I looked down at the table and tried to make sense of what Marijke was up to.

'I hope nothing is serious,' said Kiko.

I couldn't help smiling at her phrase. 'Everything is serious, Kiko. And nothing is serious. The two facts exist simultaneously in time and space.'

Kiko, being a practising Buddhist, seemed to understand that very well. 'Eat your miso soup,' she said. 'It's good for you.'

Chapter 39

I RANG HUGO. 'That American reporter really wants to meet you,' he said. 'He's on my back...'

I grunted.

'Look, he might have some information you can use. Tit for tat, you know? How about joining us for a drink this afternoon?'

'Where?'

'He wants some history. So I'm taking him to the VOC Café on Prince Hendrikkade. Is 3 PM OK?'

After Hugo, I tried calling Nassy, the academic who had been doing some sort of research for Heinke and who I had met briefly the other day with Marijke at the café by Athenaeum Books.

The number I had for him at the university never connected so I tried the central office and was told to contact the Department of Anthropology. The secretary at Anthropology said Nassy was on sabbatical but I could try the Tropical Museum as it seemed to her that he was doing some work there. I rang the Tropical Museum and after speaking with two people who had no idea in the world who Nassy was, a third suggested that he might be one of the researchers on the Siberian project. I was connected to the director of the Siberian project and finally hit pay dirt.

'Is it important?' he asked.

'Yes,' I said.

'Well, I'll check the library,' he said wearily. 'He's usually there.'

I waited a bit and then, finally, Nassy came on the line. I explained who I was and what I wanted and then he said:

'Do you know how much two sandwiches and drinks cost at De Zwart?'

I had forgotten that we had left him with the bill. 'Whatever it is, I certainly want to make it up to you,' I replied. 'And so does Marijke...'

There was a brief silence. Then he said, 'Is Marijke coming with you?'

I thought an instant, quickly weighing the pros and cons of a bald faced lie, and then said, 'Yes.'

'Oh, well,' he said. 'Maybe I could arrange a short coffee break...'

Chapter 40

THE TROPENMUSEUM WAS in the Southeast, at the far edge of Oosterpark bordering the Singel canal. It was just a short walk from there to the Plantage and the wonderful Hortus Botanicus, one of the great medicinal gardens where the coffee plant was first grown on European soil.

I didn't know the Tropenmuseum, as I had always thought of it as one of those relics from the age when the European powers put their trophies on display under glass so the world could see how virile they were. That is until Heinke had ordered me to go. Then I realised I had it wrong.

Somewhere along the line, the whole idea was turned on its head. Instead of cabinets of curiosities, a group of museum workers - in a grand coup of sorts - had developed exciting exhibits of ethnography. Little villages were constructed - not of black men with bones through their noses, but the way it really was. Huts with pages of glossy European magazines used to paper over the cracks where the rain came in. Little shops selling corn flakes by the cupful, a single comb, a single toothbrush, a tin of peas - because they couldn't afford the stock and these were luxury items anyhow. And exhibits explaining, step by step, how the economics of the former colonies really worked, how commodities like sugar and cotton and coffee and tea still enslaved them.

It could have been dreadfully boring. But it wasn't.

The museum was inside a monumental red brick structure with huge arching windows over which was draped an enormous hanging, in solid blue, with the outline of a Mongolian face looking very stoic - which was just as well, as the weather was bound to change for the worse.

My first thought, after seeing the poster and reading the sign for the featured exhibit, was that it took a fanciful imagination to place Siberia in the tropics. But, as I had learned by now, in Amsterdam, anything is possible.

I went inside and asked for Nassy at the information booth. A quizzical look and a series of phone calls later, I was informed that Nassy was engaged and that he'd meet me in twenty minutes inside the café on the second floor.

Having a bit of time, I decided to look around Siberia. At the entrance was a sign entitled, 'From Siberia to Cyberspace.' Under that was a map with 'Siberia' marked out in black, making it look as if it took up half the world. Below the map was a brief introduction which read:

'In every culture there is a prevailing awareness of the supernatural world, of the existence of a reality other than the one we know. Since ancient times there have been men and women who are able to make contact with this other world. These spiritual specialists are called shamans, a term derived from the Siberian Evankic language.

'In order to communicate with the spirits in the other world, shamans undertake a journey of the soul. This journey is only possible during a trance. The shamanistic journey of the soul to the supernatural world is not common only to the Siberian hunting and nomadic peoples. It also exists in western culture and is found among witches, old and new, among artists, new age hippies and neo-shamans. And ultimately in cyberspace as well.'

The exhibit was surrounded by a canvas enclosure making it seem like it was inside a nomadic tent. I entered via a steel walkway suspended from the floor above and ending at a circular staircase which led down to the displays below.

It was a stroke of brilliance having you enter the exhibit like that. From the steel walkway I had a bird's eye view of this strange vision of Siberia. It was as if you were descending from the heavens into a shamanistic ceremony of magical incantations.

Once inside, I was immersed in the sounds and imagery, the chants and drones, the tactile, sensual, wondrous trip through another reality that bound together the historical ages, peoples, nations in one massive, dope-induced vision of a universe that went far beyond the known, the ordinary, into the realms of the supernatural where the rigid hierarchies of life were deconstructed as effectively as undoing the strands of a DNA molecule.

Chapter 41

THE CAFÉ WAS a large room with great, green leafy plants that looked the type wild animals might graze upon. I saw Nassi at the back sitting in a wicker chair writing something furiously with one hand while holding a dripping cup of coffee in the other.

He looked up as I came over to his table and then, looking beyond me, he said, 'Where's Marijke?'

'She couldn't come,' I replied. 'It was an emergency.'

He seemed both annoyed and disappointed.

'I think she's in trouble,' I said, more as a way of focusing his attention than anything else.

The expression on his face shifted quickly to one of concern. 'What's wrong?' he asked.

I pulled out a pack of cigarettes. 'Is it OK to smoke here?' I asked.

The question seemed to rather set him back. 'I suppose so, yes.'

Lighting up, I inhaled deeply and let the smoke slowly drift out as I considered what to say. 'It has to do with her father,' I said finally. 'At least I think it does.'

'I know she was very upset about what happened,' said Nassy. He shook his head. 'But I still don't understand. What about her?'

'She's disappeared,' I said.

'Disappeared?'

I nodded.

He ran his fingers though his kinky hair as he stared down into his coffee cup. For a moment it looked as if someone had pulled the plug on his existence.

I suddenly felt more sympathetic toward him. He looked so miserable. 'I think she's all right,' I said.

I'm not really that good at offering emotional support to broken-hearted fantasy-struck crypto-adolescents. So I offered him a cigarette instead. Which he, surprisingly, accepted. I lit him up, he took a puff and then coughed his lungs out.

'How long have you known her?' I asked.

He shook his head. 'Not long,' he said, stubbing the cigarette out in his saucer. Then, looking down, he picked it back up, smoothed it out and tried again. This time the narcotic effect of the smoke seemed to calm him and he looked at me, wistfully, and said, 'Sometimes it seems like I've known her forever.'

Christ! I thought to myself. How was someone like this involved in such a brilliantly insightful exhibit like Siberia? And motioning to the room next door, I asked him what his function was.

'They needed someone to do translations,' he explained. 'I know a few esoteric languages like Evanic.'

That solved one puzzle, at least, I thought. And then, curious about several aspects of the exhibit I had seen, I asked what drug it was the Siberian shamans used.

It was, he said, the power of the mushroom. In Europe they called it Fly Agaric, that funny little toadstool with red top and white polka dots. It was found all over the continent and made its way into children's stories and picture books along with talking caterpillars and leprechauns. But in Siberia it was reserved for the shamans in order for them to make contact with the spirits and the gods. It was the divine plant, to be handled with great care and respect, for it allowed them to enter the underworlds.

'It was used in Europe as well?' I asked.

'Mainly in witchcraft and cults,' he said. 'But there's some evidence that early Christians also used this hallucinogen.'

'So from Siberia down through the Mediterranean they were having the same mushroom induced dreams?'

He took his pen and used it to write on his serviette. 'Siberia = Cyberia. It's just a state of mind, isn't it?'

'And so is love,' I said.

Chapter 42

NASSY GLANCED AT his watch and then hurriedly packed up his papers. 'I'm translating some Sumerian texts for the Jewish Museum and I'm due to give a seminar there in an hour.'

'How are you getting there?' I asked.

He looked at me curiously. 'Bicycle. How else?'

'If you don't mind walking,' I said to him, 'I'll accompany you. There's a few things I'd like to talk with you about.'

It's not that he was happy about it. No more than Marijke had been that day I forced her off her mount. But, now that Marijke was gone, I sensed he felt some curious link with me. Something that made both of us uncomfortable as well.

'You were going to tell me about the research you were doing for Heinke that afternoon at De Zwart,' I said, as we walked across Singlegracht toward the zoo.

'I never really understood it,' he said, manoeuvring his bike clumsily over the broken pavement. 'He was interested in a 18th century voyage to Suriname made by some Jewish planters...'

'There were Jewish planters in Suriname?' I asked, with a note of surprise.

'Yes,' he said. 'Quite a few.'

'They worked on plantations?'

'They ran plantations. In fact, a number of these farms were grouped together and were known as the Juden Savannah. They formed a little Israel, a tight little community with their own houses of worship, their own food supplies - all kosher, of course - and their own language.'

'That wasn't common, was it? Jewish plantations?' The idea sounded as strange as a Jewish conquistador.

'It was very unusual to have Jewish plantations worked by slaves. What happened in Suriname had to do with the special circumstances of the Jews in Amsterdam. By the 18th century, they had gained certain rights unknown in the rest of Europe...'

'One of which was to own slaves?'

'Everyone was involved in slavery back then. The Christians, the Moslems, the Jews - it didn't matter what religion you were. However, it took an enormous amount of finance to start and run a large plantation. And you needed backing from the state. Mostly the colonial plums were given to the Christian establishment...'

'So why was Suriname different?' I asked.

'Because it was such a desolate place no one really wanted to go there. But during the commodities boom of the 18th century there was a great deal of money around - at very low rates of interest. So some Jewish merchants decided to try their luck as farmers - as it seemed to them plantation owners led a very grand life. And the next thing you knew, Juden Savannah was born.'

I tried to picture a tropical plantation run under the aegis of Mosaic law - yarmulkes and candles on Friday nights, slaves serving their masters unleavened bread during Passover. Somehow the image didn't seem right.

'So the slaves learned Hebrew?'

'Hebrew, Ladino, Yiddish, Dutch. Whatever the master spoke, so spoke the slave.'

'Elisabet told me about the Bush Blacks - the slaves who ran away into the forests and started new tribes. Were any of them from Juden Savannah?'

'You know Elisabet?' he asked.

'For many years,' I said.

I sensed a change in his demeanour. It was as if the mention of her name suddenly made me more credible. He seemed to relax a bit as he spoke.

'The Jewish plantations had the reputation of being run very poorly,' he said. 'Most European Jews had never owned land let alone run large farming enterprises. Most of their slaves had more experience as planters than they did.'

'Does that mean they treated their slaves any better?'

'Not at all. They probably treated them as least as bad as the Christian owners - if not worse. The new Jewish landowners were less sure of themselves. They had more to prove. But many of them were dreadful managers, it seems, and quite a few of their slaves ran off. In fact, several of the original Bush Black tribes were mainly from Juden Savannah.'

'So they spoke Hebrew?'

'They developed their own form of Creole which was a mix of all the various languages the runaway slaves brought with them and, yes, Hebrew was among them.'

We had reached Meijerplein - the square named after the first Jewish lawyer admitted to the Amsterdam Bar in 1796. Across the road I could see the walls of the old Portuguese Synagogue.

'Do you know that statue?' asked Nassi, pointing to a monument on the square.

'The Dockworker? Of course,' I replied.

It was one of the grandest of the memorials to the European resistance. Not grand in the monumental sense - it was just a simple statue. More in what it symbolised.

It was one of the first places Heinke had taken me on our walks. And he had proudly told me the story of that one moment in February, 1941, which stood out above all others. Nothing like it happened anywhere else - even in France. The strike of the Dockworkers in protest against the Jewish deportations. The only one of its kind in occupied Europe. Broken after two days by mass arrests and executions.

I looked back at Nassy and asked, 'The slaves on the Jewish plantations - did they become Jewish?'

'That's an interesting question,' Nassy replied. 'The Jews made no attempt to convert anyone outside their religion. But by nature of the community - the number of white Jewish women was tiny - there were generations of mixed-race children sired by Jewish slave owners. Some of these children were adopted into the Jewish community. Others were ostracised. In fact there was an interesting article I was recently translating about a group of mulattos - ancestors of former slaves from Juden Savannah - who tried to start their own synagogue.'

'So there were a group of Black Jews in Suriname,' I said.

'Some. In fact, it's a very intriguing story. I tried to get the Jewish Historical Museum to do an exhibition about it, but they turned me down.'

'Why?'

He shrugged. 'I don't think they like the idea of promoting Jews as slave owners. But that's the point, isn't it? Jews - as people - are no different than anyone else.' He nodded over at the memorial. 'It's only Hitler who made them special.'

Chapter 43

I LEFT NASSY in front of the Jewish Museum feeling better about the young man than I had before.

'I want to know about Marijke,' he said, as I went. 'If she's in trouble, I'd like to help.'

I assured him that I'd keep in touch and then I walked on, through Waterlooplein and then north toward the docks.

The VOC Café was on Prins Hendrikade, overlooking Oosterdok. Hugo had wanted me to meet him there because, he said, his American reporter friend wanted a bit of local ambience. So he chose the VOC as it was old and quaint. And it overlooked the water. And it seemingly reeked of history. And it had 'VOC' - the acronym for the Dutch East India Company - in its name. Americans loved to come here because Henry Hudson launched his epic voyage thereabouts, making it, I suppose, a Mecca of sorts for them.

I wasn't delighted to come. But I needed to make contact with Hugo though I guessed he had something up his sleeve and was offering me as bait for God knows what.

It was meeting his American reporter that didn't appeal to me much. I had worked in New York for several years and came away without a great deal of love. Not that I was dreadfully chummy with the industry back home. But, at least, we didn't have an army of bloody fact checkers looking over each comma and dot.

The American notion that 'facts' are modules of truth like tiny, uncorrupted building blocks of the universe and that a reporter's job was to collect and string these little bits of matter together in short, 'objective' bursts which gave the world meaning and knowledge, seemed to me not what journalism was about. Needless to say, I fit in as well as an Indian hunting buffalo on 5th Avenue in Manhattan.

I went inside. The bar was packed but I saw Hugo at once. He was sitting by the window, laughing in thunderous peals with his American chum joining in at the chorus.

'Sacha!' Hugo called out, standing up and nearly toppling his chair and also the table, as he had been squeezed in so tightly that his bulk had nowhere to go. 'Sacha, I'd like you to meet a new friend...'

His face was already red and swollen with beer as he looked at the smiling middle-aged man across from him dressed in a rumpled suit of green corduroy. 'Sorry. What is your name again?'

The man in rumpled cords got up to shake my hand. 'Radkin. Joseph Radkin,' he said.

Recalling my last North American handshake, I grunted something and sat down.

Hugo remained standing. 'A beer, Sacha? And Radkin, a refill for you?'

I nodded. Radkin shrugged. And Hugo tried manoeuvring himself toward the bar.

'Is he always like that?' asked Radkin, seemingly bemused.

'He does tend to be a bit boisterous when he drinks.'

'Even when he doesn't,' replied Radkin. And then he chuckled. 'I sort of get the feeling he set this meeting up without your whole-hearted consent.'

The thing about Americans is they can be so bloody direct! On the other hand, they can cut through a lot of ice with a knife made for butter. I don't know what I replied. Nothing, I suspect.

Then he said, 'Look, I don't want to horn in on your territory, but Hugo was telling me about your murder investigation and I thought there were some things you should know...'

'Like how to hold my pen? Or, perhaps, what word processing program to use on my computer?'

He cringed and said, 'Can I ask you something?'

I looked over at the bar to see if I could signal Hugo for help. He was knee-deep in conversation with a young woman. I turned back. 'Maybe,' I said. 'It depends.'

'Why are you guys so fucking arrogant? I mean what the hell did they put in your Ribena when you went to school?'

'Ah,' I said. 'So you know about Ribena.'

'Yeah. And that shit-ass Marmite crap you spread on pieces of stale cardboard or oat cakes or whatever you call that stuff.'

'So you like England, do you? Ever been there or do you just watch Masterpiece Theatre on telly?'

'I worked there for a while. Nice place. Everyone wants to be a duke or an earl. I'll be back after you have a social revolution, guillotine the Queen and get some better weather.'

'The weather thing is possible, I understand, as long as you Yanks keep spraying your hair with aerosol deodorants.'

He felt for his bald spot. 'What hair?' he said.

I rolled my eyes and reached for a cigarette, lit up and blew some smoke in his direction, hoping it might have the same effect it did on his countryman.

Instead, he licked his lips. 'What kind of smokes are they?' he asked.

'Camels,' I said. 'But they give you cancer.'

'Camel Lights?'

I nodded.

'Could I have one?'

Letting out a little sigh, I tossed him the pack. He lit up and took a long and grateful drag. Then he closed his eyes, as if in ecstasy, and let the smoke drift slowly from his mouth. 'I love Amsterdam,' he said, opening his eyes again.

'You mean you can't buy cigarettes in America?'

'You can buy them. You just can't smoke them. Except in a closet or on top of very tall towers stuck away in the desert.'

'I think you're the one who needs a social revolution,' I said.

He shrugged. 'Maybe we do.'

I looked at him and said. 'You know, I never feel so English as when I'm talking with an American.'

'And I never feel so American except when I'm talking to an Englishman. Hi, I'm Radkin. Joseph Radkin,' he said, grinning and sticking out his hand.

What could I do but shake it then?

Chapter 44

HUGO HAD COME back with the beers but then excused himself again as his conversation with the young woman was still in Phase One, he said.

I took a thirsty drink and then wiping the foam from my lips and feeling a bit more sociable, I looked over at Radkin and said, 'So what are you doing here? Going on a tour of the Red Light District?'

'I guess all assignments nowadays do boil down to either sex or drugs,' he said. He drank some beer and then he added, 'Mine is more on the druggy end. But the boring druggy end. I'm covering the nark convention.'

'Sounds amusing,' I said.

'It could be but it isn't.'

'No fireworks?'

He shook his head. 'There's a real division here between the hawks and the doves - with America on one end and Holland on the other. Everyone else falls somewhere in the middle. Besides the head of the US Drug Agency making a total ass of himself - which is always fun to see - most everything else is a tired rehash of what everyone has heard before. Unless you're prepared to go behind the scenes...'

I lit up another smoke and said, 'Which you are, I suppose.'

He looked at me hungrily and I tossed him the pack.

'Thanks,' he said, putting a flame to a cigarette, and, like before, closing his eyes in ecstasy.

'Have you been off the habit for long?' I asked.

'A few months. Back home it's like being a born again Christian.' He took another drag and then letting out the smoke, he said, 'But it's so nice to sin!'

I decided to put it down to the curiosities of an Empire in decline. 'So what did you want to tell me?' I asked.

'Hugo was mentioning the story you were working on. Well - Surinamese prostitute killed by bohemian artist - the first thing someone thinks about is drugs, right?'

I shrugged.

'I figured it might make a nice little sidebar to perk up an article on a boring convention. Now this guy from the American Drug Enforcement Agency is giving a seminar where he's showing off a new computer system that he claims details all the major drug connections, world-wide - both real and suspected - and, anyway, to make a short story even shorter, just out of the blue I ask him to plug in the names of your prostitute and artist...'

I stared at him, quite flabbergasted. 'You did?'

He nodded. 'And guess what came up?'

At that very moment, Hugo came back with a refill of drinks. 'Have you got to the good part yet?' he asked Radkin.

'Almost,' Radkin replied and then, looking over at the bar, he said, 'What happened to your chickadee?'

'A little young, I think, to have left the nest,' he said, squeezing himself back into the tight space and sloshing even more beer onto the table.

I looked at Radkin. 'You were telling me about the computer,' I said somewhat impatiently.

His face took on a more serious expression. 'It turns out that the murdered Surinamese woman was a major link in the cocaine trade...'

'Then what was she doing working as a prostitute?' I asked.

'That's what the computer claimed,' Radkin said. 'But I was somewhat suspicious about it, too. There's a difference between what the Drug Enforcement Agency projects as the supply chain and what may really be the case. It's often a question of what information they want to offer and why they want to offer it. Right, Hugo?'

Hugo raised his hairy eyebrows. 'Now you don't really want me to speak against your Drugs Agency, do you, my friend? After all, I'm a cop and half my salary probably comes from them - indirectly, of course.'

'How so?' I asked.

'Through grants in aid. International drug enforcement programs where moneys trickle down to national bureaucracies. Things like that. You'd be surprised how it multiplies.'

'Keep the trough full and the pigs shut up,' said Radkin. Then glancing at the pulsating vessel on Hugo's bulbous nose, he added, 'That's what we say in America, anyhow.'

'Do you have any details?' I asked.

'Not yet,' said Radkin. 'I'll see what I can find out. But there's something else...'

'There's always something else,' said Hugo, finishing up another beer.

'While the guy from the Drug Enforcement Agency was feeding us this info from the computer, one of his colleagues comes in, sees what's up and has a fit!'

Hugo looked at me and winked. 'Our friend Frankie-boy,' he said.

'Why was he so upset?' I asked.

'He claimed the program was being misued. It was confidential material. But I don't think that's what it was about.'

'What then?' I asked.

'I think it was the names that freaked him out.'

I looked over at Hugo. Hugo shrugged.

'I'll tell you another thing. There's a buzz I'm starting to pick up on this story. And it's coming from someplace other than the drug enforcement scene,' said Radkin.

'What do you mean?' I asked.

'I can't really put my finger on it. But, you know, it's when a story starts to emerge and you wonder why it's that one and not something else, out of the millions of stories that happen in the world. And then you start to realise that somewhere, there's a power behind it, a hidden force, that's using this story for very a particular purpose...'

Chapter 45

BEFORE HUGO LEFT, I asked him to find out about an Amsterdam tough who traded under the name of 'The Ferret'. 'Definitely a user, probably a dealer,' I said.

'I'll see what I can do,' said Hugo. 'By the way, I checked on your friend's attorney - Van Houten. He's OK.'

'Where you off to?' asked Radkin, after Hugo had left.

Actually, I didn't know where I was off to. It was as if I had reached a dead end.

'I was hoping Hugo would be able to get some better information on the Rachel woman,' I mumbled, as much to myself as to him.

'The prostitute?' he asked.

I nodded.

'If you want to know about a prostitute, don't ask a cop.'

'Who do you ask?'

'Another prostitute,' he said.

It's not that he made it his business to look up prostitutes in every city he visited, Radkin told me as we walked down Warmoesstraat toward the Oude Kerk. It's just that he had been interviewing one of the organisers of Coyote - the Hooker's Union - back in San Francisco and was told about their sister group here.

'They run courses, you know.'

I looked at him strangely. 'For the women or the men?'

'For the women. Beginners and Intermediate. I'm not sure you get college credit, though.'

The Oude Kerk lies in the heart of the Red Light District. It's a rather peaceful spot surrounded by dingy buildings with signs in the windows reading *Kamer te Huur* - Room by the Hour. One of the oldest surviving buildings in the city, it faded into the surrounding shabbiness after being sacked and looted during the Reformation.

Heinke had taken me here once to visit a tomb. It was on the north side of the church and had only a number to distinguish it until recently, he said, when someone had carved the notation, 'Saskia, 19 Juni 1642.'

Then he had shown me a sketch that Rembrandt had done of her, wearing a floppy straw hat and a winsome smile. Underneath Rembrandt had written, 'This is drawn after my wife, when she was 21 years old, on the third day of our betrothal.' She died, Heinke told me, soon after the birth of their son.

I remember there was something about the sketch that I found exceptionally moving. And afterward, it left me feeling strangely bothered, as if some sort of ghostly presence had been evoked. It wasn't until later that I realised there was an unmistakable resemblance between the young Saskia and Pauline, Heinke's wife who died soon after their own marriage.

'Did you ever read Kundera's *The Unbearable Lightness of Being*?' Radkin asked me as we walked through the streets that led up to the church. 'He described the Amsterdam prostitutes sitting in their pillowed armchairs wearing bras and panties and looking like big bored cats. I don't think they look like big bored cats, do you? Some look like caged tigresses. Others like spayed kittens.'

'Not like San Francisco, I suppose,' I said.

'Oh, on the contrary,' he replied. 'Amsterdam is very much like San Francisco. A flat San Francisco - topographically, that is. I feel very much at home.' And then he asked, 'Have you ever been?'

'San Francisco?' I shook my head. 'New York was the limit of my American adventure.'

'San Francisco is about 3,500 miles west - physically and mentally.'

'It's the same country, isn't it?' I said.

'Well, if Europe ever completes its union, I'll be saying the same thing about London and Madrid.'

'Then I'm not sure you understand what the EEC is all about.'

He shrugged.

I wondered whether he might not have been right at that. Then I said, 'I guess San Francisco has its share of pot-heads. Like Amsterdam.'

'We have a sensible attitude, if that's what you mean. Except the State and Federal agencies try their damnest to stop us. We used to have Cannabis clubs where people with medical certificates could get their supply of marijuana for medicinal uses. The State closed them down for moral reasons, they said. You know, here in Amsterdam there are 350 coffee shops that legally sell hash? Anybody over eighteen years of age can walk in a buy an ounce or two of grass - no questions asked.'

'And most of our six formers do,' I said. 'Which is one of the reasons that Amsterdam frightens the hell out of European mothers.'

'Well most mothers I know were smoking pot themselves eighteen years ago.'

'You certainly do live in another America.' I muttered.

He pursed his lips and looked over at me. 'You should have been there in '68,' he said.

Chapter 46

THE PROSTITUTE INFORMATION Bureau was situated on a quiet cobblestone alley just behind the Oulde Kirk. It sat there rather sedately, I thought, almost prim with lace curtains instead of garish red lights. The only clue to what lay within its staid exterior was a book displayed in the storefront window, the title of which read, innocently enough, *How to Make Your Husband Happy: The Fine Art of Eroticism.*

'They're actually pretty nice folk,' said Radkin, as I hesitated in the doorway. Then he opened the door and walked in. I followed behind him.

Inside were display tables with books and pamphlets. Colourful bowls of condoms were placed discretely around like trays of sweeties. In the background, on wooden shelves, like an exhibit of primitive cultural artefacts were sexual aides of various size and description.

A large, pleasant-looking woman with a mane of red hair cascading down from her head to her thigh, was standing behind a counter talking with a well-dressed, Englishwoman who was busily taking notes. The words seemed to flow like her hair, passionate and lustrous, as she waxed euphoric on the psycho-sexual pleasures of the tantric communion - or something of the sort.

The Englishwoman, who was clinging to her every syllable, finally put the notebook away. Then, thanking her profusely, she left.

I watched the Englishwoman go. Turning back, I saw the woman behind the counter smiling at us - me, actually, as Radkin was thumbing through some erotic books. Her smile was so wide it formed a dimple that ran sweetly from cheek to chin. She looked at me and said, 'Another academic. The third one this month.' And then she laughed, as if sharing a joke just between the two of us. 'I've offered them on-the-job training so they could actually write something that makes sense. But...' She shrugged her shoulders and heaved her voluptuous beasts.

I was smiling, too, though a bit nervously, and scratching behind my ear, when Radkin came up and said, 'Academics call that the tyranny of experience. If they can't put it under a glass and poke it with a pin, it doesn't have any meaning for them.'

Then he stuck out his hand. 'Hi, I'm Radkin. Joseph Radkin...' He introduced me as his 'London chum', and rattled forth about his friend at Coyote and how she had said for him to call in.

Her name, the red maned lioness, was 'Tanya'. And hearing Radkin's introduction, it all seemed to make sense. To her, at least.

She took out a pen and wrote on a slip of paper. 'The Rocket Club', she said, was the place to go. 'Give this to Charlie and she'll see you have a good time, boys.'

'Right,' I said, 'except, you see, we're journalists...'

'And for that you'll get a very nice discount,' she replied.

'I'm afraid we're not much different than the academic,' I tried explaining.

'Speak for yourself!' Radkin glared at me and then looking back at her he said, 'It was more of a chat we wanted to have.'

'That's not a problem,' she nodded, understandingly. 'Everyone has their own sort of trip. Some like to touch. Other don't. We wouldn't question your fantasy or how you need to achieve it. As long as it doesn't hurt,' she said.

'Sometimes it does hurt, I expect.' I motioned outside. 'There's a rough crowd at times...'

She looked at me curiously, as if trying to make sense of what I was getting at. 'That's why we have our organisation,' she said. 'So we can protect ourselves.'

'But people do get hurt,' I said.

'People get hurt in any profession. Even doctors, lawyers and teachers.'

'But yours is a bit more dangerous,' I insisted, pleasantly.

'We don't cut anyone open and leave our scalpel inside, take half their wages for shuffling a bit of paper or fuck up their heads with half baked ideas, if that's what you mean,' she said.

'I meant the opposite. What they could do to you,' I replied.

'Well, in that case I could show you statistics comparing how many women get shit beat out of them in the privacy of their own homes with what happens in the Red Light District.'

'At least a woman has her choice of husbands,' I said.

'I'm not so sure of that,' she replied. 'And anyway, one of the demands of our organisation is that prostitutes have the right of refusal. Here they're free agents. They don't have to offer their services to anyone.'

'Except once they're in, they're in,' said Radkin. 'A thug doesn't say he's a thug.'

'I'm not telling you there aren't dangers. But there are dangers with many jobs. And there are also laws. In Amsterdam, you can't beat a woman up just because she's a prostitute. Maybe in other cities you can.'

'But things do happen,' I said. 'It's a rough trade.'

'So is coal mining. It's dirty, tiring and you end up poor and coughing your lungs out.'

'But not with AIDS,' said Radkin.

'I'll bet more miners have AIDS than prostitutes - at least in Amsterdam. We don't allow unprotected sex. We're professionals. As I told you before, we know how to handle ourselves.'

'Except sometimes not,' I said. 'Like with Rachel Desonsa...'

Suddenly her expression changed. She stared at me with cold, hard eyes. 'Who the hell are you?' she said.

Chapter 47

THE ATMOSPHERE GOT about ten degrees colder after the mention of Rachel Desonsa's name. The red-maned shopkeeper, Tanya, had lost her smile and her dimple disappeared from her face.

'Murder can happen anywhere,' she had said, 'but when it happens in the Red Light District all kinds of buzzers go off even though it's probably one of the safest areas of the city.'

'It's as if she had something to protect,' I mentioned to Radkin, later, as we sat outside the Hoppe overlooking Spui Square.

'Did you ever see Jaws?' he asked, wiping the brine from his upper lip after taking a swig from his beer.

'Sorry, I missed that one,' I said. 'But I know the story. What's the point?'

'The point is that economics often comes into conflict with purpose. If a shark attacks your beach and your beach provides your income you don't go around pushing the gory details of people eaten in the water.'

'But you do try to get rid of the shark,' I said.

'Not by talking with journalists,' he replied.

'It was your idea,' I reminded him.

'I wasn't the one who brought up the dead whore's name,' said Radkin, giving me a look which rather hurt my professional pride.

'Well, why the bloody hell did we go see her?' I asked.

He shrugged and took another swig of his beer.

I resisted the urge to call him a smug piece of bird droppings and just stared at him.

'Look,' he said, finally, 'you do something and see what results. And after that you analyse it. You don't moan about it.' Then he said, 'You know, the difference between us-uns and you-uns, is that us-uns make things happen and you-uns wait for things to happen. And wait. And wait. And wait.'

'I always thought patience was a virtue,' I said, trying to let the sarcastic tone ooze like sticky treacle.

'Everything in life has a deadline,' he said.

I took a swig of beer myself and muttered, 'I knew there was a reason I left New York.'

'And you know why I left London? Because everything turns to Jello there. No matter what you push, it always snaps right back in your face. Unless your name is Sir Piss Potter.'

I rubbed the side of my cheek as his last words made it tingle.

Then he looked at me and said, 'Hey, I'm sorry. I don't know why I came down on you like that...'

It was hard to make this character out, I thought. He seemed like a boxer who's always shifting back and forth, wrong-footing you the times you least expect it.

'There's some trouble at home...'

I cringed. The last thing in the world I wanted to hear was his life story.

'But I won't burden you with that. Actually, what I wanted you to know is there's a lot of us back in the States rooting for you...'

'For me?' I looked at him curiously.

'Not you personally,' he corrected. 'Europe. You know, The Community. It's not a bad thing to balance us out.'

'Aren't you American?' I asked.

'Yeah. And in the late 19th century I could have asked "Aren't you English?" as Britain was merrily running rampant through half the globe eating up most of the resources and imposing its sick Victorian values on innocent folk - like us!'

'In the late 19th century my seeds were either in Germany or France.'

'And mine were either in Russia or Poland. So what? Place doesn't matter but national mentalities do. I'm American because I was born and educated in the States. There's a lot I like about the country. Its diversity, its marvellous mix of cultures. Its insistence that anything is possible. But I don't like what it's become.'

'What's that?'

'Somehow we've equated freedom with monetary wealth instead of social justice. And that's a path you don't easily come back from, pal.'

'I guess you're anxious to get home then,' I said.

'Well, in a way I am,' he replied. 'I love San Francisco. There's no place in the world I'd rather be!'

'When do you leave?'

The question seemed to startle him. 'I'm glad you asked me that,' he said, reaching into his jacket pocket and pulling out a ticket. He inspected it, looked at his watch and said, 'Jesus Christ, I better go! My flight's in about two hours!'

Then he took out his wallet.

'That's all right,' I said. 'The drink's on me.'

'Oh, I wasn't' going to pay,' he replied. 'I just wanted to give you something.' He pulled out a card. 'My details - in case you want to contact me.' He held it out.

'Why?' I asked, letting his hand hang lonely in the air.

'Look,' he said, 'don't be a jerk. I happen to think you're working on an interesting story. And I wasn't kidding back there when I said something fishy was up.' He put a finger on his nose and gave it a tap. 'This shnozz of mine is rarely wrong.' Then poking the card in my direction, he said, 'Take it!'

I took it more to avoid a scene than anything else.

'Give me a ring in a couple of days,' he said, getting up. 'I'll let you know whether anything's hit the wires back in the good old US.'

Chapter 48

IT'S EASY TO get lost in the Red Light District, even for some-one who knows the area as well as me. Of course it's not the same as being lost in the woods. A few minutes of twists and turns and you're back on course. But those few minutes of disorientation often lead to something unforeseen.

After leaving the Hoppe I had walked for only several minutes, deep in thought, before realising I had no idea where I was. I had reached a bend where the narrow road I was on curved dramatically leading me back to Spui - or so I thought. But after a short time of wandering through a maze of tiny alleys, I had lost all notion of direction and resigned myself to playing the tourist and asking someone to guide me out.

However, the backstreet I was on was deserted. What's more, the sky had darkened and the first drops of rain promised more to come. I quickened my pace, searching the side streets, hoping to find a recognisable name. I passed several dark and uninviting roads, but nothing registered until I came to a tiny alleyway. Searching the opposite wall for a street sign and then, finding it, something twigged inside my brain.

I had seen this name somewhere before. Recently. A fleeting glance, perhaps, but it had stuck in my head. And then I remembered. I reached into my pocket and pulled out the slip of paper the lioness had written at the Prostitute's Information Bureau. I had stuck it in the pocket of my trousers in lieu of a rubbish bin and now, unfolding it and reading it again, I realised I was on the very street that she had written as the address for the Rocket Club.

It was a quiet street of elderly buildings with facades that looked rather unpretentious, even a bit drab. Certainly nothing that appeared to be a night club. There were no marquees. No signposts. Not even the appearance of a shop could be seen as I walked around a very sharp bend. In fact, the only thing I discovered was that I had walked into a hidden impasse as a few yards further on the street suddenly stopped and became instead a sheer brick wall which, on closer inspection, was the windowless side of a very large building.

There was a number on the wall - 96. Below the number was a door, brightly painted green. I took the card out of my pocket again and checked it. The number was the same. I thought for a minute and then I reached up and pressed the buzzer.

It was an impulsive act that I immediately regretted. And I had turned to leave when I heard a voice behind call out, 'Hello?'

I turned back. There was a young woman standing in the doorway. Slim, auburn hair pulled high on her head in a bun, casually dressed with a pair of wire glasses perched hesitantly on her nose, she looked at me enquiringly and said, 'German? Italian? English, perhaps?' She smiled. 'Usually I can tell.'

'English,' I said. And then (with a bit of a cringe, I must admit) I asked, 'Is this the Rocket Club?'

She looked at her watch wrapped daintily around her wrist in soft brown leather. 'It's quite early yet.' And then looking at me, she smiled, 'What time does your invitation say?'

I took the slip of paper and showed it to her. 'This is all I have,' I said. And then I added, 'Are you Charlie?'

She thought that was very funny. Anyway, she laughed, 'No, I'm not Charlie.' And then she shrugged, 'I guess you better come in.'

'I can always come back,' I said.

'Did you want to see Charlie?' she asked.

'I suppose there are a few questions...'

She opened the door wider. 'Well, come in then.'

Taking a deep breath, I walked inside. She closed the door behind and led me into the vestibule. It wasn't what I expected.

In the centre of the vestibule was a large, ornate fountain in the middle of which was an enormously erect penis spewing out cascades of coloured water. Around the periphery were smaller statues of angels - the kind that were popular during the renaissance, except these angels were all having various and inventive forms of sexual intercourse.

'Aren't they cute?' she giggled, noticing that my eyes were focused on that strange erotic construction. 'I especially like the one over there,' she said, pointing to a plaster couple doing an intricate act of copulation which had them tied together head to toe in what looked like a figure eight knot.

I followed her up a flight of circular stairs to a rather ornate sitting room of the type one might find in a second class hotel trying to appear like a first - everything was a bit too plush, the colours a bit too garish. Even the chandeliers above gloried in their fakeness. The whole thing seemed to have the indelible stamp of 'whore house' which, of course, is exactly what it was.

She had me sit down on a black satin sofa which swallowed me half-way into its depths and then handed me a bowl of salty nuts which had been sitting on the adjoining side table.

'Here, munch on these,' she said. And then looking at me questioningly she asked, 'What was your name again?'

'Do people really give their names in places like this?' I said.

'It doesn't have to be the name on your passport,' she said with a knowing smile. 'Just something we can call you with.'

'Well how about Farquart?' I asked.

She tried it several times and then shook her head. 'Too difficult.'

'What name do you use?' I asked.

'Suzie,' she said. 'It's easy to say and has an equivalent in all the major European languages.'

'Then how about calling me 'Euro', I said.

'Euro?' She laughed. Then she shrugged her delicate shoulders. 'OK, Euro. Is that your surname or your first?'

'I don't know,' I said. 'How about both?'

'Mr Euro Euro? Is there a middle initial?'

'Yes,' I said. 'E.'

'Mr. Euro E. Euro. OK. I'll get Charlie for you.' And then she walked to the other side of the room and disappeared through a passageway.

I ate a few of the nuts which I found incredibly salty, put them back, and then took them again and ate a few more.

Suzie returned quickly and said, 'Charlie will be with you in a minute. She's just freshening up. Did anyone go over the pricing scheme? Will you be paying cash or using a credit card?'

'Actually, I just want to talk,' I said.

'Whatever,' she replied. 'There's an hourly rate.'

'Cash, I guess,' I replied. 'It shouldn't be more than an hour.'

'An hour's good,' she said. 'Sometimes it only takes ten seconds. But guys tend to last longer as they get older.' She winked. 'That's why I like older guys.'

It might have been my protected upbringing but I couldn't really see her as a whore. She looked a bit too innocent.

'Been at it long?' I asked.

'The job?' She shook her head. 'No. Actually I only work part-time. I'm a student,' she said, lifting up a book she was holding. 'Developmental Psychology.'

'No kidding?'

'You learn lots about human nature here,' she said.

Chapter 49

CHARLIE DIDN'T LOOK exactly as I imagined, though I'm not quite sure what I imagined, actually. But whatever it was, it wasn't that.

She was built - constructed, more likely - in a high-tech gymnasium and her oiled-up muscles glistened to prove it. She was wearing an extra-tight T-shirt that showed off her bi-cepts more than her breasts. And her legs bulging out from her shorts where so taut you could count every ligament. Her face appeared hewn from the hardest of boulders. Her hair was cropped so close you could see the sinews flexing in her temples as she spoke.

'Hi,' she said. 'I'm Charlie.'

'I'm Euro,' I replied.

'Yes,' she said. 'Suzie told me. Do you want to come with me?'

'Do you mind if we stay here?' I replied.

'Here?'

'I just want to talk.'

She glanced at her watch. 'I guess we have time.' Then she said, 'Do you want to humiliate me, me to humiliate you or do you want me to talk dirty?'

'No, I'm afraid you don't understand...'

'Whatever. Just tell me the scenario so I can dress appropriately,' she said.

'I'm a journalist,' I explained.

'So you want a discount?'

'A discount would be nice. But I wanted to ask you a few journalistic questions...'

'How should I dress?'

'What you have on is fine. I wanted to ask you about a murder...'

'I don't mind fantasy violence,' she said, 'but we have rules. Did Suzie go over them with you?'

'I wanted to ask you about Rachel Desonsa...'

'Rachel Desonsa?'

'The Surinames prostitute who was killed a few weeks ago. I'd also like to ask whether you know a man who calls himself "The Ferret".'

She looked at me curiously. 'Who sent you here?'

'Tanya,' I replied.

'Tanya sent you here to ask me about Rachel Desonsa and "The Ferret"?'

'Well, she gave me your name,' I said.

'Would you wait here for just a minute?' she asked. And then she walked out the same passageway she had recently walked in.

I ate some more salty nuts as I waited and then realising I was eating them out of nervousness and they were making me incredibly thirsty, I put them back.

At that moment Suzie came in carrying a tray with a drink which she offered and I thankfully took.

'Where are you from?' she asked, sitting down across from me and watching as I thirstily guzzled the drink down.

'London,' I said.

'Do you come to Amsterdam often?'

'On occasion.'

'Do you like it?'

'Yes.'

Suddenly I felt my head start to spin and my eyes start to blur. I looked at the glass, now sitting empty on the table, and then at her.

'What did you put in that drink?' I asked.

'Oh, a little Amyl Nitrate,' she said. 'You'll be asleep in a minute or two. I should warn you that you might wake up with a slight headache, but it really won't last.'

Chapter 50

MY HEAD WAS throbbing and there was a blistering pain in the space between my ears that once contained my brain. I opened my eyes. Everything was white. The ceiling. The walls. Even the bed I was in. In the corner was a white piano with a white candelabra and a white vase containing white flowers. On the walls were picture frames, white, containing empty white canvases.

The strains of a melancholy piano concerto filtered through the air. I recognised it as Gymnopedies.

I pushed back the covers and tried to get up. And then I realised I was stark, bone naked.

'How's your head?'

I looked over to my side and saw the young woman who had first let me in. She was sitting on a chair against the wall and smiling, rather benignly, I thought.

'How did I get here?' I asked.

'Charile carried you in,' she said, sweetly.

'Where the bloody hell are my clothes?'

'Being ironed. But don't worry. They've taken a complete inventory. Are you comfortable? They put you in the Eric Satie suite, one of my favourite rooms...'

Then Charlie came in. She was carrying a portfolio which she tossed onto the white bedside table. 'You're up,' she said. 'Very good.' And then, pointing to the portfolio, she said, 'Take a look. They're straight out of the darkroom so be careful, they're still a bit wet.'

I sat up in bed, took the portfolio and opened it. Inside were large glossy print photos. I took them out and examined them one by one. They were quite remarkable shots of Suzie and myself doing some extraordinary things that I really don't recall. However, since she was on top and my eyes were shut, I could either have been asleep or in some sort of rapture that deletes itself from your brain as soon as it's done.

'I especially like that one,' said Suzie coming over and pointing to a photo that contained a rather awkward pose, on my part at least, but did answer the question of whether a full erection could be obtained in an unconscious state.

I put the photos down and yawned. My head ached ever more. 'What's this about?' I asked.

'We're in a very delicate position, Mr Dumont - sorry, but we did need to get some details about you...'

'I really prefer the name 'Sacha' over 'Euro', said Suzie. 'It's very sweet. Is it Russian?'

'Look...' I said, rather angrily but quickly moderating my tone because of the pain in my head. 'Look, I just wanted to ask a few simple questions. Nothing to merit this...' I glanced over at the photos. 'What the hell is this all about, anyway?'

'The photos? Just a bit of protection,' said Charlie. 'If you don't behave, we send them to your wife.'

'I'm not married,' I said.

'To your employer then.'

'My employer would just ask me for your address.'

Charlie stared at me. 'Are you sure you're English?'

'We wouldn't have done it if you were French or German,' said Suzie. 'It wouldn't have been any use. A Frenchman would frame them and put them in his study. A German would ask for duplicates to hand out to his friends. But Englishmen usually fall to pieces. Americans are worse - or better if what you're trying to do is blackmail them.'

'Is that what this is about? Blackmail?' I said.

'Not in the least,' said Charlie. 'It's just our form of insurance.'

'Could I have my clothes?' I asked.

They brought me my clothes and had me check through a detailed inventory list and then sign a statement saying I had received everything back in good order.

'You don't mind if I go?' I said in a tone I usually held in reserve for football hooligans.

'Go or stay,' said Charlie. 'If you want, we'll give you an hour without charge as compensation. So maybe you could finish what she started...'

Suzie looked at me and smiled.

'Thanks, but I've got a splitting headache. Maybe some other time,' I said.

I put on my clothes, checked my wallet and Suzie walked me to the door. 'I still don't understand,' I said to her as I left (though it's strange speaking to someone who knows you intimately without you knowing her), 'what is it about Rachel Desonsa that makes all your friends so jumpy?'

'There's a real difference between the girls in the shop windows and us,' she said. 'We have more security and they have more independence. But when something like that happens, it sends a shock wave through the community, you know? People get edgy...'

'Did you know her?' I asked.

She shook her head. 'I don't know anyone who did know her. But we all felt terrible about it. She wasn't a girl. She was older than my mother. She shouldn't have been on the street...'

'But she was,' I said.

'We had a little memorial, you know. We walked past her shop. Each of us carried a flower. By the end, there was a mound of flowers by her door. The next day they were gone...' She looked down at the ground and then back up at me. Her eyes were different. There was a trace of sadness, like the haunting strains of Satie's sonata.

'But why did Charlie react that way when I asked about her?'

'It wasn't her, I think.'

'What was it then?'

'It was when you asked about "The Ferret",' she said.

Chapter 51

BACK IN MY hotel I stood under the shower, lathering my body in soap and letting the spray slowly rinse off the suds and then starting the process again until I felt - not clean but perhaps less dirty.

Wrapping myself in a towel, I lay down on the bed. My body still felt ungainly, cumbersome, painful as if along with being drugged it had been beaten as well.

I picked up the remote from the beside table and switched on the TV. I never watch TV except at moments when I need some mental anaesthesia. I don't care what the program is. The alpha waves themselves seem to do the trick. In fact, it could just be a stationary camera focused on a piece of bread watching it mould. It wouldn't matter.

The images on the screen, however, were somewhat more frantic. The camera was following a parade of youth in the Amsterdam Woods, half clothed, totally zonked, moving hypnotically to the rhythms of a band whose only purpose, it seemed, was to emulate the sounds of people fucking.

I turned it off and gazed up at the ceiling.

The telephone rang. It rang again. Reluctantly I answered it.

'Dumont, I've been trying to reach you forever. Why don't you get a mobile phone?'

I recognised the voice as that of Tompkins, the editor of my London newspaper.

'How's the weather?' I asked.

'Probably better than where you are,' he said. 'That story you're working on - how's it going?'

'It's going,' I said.

'You know we're starting to pick up some things on the wire about that murder case. Seems like there's interest. I didn't realise he was a famous painter and she was working for the drug lords...'

'Where are you getting this?'

'I told you, it's coming down the wire. When do you think you can send us something?'

'Soon.'

'When?'

'In a few days.'

'OK, but don't let it grow cold,' he said.

I put down the phone and stared back at the ceiling. Then I closed my eyes, opened them again, took a deep breath, got out of bed and dressed.

Chapter 52

I HAD BORROWED a magnifying glass from Joop, the hotel relief clerk who was using it to inspect his stash of old 45 rpm discs for scratches.

'What do you want it for?' he asked.

'My eyes are getting bad,' I said.

'Maybe you need glasses,' he suggested.

'Maybe I need a new head,' I replied.

I took it to Heinke's boat.

I was tired, angry, frustrated, annoyed and generally peeved - at the world, at my job, at myself and the fix I was in. I don't like being left in a field full of time bombs and invisible incendiaries especially when it's me who left myself.

I was tired of Heinke boat. And even Heinke.

It was getting dark when I climbed down into the hold. I lit a candle and took out the bottle of rum I had purchased on the way, wiped a glass clean and poured myself a hefty shot.

I swung the easy chair around, the one with the stuffing sticking out, so it faced the wall with the COBRA pictures. I lit up a cigarette and had a drink. Then I sat back and gazed at the photos, trying to project myself inside them.

COBRA 1 and COBRA II. One lasted two years. The other fifteen seconds. One had a brilliant museum to display their works, the other had Heinke's boat. One came out of the war and the resistance. The other from anarchy and guilt.

I took another drink and stared closer. There was Vanderzee above and Heinke below. Father and son. So alike yet so dissimilar. And the people I had known in my youth, the young Elisabet, Johannes and all the rest of them.

Moving closer, I placed the flickering candle on a shelf by the photos and took out Joop's magnifying glass. I used it to study COBRA II, face by face, moving it back and forth till I could pick out every pixel, every dot. It came to rest on the mystery woman - the Surinamese girl sitting at Heinke's feet.

I examined her face through the magnifying glass. I took another drink and examined it again. It was a beautiful face, I thought. Magnificently radiant in white and black. Something shone through even the dots. Something was captured in that fleeting moment when the flashbulb flashed and the shutter snapped shut. Something rare and extraordinary.

I took another drink and then studied it again, letting the magnifying glass slowly descend from her face to her neck to her torso where it lingered.

I squinted my eye and inspected it closer. The dots had begun to pulsate. I stared harder till I saw through the dress. Till I saw through the belly. Till I saw...

And then I remembered. What Elisabet really whispered in my ear. Just before the train pulled out.

'You couldn't see it, Sacha. Because you're a man. But I could tell. The young woman, the Surinamese girl. She was pregnant.'

Chapter 53

I HEARD A noise on the deck above. I quickly extinguished the candle and retreated to the back of the cabin where I hid behind the curtain that divided off the galley from the sitting room.

In a minute or so I heard the hatch creek open. A beam of light glared down from above, sweeping through the cabin on a searching mission. A moment later I heard him climbing down the ladder.

And then, in the faint light, I saw him. Lithe, sinewy, primed as a leopard. He sniffed the air. Maybe it was odour of burnt tallow. Maybe he picked up my smell. Whatever it was, his body stiffened, his ears pricked up, his nostrils twitched. His eyes darted from here to there, around the room.

He noticed the candle which I had lit and extinguished. Moving toward it, he reached out his fingers and touched the wick. His eyes darted round the room again. He sniffed. The muscles of his face tightened. It was clear he had sensed I was there.

I flung myself forward just as he reached the stairs. He was quicker than me, much quicker, but fortunately he momentarily lost his grip falling back a rung just as I reached him.

Grabbing onto his sleeve, I held tight, pulling him back toward me. But he gripped fast to the ladder and with an enormous burst of strength, tore himself free, propelling himself forward and then lurching upwards as I fell back, still clinging to his garment.

In a moment he was gone. I was on the cabin floor. His jacket was on top of me.

I sat up, rubbed my head and cursed. Not only did I lose him again, but I probably had the only heavy piece of clothing that stood between his body and the elements.

Getting up, I went over and relit the candle, poured myself another drink and cursed again.

I looked over at the jacket on the floor. It was brown like his skin. I went over and picked it up. I looked through the pockets, taking out bits and pieces of things. Paper, string, ragged stuff, things you'd throw away - things of no value.

I spread it out on the table and inspected it, unfolding pieces of paper - old candy wrappers, butts of cigarettes. Nothing. Nothing. Nothing. And then, something. Maybe. Perhaps.

A card. Folded in half. Crumpled. Torn. Mutilated. 'Outer Limits Coffee Shop', it read. And there was an address. And on the back was a name - scribbled. But it was a name I knew well.

Pocketing the card, I left.

Chapter 54

HANS MARKER WAS one of the people in the COBRA II photograph. In the picture, he was standing next to Heinke, to his left, wide eyed and innocent. He was younger than us by about five or six years and had come to Amsterdam from Germany as a teenager on a trip, liked it and stayed on. When I had known him, he had already been there for a while - one of those lost sheep Heinke occasionally found.

I remembered him as a nice young lad with eyes that seemed constantly dilated and a puppy-like smile permanently attached to his lips. In the army he would have been one of those kids who was the first to volunteer when an impossible mission was mounted. However, this being Amsterdam, he battled the police instead.

He was always on the boat, a fixture of sorts, but usually in the background. He hardly ever spoke. And when he did, it was usually to agree with something Heinke said.

And then one day he disappeared. It seemed to happen just like that. I came back one year and found he wasn't around. And the only explanation Heinke would give was just to announce tersely - 'He left.'

Much later I heard that he had opened a small coffee shop. I never went there - it really wasn't my scene. But for Hans, it had seemed fitting, somehow.

Chapter 55

THE OUTER LIMITS Coffee Shop was located in the Western side town on a side street off one of the main boulevards that runs by the Plantage, not too far from the old Jewish quarter. It was isolated and out of the way no matter where you were going. If you hadn't known it was there, you wouldn't have found it.

The shop was quite ordinary looking for a den of iniquity, I thought. At first glance there wasn't much to establish it as a cannabis café. Except on closer examination the little spacemen climbing out of the flying saucers painted on the shop window did, indeed, look like they might have imbibed some mind-altering substance.

I walked inside. The place was small. Only three or four tables on one side and a long counter on the other. At the far end was a pin ball machine. Behind the counter was a curtained doorway that led to an inner sanctum.

Hans was standing behind the counter. I recognised him at once, even though I hadn't seen him for fifteen years. Lanky build, long face, bright eyes, hair down to his shoulders - he looked just the same. Maybe there was a bald patch, maybe a grey hair or two, maybe his skin wasn't quite as boyish, maybe his eyes not quite so eager. But he was the same. Almost.

I sat down at the counter. He didn't seem to notice me at first. He was engaged in conversation with a young lad who might have been himself many years before. From the gist of the conversation, I realised the kid was from England, some small town in Cornwall, had recently arrived, was looking for a place to stay and had just found a job loading barrels at the Heiniken brewery. He had already decided Amsterdam was his home.

I let them chat for a while. Hans was offering some fatherly advice on where not to live and what not to inject into his system. Then, turning to me, he looked inquisitively.

I ordered a coffee. He made it at a small machine - not one of those gorgeous Italian jobs with gold plated eagles but just a simple, one-handled apparatus that said a lot about his state of affairs. He ground some coffee, packed it into the holder, screwed the holder in, pumped out the essence, frothed some milk, poured it into the cup - all the while continuing his conversation with the kid.

Then he brought me over the steaming brew and offered me a biscuit from a little tin.

'How much?' I asked.

'One guilder fifty.'

'For the biscuit?'

'For the coffee. The biscuit's on the house.'

'How the hell can you afford to run this place charging one guilder fifty for coffee and biscuits?' I asked.

He shrugged. 'You want to pay more?'

'You never did have much sense of economics,' I said.

'If I had any sense of economics, I'd have left this place long ago,' he replied. Then, looking at me closer, he said, 'Do I know you?'

'It depends on what you mean by "know".'

'Fucking hell! You're Sacha-the-philosopher,' he said.

'The philosopher?' I hadn't heard that one before.

'Isn't that what we called you back then?'

'I hope not,' I said.

'Maybe you weren't listening.' He laughed and stuck out his hand. 'Good to see you, man!'

I shook his hand and then glanced around. 'Nice place,' I said. 'How long have you had it?'

'Quite a while,' he said.

'You must have been one of the first.'

He nodded. 'Back when it was more of a calling than a business. It's not the same, man.'

'How so?' I asked.

'Haven't you seen those multi-story jobs? They've been taken over by corporations, man. It's big business. Big guilders. Less and less room for guys like me who just wanted a quiet little place where people could come and smoke pot.'

'Why? You probably appeal to a different clientele, don't you?'

'They're trying to squeeze the small guy out. Lots of restrictions and regulations. Like they're no longer giving coffee shops permits to serve alcohol. I don't mind that. But everyone is under constant observation. You sneeze the wrong way and they grab your licence.'

'You mean for hard drugs...'

'On the face of it, yes. But really they're under obligation to the EEC.'

'For what?'

'To cut back on the numbers. There's over 350 coffee shops in Amsterdam now. In two years they want the numbers cut to around 200. So if it isn't by natural attrition - you can't sell your permit any more - it has to be cut and slash. Find a reason, shut it down. So who has money to fight them in court? Not me. But the Grasshopper or Bulldog, they've got clout.'

'I thought Europe was swinging the other way,' I said. 'Places like Germany and Spain have made it almost legal, haven't they?'

'Ignoring it is one thing. Having it in your face is another. Besides, there's the pressure from America. The more we try to divide off hard from soft, the more they try to link them together.'

'It's worse in England,' the kid chirped in. I looked over at him. He couldn't have been much over eighteen, I thought. 'Cops just use it as an excuse to roust you,' he continued. 'They nicked me for possession, let me off with a warning, sent a note to my headmaster and my college kicked me out.'

'So here you are in Amsterdam,' I said.

He grinned. 'Yeah. It's great!' And then taking his bag of hash, he stuffed it in his shirt pocket along with his pouch of tobacco, his papers and his pipe, gave a little boyish wave saying 'See you tomorrow, huh?' and walked out.

'I had to check his ID,' said Hans after he left. 'They'd have my ass if I sold him hash and he was under age.'

'How many kids like that do you find coming in?' I asked.

'From England? More than you think. The wealthier ones go to the tourist cafés in the centre, have a few laughs and go home with their pockets stuffed with things they bought in head shops. Then there's the others. Lonely and lost. They come here without much money and expect to find a job and a place to live. But it's not so easy. Some of them get into trouble. Some of them not. A few of them actually find a home for themselves here.'

'Like you?' I said.

'Yeah,' he said. 'Why not?'

Chapter 56

NOW THERE WAS only the two of us. Hans made himself a coffee and joined me at a table. I lit up a cigarette and offered him one.

'No thanks, I've got some of my own,' he said taking a roll-up from his shirt pocket and lighting it.

There was a sweet, tell-tale fragrance that enveloped the room. Hans inhaled deeply, taking a sharp quick breath. He held in the smoke for a moment and then slowly let it out.

He tried handing the roll-up to me. I shook my head. 'That's OK,' I said, taking another puff on my cigarette. 'I'll stick with this.'

'You'll live longer with this one than that one,' he said.

'We each die our appropriate death,' I replied.

'Maybe, but I've seen enough people die of lung cancer.'

'You mean you can't get cancer from that?' I asked, pointing to his smoke.

'No,' he said. 'This cures it.' Then, looking at me curiously, he said, 'Don't tell me back in the 70's you never turned on.'

I shrugged. 'All you had to do was breathe the air back then.'

'Especially on the boat. Come on Sacha, don't tell me you didn't smoke!'

'I tried once or twice. But, really, I preferred alcohol. Still do, in fact.'

'Bad scene,' he said. 'Alcohol's a depresent. Very toxic after a while. I'd rather be hooked on heroin.'

'No you wouldn't,' I said.

'Pure heroin's not so bad. It's all the impurities that fuck you up. Look at people like Burroughs.'

'Listen,' I said, 'I've done enough stories on the death and destruction in housing estates to last me a lifetime. Heroin kills,' I said. 'One way or another.'

'Poverty kills,' Hans said. 'Heroin's just a drug. I know people who live normal, functional lives on it. Any drug's like that. You can use them or misuse them whether it's prosac or aspirin. A hundred years ago everyone took opiates in one form or another. Cocaine was the most common medication. It was in everything - from sodas to tonics. Nobody saw it as evil. It was a panicea back then.'

'That was then and now is now,' I said. 'They had their own problems. We have ours. Sure, an intelligent, knowledgable person can get away with taking almost anything - for a while. But plagues are plagues. And heroin, cocaine or anything else like that doesn't help people get out of the poverty trap. It just makes them forget they're in it. Besides,' I said, giving him a curious look, 'I thought you made a distinction between hard drugs and soft ones.'

'I don't. They do,' he said. 'And as a good, honourable merchant, I follow the rules and guidelines they've set. But not without question. I'd much rather have centres of experimentation and education where young people could be taught the realities of drugs, not fill them with half-truths and stories of hell fire and damnation.'

'I could just imagine what the EEC commissioners would say about that.'

'Well, of course, it can't be done. Not now. Besides, it's not only the commissioners to worry about. Drugs are a trillion dollar business. Probably up there with oil in the commodity trade. Think of what it would do to the pricing structure if they were suddenly legalised!'

'You'd legalise everything?'

'Everything. And you know what? Most intelligent policemen agree with me. Legalise. Control the distribution. And tax the lot. In one great swoop you'd get rid of half the crime. Half the prisoners in jail are in there for drug related offenses. Half the burglaries are done by fucked-up kids trying to get the money for their next fix. Half the murders have to do with drugs.'

'But drugs would still be a problem. There wouldn't be less of them around. There'd be more.'

'Who cares? Look what's happened here with pot. In Amsterdam you can have all the hash you want. But the incidence of young Dutch people smoking has actually gone down ever since the advent of the coffee shops. Some of them smoke. Some don't. It's no longer a way to prove you're cool. Because it's ordinary, there's no dangerous allure. Smoke or not. No one gives a damn.'

'But hash is relatively safe. I wouldn't say that about crack cocaine.'

'No drug is safe when it's kept underground. The only way to use drugs is to take them with full knowledge and understanding of what they do. They can open up the doors of perception or close them down. It's up to you. But you have to know what you're taking, when to take it and how much. A thousand years ago people were better educated about drugs than they are today.'

'When the American Indians took mescalin, they did it as part of an organised ritual. No one took it for fun. It was serious business,' I said.

'And we have a lot to learn from them,' said Hans. 'Just like you have a lot to learn from us.'

Chapter 57

'I DON'T THINK you came here to talk to me about drugs,' said Hans.

I thought that maybe I was wrong about him being just the same. There was something about his eyes. No longer innocent and adoring as I remembered. They were probing. It made him look wiser.

I showed him the photo I carried in my wallet. The picture of the wild man.

He gazed at it for a moment and put it down. 'Solomon,' he said. Then, looking at the photo again, he asked, 'Where did you find it?'

'Marijke gave it to me,' I said. 'She found it on the boat.'

'I'm surprised Heinke kept his picture,' said Hans.

'Why?'

Hans shrugged.

'Who is he?' I asked.

'The son of a woman I once knew. Rachel Desonsa.' He closed his eyes for a moment and then opened them again. 'She's dead. You knew her, didn't you?'

I shook my head.

'But she was around the boat. Remember?'

'It was a little before my time. I came later.'

'You should have known her then. She was beautiful.'

'I saw her photograph,' I said.

'Where?'

'A group picture. On the cabin wall. You were in it too.'

He nodded. Then lighting his roll-up he took a puff and stared up at the ceiling in contemplation. 'If only I could be transported back,' he said, finally, 'things might have been different.'

'Like what?'

'Like maybe I could have convinced her to stay. To have her child in Amsterdam. Instead she went back.'

'To join the revolution?'

'Yes.' He made an ironic laugh. 'The revolution that never was. We filled her head with dreams and gave her money for guns and sent her back to the jungle. Her and her foetus.'

'Did you know she was pregnant?'

'Not then. She didn't tell anyone.' He rubbed the bristles on his chin. 'She might have told Heinke. She was so crazy about him.'

'Was he in love with her?'

'Heinke? Ha! Heinke in love with anyone? With himself, perhaps!'

'With Pauline,' I said.

'Maybe. But she died, didn't she? Very shortly afterward.'

I stared at him. His bitterness was clearly stored so long it was becoming rancid.

'Was it Heinke's child?' I asked.

'She wouldn't say.'

'You kept contact with her though.'

'For a while, yes. I even went to Suriname.'

'You did?'

'After things fell apart there. It was really bad. No work. No food. I tried to convince her to come back. She wouldn't hear of it.'

'Why not?'

'Because of Solomon. She was devoted to the boy. He wanted to stay. And she still had faith in the country, in the land. But then it got too much. And when she did come back, finally, it was because of him too. So he could get a decent education.'

'In Amsterdam.'

'Yes. But it was too late. She left it for too long. Things weren't the same when she came back. By then there were more

Surinamese in Amsterdam than in Paramaribo. She had no contacts any more. No friends.'

'Except you. And Heinke, perhaps.'

'We had lost touch. And Heinke - she didn't want to see him.'

'Why not?'

'Ask her,' he said.

'So she ended up in Bijlmermeer.'

'In Bijlmermeer. Yes.'

'And Solomon?'

'What do you expect? Fell in with the wrong sort. Petty thieves. Crooks. Dealers.'

'Is that where you come in?'

'She managed to track me down,' he said. 'She was worried about him.'

'Solomon.'

'Yes. I let them hang out here. Him and his friends. As long as they were clean. We got along OK. I liked him. He liked me. I introduced him to some people I knew in the music scene. He and his friends were going to start a band...'

'What about Rachel?'

'She got a job working as a waitress. The pay was lousy and the work was hard but she was making out OK. She even started night school. She wanted to be a journalist.'

'And then?'

'And then something happened. Something very bad...'

Chapter 58

'THE EL AL crash. You heard about it?' he asked.

'Yes. A housing block completely destroyed,' I said. 'In Bijlmermeer.'

'Wiped from the face of the earth. The noise was so great it shattered glass for miles. It was like a nuclear explosion. The heat of a thousand furnaces. A blinding flash of light. People swore they saw a mushroom cloud rise up afterwards.'

'Rachel and her son - where were they?'

'He was with his band in Amsterdam. She was with some neighbours. But close enough to feel the heat of the blast, to smell the fumes, to be deafened by the explosion.'

'At least they weren't in their flat.'

'It might have been better if they were,' he said.

'You don't mean that.'

'Maybe I do.'

He had gone behind the counter to make some more coffee. I went up to the bar, sat down on a stool and watched him.

'Nobody understands what happened to those people - afterward...'

'You mean post-traumatic stress?'

'That's just a term. No, I mean hell.'

'People survive bomb blasts and live on,' I said. 'I was in Sarajevo during the shelling. It was terrible. But people survived and went on with their lives afterward.'

'This was different.'

'Bigger and louder, perhaps.'

He put the milk jug under the steamer and turned it on full blast. There was an eruption of foam which splattered over him. He turned. I saw the hot foam dripping from his face.

'Sacha, this was different. It melted steel. It made lava out of rock. That El Al plane was carrying something lethal!'

'Are you sure?'

'Yes.' He took a towel and wiped his face. 'I don't know what it was. But afterward people began to suffer. They were sick. Very sick. And they didn't seem to get any better.'

'What happened to Rachel?'

'She was in bed for a month. When she finally got up, she wasn't herself anymore. You should have known her before, Sacha. You should have seen the fire in her eyes. That woman had soul!'

He poured the foamy milk into the coffees and handed me a cup.

'She didn't get better?' I asked, taking some sugar and stirring it in.

'Not really. Sometimes she seemed OK. Sometimes not. She quit her job, withdrew from school...'

'And become a prostitute?'

He took a sip of his coffee and looked at me over the rim. 'Eventually.'

I shook my head. 'I don't get it.'

'I don't either,' he said. 'It wasn't her. It was someone else.'

'Who set her up? I mean it's not something you go apply for, is it?'

'It seems she owed a great deal of money to someone. I don't know who. I leant her some myself but never expected it back. But she needed more. And in Amsterdam, a woman's always got an option.'

'Even if she's ill?'

'It's one of the few jobs you can make money lying on your back.'

'For what?'

He shrugged. 'She needed big money. She needed it fast. I think it had to do with her son,' he said.

'Solomon? What happened to him?'

'He was cool for a while. Then something snapped.'

'Something snapped?'

'Yeah, something snapped. And the kid went bonkers.'

Chapter 59

IT WAS LATE when I got back to the hotel. Joop, the relief clerk, was playing some mellow jazz. He offered me a drink but I took a rain check.

I needed a chance to think. To be alone with my thoughts. I went up to the room, locked the door, got into bed, lit up a smoke and stared at the wall.

I tried to picture what Hans had told me right before I left. It was powerful. I wanted to capture the imagery.

The kid, it seemed, had landed on his feet and was on his way up as Rachel was on her way down. Their lives grew more and more apart.

And then one day it happened. Hans heard the story later from one of Solomon's chums. They were out on the town, some of the members of the band - three of them, he said. They had a few drinks and something to smoke. They were walking through town. Cracking jokes. Making fun of the Johns, the lonely guys from all over the world who congregated on those streets at night. Searching for pleasures of illicit love. Nervously eyeing the girls, each other, girls, each other, girls, whores, girls. And, after enough alcohol, bolstering courage, hesitantly knocking on windows and doors.

The boys were high. Bathing in lights, throbbing red. They laughed. They joked. Pointing their fingers, they whistled and winked and bellowed and roared.

Until they got to a little alley off Monnikenstraat.

There was a game. A shell game. Run by the Turks. They pushed their way through the motley crowd and took some guilders out.

The shells moved quicker than the eye. Where was the ball? Under three or under two? Ten guilders on three. Fuck! It was two!

A few more goes and he was skint. But what the hell? Another night on the town. So what?

And then it happened. As he moved away, back out of the crowd. He glanced over at the one storey shack and saw her under the neon strip light pulsating red. Standing in the window.

At first he didn't recognise her. Just another whore. One of those older, pathetic ones. He looked away. Then he looked back.

A John had come up. She opened the door. They had a few words. Then the John went in and the curtain closed.

They found him, his mates. Standing there. Rigid. Staring. Unmoving. Just a muscle twitching in his forehead.

They took him home. He went to bed. And that's the last they saw of him, Hans said.

Chapter 60

IN THE MORNING I rang my contact at De Volkstrant to ask him what information he had about the plane that crashed into Bijlmermeer.

'You know, of course, it's back in the news.'

'I didn't,' I said.

'But it's made the wire services! Certainly you've heard! The El Al flight that crashed was carrying lethal cargo...'

'Like what?'

'Like substances used for biological war.'

'But that was more than six years ago,' I said. 'Why is it coming up now?'

'Rumours have been circulating for many years,' he said. 'The people in the surrounding area have been showing signs of mysterious diseases for quite a while. There have been a number of reports suggesting a toxic spill could be to blame, but the government has been very hush, hush. It's a very sensitive issue for them. But there's been a persistent investigation. And now there's something more...'

'What's that?'

'New reports have come out saying the plane may have been carrying plutonium...'

After the phone call I went downstairs for breakfast. I had a double helping of miso soup, remembering a story I had once read about the survivors of Hiroshima. They had claimed a diet of miso soup saved them from radiation poisoning. Not that I had been consciously exposed, it's just that, by now, I had plutonium on the brain - and whether or not it was in my head I felt a little miso soup might have a therapeutic effect. Anyway, it couldn't hurt, I thought.

The morning sky was blue. The sun was out. I decided to take a stroll in Vondelpark hoping the open space would give me some perspective. It had come time to face up to some facts that had be preying on me for a while. It wasn't just a whore Heinke was accused of killing. It was a woman whose life had connected with his before. And she had a son who may have been Heinke's. A son, it turns out, who was once a petty dealer and crook.

What's more, according to Hans, Rachel had owned a great deal of money. More than he could lend her. And the American journalist I met said the Drug Enforcement Agency accused her of being a major drug connection.

But the pieces didn't add up. She didn't have money, she was broke. And Hans had portrayed her as a wide-eyed idealist, not a cynical drug dealer. So where did that leave Heinke? And why did Marijke suddenly run off with a cocaine addict?

Nothing seemed to make sense. Yet there was something lurking in the background. I hated to admit it, but that's what the American journalist had said. And, suddenly, I realised I needed to talk with him.

There was a phone box near the Film Museum. I headed in that direction and when I got there I searched for his card - the one he had given me before he left.

I found it, crumpled in my pocket. Then, inserting my plastic, I dialled one of the numbers - the one for his mobile - and waited as it rang.

It rang for a while. I was about to hang up when a gruff voice finally answered.

'Yeah! What do you want?'

'Radkin?' I said. 'Is this Joseph Radkin?'

'Who's that?'

'This is Sacha Dumont. I'm ringing you from Amsterdam...'

'Fucking hell! Do you know what time it is, Dumont?'

I looked at my watch. 'About 10AM,' I said.

'I mean here! It's fuckin' two! In the morning!'

'Oh, sorry,' I said. 'I forgot about the time difference. I need to talk to you.'

'Call me at the office,' he said. 'In about eight hours!'

'I reached an impasse,' I said. 'I remembered you were saying something about noises in the background.'

'Look,' he said, his voice a little calmer now, 'I told you I'd read the wires. I haven't done that yet. Call me back...'

'But I've reached an impasse,' I said, again.

'There's only one guy who can help you with that,' he said. 'And you know who that is...'

'Who?'

'You're fucking artist friend, damn it! What's his name again?'

'Heinke.'

'Yeah. Him.'

'Well, that's the trouble. I can't talk with him.'

'Why the hell not?'

'He's in prison.'

'So what?'

'He won't talk with me. He won't talk with anyone.'

'Then force him to talk!'

'How can I do that?'

'Shit, man! How do you guys survive without us? I'm going to bed! Call me back later! Fuck!' And then he hung up.

Chapter 61

I MADE A second call from the Vondelpark phone box. It was to the office of Van Houten, Heinke's lawyer.

It wasn't his secretary who answered the phone - not the clumsy one I had met anyhow - it was a man with a strong English accent.

'What can I do for you?' he asked.

'I'd like to speak with Van Houten,' I said.

'Is it about the auction?'

I hesitated for a moment and then I said, 'Yes.'

'Well maybe I can help you with that. Is it the preview you need to know about?'

'Yes.'

'Well it hasn't been set up yet.'

'Why not?' I asked.

'There's been a slight delay...'

'But it's still at...'

'Yes. De Koning, gallery. New York. And you are?'

'Thanks,' I said, hanging up the phone.

I stood there for a moment and rubbed my head. Then I picked back up the phone and dialled the number again.

The same man answered.

'Is Van Houten there?' I asked, in a slightly different voice.

'Is this about the auction?' he said.

'No. It's about a case he's working on. It's urgent I speak with him.'

'Who should I say is calling?'

'I'm calling for Marijke, Heinke's daughter,' I said.

I waited a few minutes to be connected. Then Van Houten came on the line. His voice was brusque. 'What can I do for you?' he said.

'This is Sacha Dumont,' I said. 'I need to see you.'

'I'm extremely busy, Dumont...'

'It's vital I see you today.'

'Impossible!'

'I have some information crucial to your case,' I said. 'Something I just found out...'

'Well, give it to me over the phone.'

'I can't,' I said. 'I need to show it to you.'

'Show it to my assistant - tomorrow.'

'I have to show it to you. Today.'

'Sorry...'

'Listen carefully,' I said. 'I'm writing a story. It's going out today. It contains information that might disbar you. Might even send you to jail...'

'What the hell are you talking about?'

'I'm sending it out at noon. What time can we meet?'

There was silence on the other end.

'Really. It's all the same to me, Van Houten. It's Heinke I'm thinking about...'

There was an audible sigh on the other end. 'I'll see you in half an hour,' he said.

Chapter 62

THE PROBLEM WITH bluff is that, in the end, you need something to back it up. Not only that, you need to know what you're bluffing.

I was thinking of that as I rounded the corner, heading for Van Houten's office. I was just a few doors away, passing a neighbourhood café, when I heard the crash - the splattering of glass, the smashing of china. I don't think it was so much the noise as the groan that followed it that made me recall her.

The poor woman was truly flustered as she stood staring down at the mess. The customers sitting at the outside table, looked sadly at the remains of their late morning snack - coffee, toast and assorted jams - now a melange of soggy bread, coffee dregs and broken crockery lying on the pavement.

The proprietor, a heavy man with a walrus moustache wearing a great white apron wrapped around his bulging middle, came out, looked at the mess, looked at her - simpering - and then, kindly, told her to sit down and relax while he sent someone to clean up.

'Didn't you work over there?' I asked, coming up to her and pointing to the office several buildings down.

Tears were streaming down her eyes as she nodded.

The proprietor came back out with a tray full of coffees. He gave the outside customers each a cup and then brought her over one, telling her to take a break until she calmed herself.

'Do you mind if I join you?' I asked her after the proprietor left.

She shrugged her shoulders, wiped her tears with a paper serviette and then took a sip of her coffee.

'What happened?' I asked.

She looked at me. Her eyes were very red. And suddenly the tears began to flow again.

I handed her my hankie as the paper napkin had reached the end of its brief service. She took it, gratefully, and used it as a facial mop.

She dried her face and then squeezing the hankie she handed it back saying, 'Sorry. It's very wet.'

'Keep it,' I said. 'I've got another.' Then motioning toward Van Houten's office again, I said, 'When did you leave there?'

'Just yesterday,' she said. 'He's a horrible man!'

'He gave you the sack?'

She looked at me questioningly.

'Fired you? Made you redundant?'

She nodded.

'Because you kept dropping things?'

'Because there were things I didn't want to do,' she said. 'I was supposed to be a legal secretary, not a person who makes deals with galleries and writes stupid press releases.'

'But that sounds like interesting work,' I said. 'More interesting dealing with the world of art than the world of mortgages.'

'There's art and crooked art,' she said.

'Crooked art? What's that?'

Then, realising she had said more than she had wanted to, she got up. 'Thanks for the handkerchief. I better get back to work,' she said.

Chapter 63

THE DOOR TO Van Houten's offices was open. I walked up the stairs and into the reception room as I had done before. Except the clumsy secretary was now serving drinks down the road. In her place was a well dressed man with a neatly trimmed moustache that spelt trouble.

'Sacha Dumont to see Mr. Van Houten,' I said to him as I came in.

'Ah, yes. Dumont,' he said, standing up and holding out his hand. 'John Parkins. Nice to meet you.'

Nine words out of his mouth and I had him sized up. Home counties. Minor public school. Third class degree from Oxford or Cambridge in some very useless subject. Then off to the world of Media with a capital 'M'. Definitely spent time in the States and gloried in his trans-Atlantic accent.

'Could you tell Van Houten I'm here?' I said.

'Right,' said Parkins.

He went over to Van Houten's door, opened it and walked in. A few minutes later he came back to the desk and with an ingratiating grin said, 'Van Houten will see you in a sec. How about a drink? It's a little early for brandy...' And then he winked. 'But maybe not.'

'That's OK,' I said. 'I'm fine.'

He tapped his finger on the side of his head. 'Sacha Dumont...I know that name. Didn't you do a series on Sarajevo a few years back?'

He caught me by surprise. 'Yes,' I said. 'You read it?'

'Bits and pieces. I was a journalist myself...'

'London?'

He nodded. 'For a while.'

'And now?'

'I'm based mainly in New York.'

'Doing what?'

'Public relations.'

'How did you hook up with Van Houten?' I asked.

'We met at the COBRA exhibit. I was doing PR for a gallery that has some Dutch connections. We were interested in COBRA art and he was representing the estate of some of the artists.'

'And now?'

'We're trying to co-ordinate a major retrospective in New York. The first one of its kind there. It's tons of work...'

Just then Van Houten came out from his office. 'Nice to see you again, Dumont,' he said, coming over to me, shaking hands and trying his best to smile as he did.

'Let's go into my office,' he said, leading me to his inner sanctum.

I noticed Parkins had followed us inside. 'I was hoping we could talk in private,' I said.

'I'd like Parkins to stay, if you don't mind,' said Van Houten. 'I suspect what you have to say has as much to do with him...'

I looked over at Parkins. He smiled in a PR-ish sort of way. I looked back at Van Houten and shrugged. 'OK.'

I sat down in a chair facing Van Houten's desk. Parkins pulled a chair between mine and the desk so he was facing both of us.

'So what's this about?' said Van Houten.

I was afraid he was going to ask that question first. And I had prepared my response in the manner of my American friend - namely, always attack whenever in doubt. Mercilessly.

'I want to see Heinke,' I said. 'Today. I want you to arrange it.'

'Why?' Van Houten asked.

'Because I'm afraid what I've written will land him in worse trouble than he's already in.'

'You can't be in much worse trouble than being accused of murder,' said Parkins.

'No, I guess not,' I said, looking at Van Houten. 'But you can.'

'Look,' said Van Houten, 'I'm afraid you've got this all wrong...'

'What exactly have you written?' Parkins asked, cutting in.

'You know better than to ask me that,' I said, throwing Parkins a harsh look even though it was a perfectly reasonable question.

'It seems to me, Mr Dumont, that you're trying to blackmail us without any blackmail,' Van Houten said with a smile that made me feel slightly queasy.

'I'm not trying to blackmail you,' I replied. 'I just want to see Heinke. Today. As soon as you can set it up.'

'Impossible,' said Van Houten. 'I told you that before.'

'Perhaps you could just give us some idea as to the tenor of your story,' said Parkins, trying to be placating.

I glanced over at the Vanderzee hanging on the wall. The Orange Dog. 'It has to do with a Dutch lawyer using the plight of his client to manipulate the price of some works of art under his control.'

'What organisation are you working for?' Parkins asked.

'Global Media, London,' I said.

'They'll never run it,' said Parkins looking over at Van Houten. 'It's not big enough for them to risk the threat of libel.'

'I'm not writing it for them,' I said.

'Then who are you writing it for?' asked Parkins.

'For Pacific New Service,' I said, pulling out Radkin's card. 'They're on the wire.'

'What do you know about them?' asked Van Houten, looking at Parkins.

Parkins shrugged.

'They're used by over a thousand US papers,' I said.

'Not bad,' said Parkins. 'Not bad.' Then he glanced over at Van Houten. Van Houten made a little nod.

'Maybe we can cut a deal,' said Parkins.

'What kind of a deal?' I asked.

'We actually don't care what kind of article you write as long as you get your facts straight...'

'Why wouldn't I do that?' I asked.

'Yes,' said Parkins. 'We won't go into it. But you're barking up the wrong bush.' Shooting a glance in Van Houten's direction and then looking at me, he said. 'It might actually help if you did speak with your friend.'

He looked back at Van Houten. 'Is it possible?' he asked.

'I have a court appearance at three for a preliminary hearing,' said Van Houten. 'I can say you're my assistant.'

'I'd want to talk with him alone,' I said.

'You wouldn't have long,' Van Houten replied.

'How long?' I asked.

'No more than fifteen minutes.'

Chapter 64

I LEFT VAN Houten's office feeling very pleased with myself. Not that I completely understood his sudden change of heart in letting me see Heinke that day - in only a few hours, actually, I noted looking down at my watch. But I wasn't going to question it. However, I couldn't help considering that perhaps there was some elusive undercurrent which not only had caused this to happen but had also swept me up with it.

I wanted to walk. To walk and think. So I followed the route of the Number 2 Tram. Up past the museums, over the Singel, through Leidseplein, down Leidsestraat. Then, jumping the tracks, over the Amstel and down Kloveniersburgwal following the canal.

I made my way to the Literary Café. I wanted to be someplace familiar. Van Houten had promised me fifteen minutes. I needed to make best use of that time, so I wanted to write down some notes.

It was still early enough to have avoided the lunch-time crowd. The place was nearly empty by the time I arrived and I found my favourite table, tucked away in a corner by the front window, overlooking the canal.

I ordered a beer and lit up a smoke. Then I took my pen and notebook out and placed them on the table. I took a drink, had a smoke and peered out the window.

Heinke and I had spent so many hours here before. Sitting, drinking, smoking, talking. What the hell did we talk about? Lots of things. But it was hard to remember.

Mostly it was Heinke spouting off. Waxing on about this thing and that. So much of it was crap, thinking back. But it all came from the heart. And through his mouth even the crap seemed interesting. Back then.

I looked down at my watch again. It wasn't long before I would see him. What was I going to say in fifteen minutes? And why was I so angry at him?

It was almost like catching yourself unaware. I suddenly realised I was angry. But why? Was it the thought that he actually might have killed her? I still couldn't bring myself to believe that. Was it Marijke? Perhaps it was partly that. But the sense of hurt I felt was lingering. Lingering somewhere in the past.

I looked down at my notebook. The page that was open was still empty. I closed it up, took my pen and put them both back in my pocket. I finished my beer, got up and left.

Outside the air was crisp. Inside it was getting stuffy. I felt I could breathe better out here.

I walked over to Nieuwmarkt Square and sat down on a bench. I lit up a smoke and pondered the scene. The market was bustling with people queued up to buy breads and cheese and fish and veggies. People buying. People selling. People interacting - chatting, laughing, bargaining.

And then I had a vision. We were here, weren't we? It was here, wasn't it? When he told me that story that stayed in my mind but that I tried to repress because I really didn't want to think about it.

'I want to tell you something,' he said. It was a different voice. Without the brusque bravado. I looked at him. It was a different face. Without the tiresome certainty in it.

'What?' I asked.

'I've wanted to tell you for a long time but I was afraid...'

'I didn't think you were afraid of anything,' I said.

He looked at me seriously. 'I was afraid of losing your friendship.'

'Our friendship has withstood a lot,' I said, thinking of Pauline. And it was Pauline I thought he was speaking about. But it wasn't.

'It's been eating at me,' he said. 'Like an ulcer. I don't think about it all the time, but it's a pain that never goes away.'

'Then tell me I said.'

'It's about my father,' he replied.

'I didn't know your father very well,' I said.

'Neither did I.' He gazed out into the square. Then he looked at me. 'Things happened in the war. Things I can't understand.'

'Nor can I,' I said.

'Your grandfather,' he said. 'Do you ever think of him?'

I nodded my head.

'Do you know how he ended up at Auschwitz?'

'Like thousands of others. Because his ancestors were Jewish.'

'But how? He was hidden, wasn't he?'

'Yes. Like my mother. At your father's place.'

'But your mother escaped.'

'Yes.'

'And your grandfather didn't.'

'What are you trying to say?' I asked.

'No one knew he was hiding there.'

'Well, someone did.'

'And then, one day, they came. I was just a little kid. They took him away. They also took my father away.'

'I didn't know,' I said.

'But my father came back.'

'Your father wasn't Jewish.'

'But he came back. They didn't send you back if you were hiding Jews. Not if you were caught. Unless...'

'Unless what?' I said.

'Unless...' He looked down at the ground.

Suddenly I understood what he was getting at.

'Listen,' I said, 'I owe my life to your father. I wouldn't be here if he hadn't helped my mother escape.'

'It's not your mother I'm talking about,' he said.

'You don't have any evidence.'

'I'm talking about feelings. I'm talking about intuition. I'm talking about something that's eating me up inside, Sacha.' He stared at me. His eyes were so very different. They were pleading for me to understand.

'Did you ever read the report of the commission that investigated the arrest of Ann Frank and her family?' I asked.

He shook his head.

'They studied the case for years. They interviewed hundreds of witnesses. The more they interviewed the more complex it got. There were suspects, yes. Good suspects. But the more they dug, the more everyone became tainted with suspicion. Because in that world everyone was suspect. No matter what you did, you could never do enough. Because in the end, Ann Frank was killed along with six million others.'

'But who pointed the finger, Sacha? Who pointed the finger. We need to know.'

'Maybe you need to know,' I said. 'I don't. And I'll tell you why. I once met a man. An elderly man. He was a young man during the war just starting university. It was a small town they were in. A small university. There were only fifty in his class. Just fifty. Some of them were Jews. When the Nazis came and took the Jews the students rebelled. They had a strike. They demanded the Jews be brought back or they wouldn't go to class. There were acts of sabotage. So the Nazis rounded them up. They lined them up and had them count. They counted off - one, two, three, four. And when they got to four, the fourth young man was shot. Then they had them count again. This time they shot at two. The next time they shot at six. And so on.

'The man who was telling me the story was near the end of the row. The students were counting off and he knew what number would be his but he didn't know if he would be shot. And it was all the more terrifying because he couldn't prepare himself. One, two - bang! One, two, three, four - bang! One, two, three - bang! At each shot, he'd feel an explosion inside his head. He'd see a friend, a fellow student fall and lie twitching on the ground. But he never knew whether he'd be shot or if they'd shoot the boys on either side of him...'

'What does this have to do with my father?' Heinke asked.

'Because that's the mind-fuck of terror,' I said. 'If they had stopped the count-off and said everyone would be exempt if they betrayed their mother, how could you blame someone if they did? I couldn't say how I'd respond, Heinke. Nor could you. The Resistance understood that. And that's why they expected anyone who was captured by the Gestapo would talk. And most people did.'

'My father wasn't captured by the Gestapo,' he said.

'And you have absolutely no evidence that he betrayed anyone. But we know he saved the life of my mother. Isn't that good enough for you?'

'No, it isn't, he said. 'But I'm glad I finally told you.' And then looking at me closely, he said, 'It's not going to make any difference to our friendship is it?'

'Of course not,' I said.

But it did. Unconsciously, perhaps. That's the problem with planting a seed of doubt. It's only a little seed that's planted, but it grows within you.

Chapter 65

I WANTED TO phone Radkin before my meeting but it was still too early to call San Francisco. I did, however, get in touch with Hugo.

'The man you wanted to know about is Karl Troost, known sometimes as "The Ferret". He's a small time dealer with big ideas. Likes to hang out with the arty set. Works as their procurer. Pretends he's a musician.'

After my phone call I had a quick bite to eat and then headed for the Central Court House.

Van Houten was waiting for me in the lobby, as we had arranged, and led me to a private room reserved for lawyers and their clients.

'Remember,' he said, 'fifteen minutes.'

'It might take longer,' I said.

He shook his head. 'Fifteen minutes.' Then, after having a quick word with the officer on duty, he left.

I was sitting on a straight back chair at a wooden table when Heinke was escorted in. I hardly recognised him. Pale, his skin drawn tightly over his thinning face, it was someone else. Heinke always bathed himself in light. And light radiated from him. This person who came toward me was subdued. And dull. What's more he was dressed in a suit. I had never seen Heinke in a suit before.

I got up and stood by the side of the table. I noticed he was walking with a slight limp. He came over to where I stood. Then, when he was just inches away, he stopped. He looked at me and smiled.

'Sacha,' he said. And then he made a little gesture, with his face, with his head. It was a gesture of gentle irony, full of wonder and was done in a way that said, 'How did we end up like this?'

And suddenly it was him. I stepped forward and embraced. My friend. My comrade. My brother.

Chapter 66

WE WERE SITTING opposite one another at the wooden table.

'Did you kill her?' I asked.

He shook his head. 'No, but I was going to.'

I looked at him, puzzled. 'Why?'

'She wanted to die. She asked me to help her. She was ill, Sacha. Very ill. Something was going on inside of her, sapping her essence. The doctors didn't know what it was. Some kind of auto-immune deficiency, they said. They held out very little hope. She struggled on. Day by day. Until, finally, she had enough...'

'How did she continue working then?'

'Cocaine. The magic of pharmaceuticals. It gave her a little burst right up to the end. I'd watch her sometimes, in amazement, making up her face, in so much pain she could hardly use her hands and then, a little snort, a little pill and she'd start to glow again.'

'So she contacted you when she got back from Suriname?'

'No. Afterward. She was living in Bijlmermeer. You heard about the plane crash?'

I nodded.

'She contacted me soon after that. She needed help. She had a son, you know...'

'Yes. Solomon.'

'A nice young man. She was worried about him. She wanted to connect the two of us...'

'She didn't tell you why?'

He shrugged. 'She was concerned. He was confused, a little wild. I told her to let him be. That he'd soon find himself. Then one day he came to the boat. And then again. And again. He'd sit there watching me work. Just watch. I asked him what he wanted to do. He said he wanted to fly. Then fly, I told him. Fly if you want...'

'How did you tell him to do it?'

'I gave him books on people who flew. I told him to examine his roots. And then he went off...'

'Where to?'

'On a voyage of discovery,' he said.

'And Rachel?'

'I had some friends who were setting up a squat on the Western Isles. I helped her move in. But she was already ill by then. She lost her job. She needed money, she said.'

'What did she need it for?'

'I didn't ask but I assumed it was drugs.'

'Is that where Karl Troost came in?'

'You know him?' asked Heinke.

'I met him once,' I replied. 'Where do you know him from?'

'He's a jazz man. Plays the sax. Hung around the Boom! Boom! Club. People used him for supplies. I made the mistake of introducing Rachel to him. He let you have stuff on credit...'

'He set her up?'

'In a way. I'm not sure they didn't know each other before.'

'How so?'

'They had some connection. Didn't you get the article I sent you?'

'What article?' I asked.

'An article she wrote. I sent it to your office.'

I shook my head. 'Things take a year to reach me there.' Then, looking down at my watch, I said, 'Listen, we don't have much time.' I looked straight in his eyes. 'Tell me what happened that night.'

'We had talked about it before,' he said. 'She wanted me to help her when it came time. I said I would, as long as she had thought it out. As long as it wasn't impulse. We decided on a morphine overdose. But I needed some supplies...'

'So you asked Troost?'

'Yes. He was the only one I knew who might be able to get it. It took him a while, but finally he called...'

'You picked up the supplies. What happened next?'

'We had arranged to do it right away, as soon as the supplies came in. I picked up the stuff and went to her shop. She wanted to do it there, she said...'

'Who knew you were going there?'

'No one,' he said. 'Just her.'

'And Troost?'

'Yes, Troost.'

'And when you got there?'

'She'd been shot. She was lying in a pool of blood...'

'What did you do then?'

'I got into bed with her. I took her in my arms. I caressed her...'

'But she was already dead?'

He nodded.

'And then what happened?'

'The police arrived.'

'Someone called them? Who?'

'I don't know.'

'Why would someone want to shoot a woman who's already dying?'

'I don't know that either,' he said.

'Unless it was actually directed against someone else...'

'Like who?' he asked.

'Like you,' I said.

I looked down at my watch again. 'We only have a couple of minutes,' I said. 'What did you tell the police?'

'Nothing,' he said.

'On the advice of your attorney?'

He nodded. 'We had it worked out.'

'But you put yourself in a terrible position!'

'Not really. I gave Van Houten Rachel's sworn statement saying she wanted me to perform an act of euthanasia. There's also a statement from her doctor giving details of her medical condition.'

'So why wouldn't you see anyone?' I asked. 'Not Marijke, not me...'

'I'm sorry. Van Houten said it would be better not to yet. He told me to keep still until the time was right...'

'For what?'

He rubbed the side of his face. 'I needed money, Sacha.'

'I thought you had money,' I said. 'Didn't your father leave you some?'

He made a little laugh. 'My father? He died nearly broke. He was an artist, remember?'

'His house?'

'It wasn't his.'

'So you thought by keeping mum you'd up the price of his pictures?'

'I told you, Sacha, art has no monetary value unless there's a story behind it. But it has to be the right story. It needed to evolve. But I don't own any of Vanderzees paintings any more. I sold them to Van Houten for a song...'

'So whose pictures are we talking about?'

'Mine,' he said.

'Yours?' I looked at him incredulously.

'I've worked out a deal with him. We've got a contract. I've given over my paintings to him and he's footing my legal bill plus a monthly salary when I start painting again.'

'How much?'

'It depends on the worth of the paintings.'

There was a knock at the door. A guard came into the room, signalled to us and pointed to his watch.

Heinke got up. There was a worried look in his eye. 'Sacha, my friend, I need your help,' he said.

'I'll do what I can,' I replied. 'But I'm a journalist not a lawyer or a cop.'

'It's Marijke,' he said. He took out a letter from his shirt pocket and unfolded it. 'She's in Paris...'

'With Troost, I know...'

'She thinks she's helping, but she's just going to get herself into very bad trouble.' He looked at me, pleadingly. 'I need your help,' he said.

'If you're so worried, why don't you just instruct Van Houten to ask the court to set bail. Certainly they'd let you out if they knew the circumstances...'

He ran his fingers through his hair, nervously. 'It's not so easy,' he said. 'I just received her letter - right after the preliminary hearing was held. I've asked Van Houten. He says a new hearing will take at least a week.'

He handed me the letter.

'I want to know something,' I said. 'Is Solomon your son?'

'I've accepted responsibility for him. Yes.'

'Does Marijke know she has a brother?'

He shook his head. 'I haven't talked to her about him.'

'Why not?'

'I was waiting for the right time,' he said.

'Do you know why she'd go off with Troost?' I asked.

The expression in his eyes was so heartrending I could hardly bear to look. 'She had a relationship with Troost. She doesn't love him. I know that. But Troost has some strange power over her. She knows there's danger. I don't know why she went off with him.'

The guard came forward and tapped him on the shoulder.

We embraced and then he began walking away. Just as he reached the door, he turned and said, 'I depend on you, Sacha.'

The guard opened the door. Heinke walked out. The door closed leaving a metallic echo which reverberated through the room.

'I'll do my best,' I said into the emptiness.

Chapter 67

IT DIDN'T MAKE sense, I thought as I left the court house. It didn't fit together. But puzzles are games. In real life things never fit together the way you'd like them to fit.

I headed for the nearest telephone kiosk and dialled the number for my London newspaper. I connected with Janet, one of the sub editors I was quite friendly with, and asked her to see if there was any mail from Amsterdam on my desk. I told her to fax anything she found to my hotel. Then I walked back to the Literary Café to write my article and to get drunk.

The article started easy enough. I wrote about COBRA, about Vanderzee, the little-known artist, about his son, Heinke, who was carrying on the COBRA tradition and about Rachel, the revolutionary whore and her son, Solomon, the wild boy searching for his roots.

But something was missing. Part of the melody was there but it was as if a phantom tune was lingering, silently, just out of ear-shot. And there was something else. Something that was weighing on me. Heinke had been obsessed in the last few months. With ships, plantations and Suriname. What was all that research about?

I mulled it over in my mind as I left the Literary Café (realising I didn't want to get drunk - at least not yet). I strolled across town and then over to Prinsengracht, along the canal. I found a bench, sat down and had a smoke. I looked across, at the boats, at the line of shade trees. And then it struck me like a thunderbolt. I remembered. The Leaf!

It had been years ago. Not far from here. We had been sitting on a bench like this. It was Autumn. The leaves had turned. The chestnuts were beginning to brown. We were smoking. Chatting about something unimportant when a leaf fell from a branch above us and slowly wafted its way down, landing, finally, on Heinke's lap.

He picked it up and looked at it. He held it to the light. He ran his fingers over the ribs and the veins feeling the roughness of its texture, of its skin. He put it to his mouth. He tasted it. And then, opening his briefcase, he carefully stuck it in.

The next day when I visited him, he was engrossed in work. Books were strewn on the table along with pictures from natural history magazines - all of leaves.

In a while he had amassed a great leaf collection from all over Amsterdam. We would take forays into the woods. He was always on the lookout, searching for leaves of different colours, different textures.

Some he waxed and pressed, some he let dry and crinkle, some he ground and mashed and formed into a liquid which he tasted. Some he plastered to the walls. In the course of a month there were leaves everywhere in his cabin, tons of them of every size, shape and description.

And he read everything about them. How they functioned. Why they were shaped the way they were. When they changed colour. When they fell.

Then, one day, he began to paint. He didn't speak, he didn't go out, he would hardly ever eat. He was in a world of his own.

I came sometimes to see him. He didn't mind me coming. He just wouldn't speak. Marijke would bring him tea and food. She would place it on a stool next to him and leave. Sometimes it would stay for hours, getting cold. Then it would mysteriously disappear, she said.

I asked her if she minded living with him like that.

'Oh, not at all,' she said. 'It's like him leaving on a trip. Except he's there.'

And then he was finished. All the leaves, all the books, all the natural history magazines - they all had vanished.

'Where's the painting?' I asked, when I came in and saw the cabin back to normal.

'What painting?' he asked.

'The painting of the leaf,' I said.

'Oh, somewhere over there,' he said, making a vague gesture toward a pile of canvases stacked against the wall.

It was then I realised something I had never understood before. It wasn't the painting that had meaning for Heinke. For it became a relic as soon as it was done. It wasn't the painting itself, it was the process that had meaning for him.

That leaf which had fallen into his lap when we had been sitting on the bench that day became the impetus for a journey - a curious, convoluted journey which led him through a different universe. And what came out at the end, the painting, that synthesis of feelings, of ideas, of questions - that essence of leaf - was simply the product of the journey itself.

Perhaps I understood a little more about the nature of art that day. Perhaps not. But I did understand a little more about Heinke.

And then it twigged. There was something that needed to be done before it was too late. I finished my cigarette and then walked further down the canal to Heinke's boat.

Chapter 68

I KNEW SOMETHINg was wrong as soon as I got there. It was more a feeling than anything else. I climbed down the ladder, turned around and realised at once. The paintings were gone. All of them.

It was like the bowels of the boat had been gutted and left to rot without the preservative of all that art. Now it was barren, just an empty shell.

There was no reason for me to stay. I couldn't, anyway. I climbed back out, took a deep breath and felt my body, heavy, ungainly, older somehow.

And then I saw him. Like so often before. Only this time he was off the boat and I was on. He was staring at me. Watching. But it was different now. It was if he had been waiting for me to come, to see.

I called out to him. For now, at least, I knew his name. 'Solomon!'

He responded by moving further away. But then stopping and waiting again.

I climbed down the gangplank, off the boat and walked in his direction. He turned and loped toward one of the side streets that led into the centre of town.

Afraid of losing sight of him I ran to where I saw him turn. I thought I had lost him, yet again. But no. He had waited. Close enough for me to see him but still keeping a healthy distance away.

It was clear now that he wanted me to follow. And I did. He took me on a long and twisty trek that led through the centre of town, and eastward, past Nieuwmarkt, through the old Jewish quarter, across Waterlooplein and Mr. Visserplein and down through the Plantage.

He kept such a distance ahead of me that it was often hard to see which way he went. Several times I lost him and thought the chase was over, but each time he would double back and wait till I caught sight of him again. And then he'd be off. Not walking but loping slowly, steadily, effortlessly. Ignoring the people and the traffic, the bikes, the cars, as if they were just part of his magical forest.

He led me to the Plantage, through the greenery and past the wild animal enclosures and then crossing the Muider canal, further east again, till we came within sight of the old windmill, the last of those very Dutch trademarks in Amsterdam, and then a dog-leg north and east again into the derelict docklands at the Eastern reaches of the IJ.

We had circumvented the Plantage, which was just on the other side of the water. I could still hear the low, ominous growls of the lions and the occasional bellowing of elephants. The sounds lingered in the air even though we were now beyond sight of the zoo. We had reached a maze of little streets and alleys across from Kromhout Wharf, with the old windmill still visible to the south.

The tiny alley he had led me to was just behind an abandoned pier overlooking the enormous waterway that emptied into IJmeer bay. The buildings were mainly small warehouses, most in dire need of repair but all left to rot till the next phase of urban renewal reached out to them.

I saw him turn the corner and then he disappeared. For a moment I was lost in the dark, encroaching shadows that began to fill the narrow space between the buildings due to the quickly setting sun. I couldn't make out where he had gone. And then I saw a passageway that led along the side of a small warehouse. I noticed that the door, a few feet down, was slightly ajar.

I walked down the passage to the door. I could tell that it had been recently forced open as the rotting wood was freshly split at the latch. A rusty padlock which once might have prevented forced entry before the woodworms had eaten through the frame, lay, helplessly on the ground.

I pushed the door slightly and stared into the darkness of the warehouse. 'Solomon?' I called out in a throaty whisper that echoed back.

There was no response. Just darkness. Emptiness. And then, all at once, a brilliant flood of lights. Blinding me. I rubbed my eyes. The storeroom was aglow from the brilliant wattage of the overhead lamps.

I looked around and saw that Solomon was standing by the front doors of the warehouse. His hand was still poised by the great metal switch of the mains supply that was mounted on a pillar.

The room was nearly empty. Just some pallets and some crates and several tables with tools and a large workbench.

I went over to where the crates were stacked and saw they had either been undone or else hadn't been nailed shut yet. It was a professional job, I thought. Packed snugly and safely for a distant voyage. I knew where. I didn't have to look. But I saw the label, anyhow.

I took the paintings out, one by one, till I found the one I wanted. I knew it would be there, though I had never seen it before. I placed it against one of the crates, so that it faced the front.

The painting was of Rachel. She was dressed in flowing robes like a classical goddess with one side of her dress dangling down over her shoulder exposing a perfectly shaped breast. Her hair, thick, black and lustrous had been taken up by a pictorial breeze and was flowing like the ripples of a brook.

She was standing in some Elysian field across a river which established a metaphorical dividing line behind which, as the perspective moved slowly back toward the graphical point of infinity, were jungles, plantations, an ocean with sailing ships and, finally, a distant representation of the city of Amsterdam.

Her hands were outstretched as if making an offering. One hand held coffee, the other held white, crystalline granules - of sugar, perhaps, but it could have been something else.

As I gazed at the painting, at the face, so proud, so dignified and at the body, so womanly, so full of life, I slowly began to realise there was something Heinke had painted on the material that hung loosely from her chest. It was a patch of yellow, a raged patch. On the yellow was the Star of David. It was the badge the Nazis made my Grandfather wear right before he was deported to the death camps.

I moved toward the side door, far enough so that Solomon could observe the painting safely, without me being in the way. I watched him come forward. Slowly. Hesitantly. And then he stopped. But I could tell his eyes were devouring her.

'A portrait of your mother,' I said, softly, so that I wouldn't frighten him. 'Painted by your father...'

He had got down on his haunches. Crouching in a position that gave him a look of concentration.

'I think she was a remarkable woman,' I said.

He didn't move. He wasn't rigid. His body wasn't tense. He seemed to be in a meditative trance. His face was calm and placid. There was no emotion I could see. And then a little tear ran from the corner of an eye down his cheek and lingered on his chin.

I stood there, watching for a while until it struck me. Something wasn't right, I thought.

'Solomon. Wait here. I'll be back in five minutes.' And saying that I turned and hurried out the side door where I had entered from.

Chapter 69

I HAD REMEMBERED seeing a telephone as I passed the old windmill while following Solomon to the warehouse. It wasn't far, just several minutes. When I got there, I rang Hugo on his mobile. He didn't pick it up but the call was connected to an answering device. I left a message and then went back to the warehouse where I had left Solomon.

As I walked, I thought about the great trek he had led me on. How did he find the place? I wondered. I tried to imagine it. He was always lingering around the boat. He must have been there when they took the paintings and loaded them into some sort of transit van. Maybe he ran behind. But it was quite a distance. More likely he managed to cling onto the back and then jumped off without being seen when they got there.

I wondered how to ask him and how to get him to respond. But by the time I returned he had vanished. Along with the painting of his mother.

Alone in that vast open space with just Heinke's paintings to provide familiarity, I felt rather cold and vulnerable. I went over to the crates that I had stacked the pictures against after having unpacked them. They were being shipped off to New York - something I had assumed would happen after speaking with Heinke and his lawyer. But something was curious. Something I had spotted that hadn't seemed right.

The paintings had been reframed. Someone had taken the originals off. Not that the old ones had been anything special. Just simple wood constructions, stained in various shades appropriate to the colours of the work. But the new frames were awful - ungainly and totally out of keeping with Heinke's style.

I went over to one of the pictures and ran my finger over the edge. Why would someone go to all the trouble before they were shipped? I wondered. It was something that could have more easily been done afterwards as the new frames made the paintings even more difficult to pack.

It had struck me what the answer was as I had stood there watching Solomon gazing at the portrait of his mother. When I realised, I knew it wasn't safe to hang around. So, in a way, I was glad Solomon had buggered off. And, actually, I was glad he took the painting. Even though, by that time, I had come to suspect he got more than he had bargained for.

Taking a screw driver from the workbench, I turned one of the paintings around and dug into the back, where the frame met the canvas. I pried enough of it off so I could stick my fingers into the hollow within the frame itself. I felt something and pulled it. A plastic bag spilt out, dropping by my feet and covering the ground around me with a fine, white powder.

I stared down at the powdery mess, dumb struck. Suspecting it is one thing. Seeing it is quite another.

Suddenly the front doors of the warehouse flew open letting in a gust of wind. Startled, I turned. I saw him walk in from the darkness.

It took a moment before he saw me. Before he was aware. And then his jaw dropped. He looked stunned. He stood there for a moment, staring. Then he began to curse. 'Dumont! You filthy piece of scum! What are you doing here?'

'Just doing my job,' I said. He had caught me as unaware as I caught him.

'You bloody rotten meddler!' He shouted, 'Do you know what you've done?'

'Calm down, Parkins. Maybe I've done you a favour,' I said, trying to stay cool myself. To tell the truth, I was pretty frightened. You can never be certain what someone might do if you've just exposed them as a drug runner. Except I knew his type. He was essentially a coward.

'Why the hell did you do such a stupid thing?' I asked.

He looked at me with as much hatred as he could muster. 'Why the hell do you think? I need the money. New York is bloody expensive. The drug market's up. The Art market's down. I've got a condo with a million dollar mortgage and a wife who thinks diamonds are a girl's best friend.'

'You've done this before?' I asked. The scam was so obvious. I couldn't believe he actually did it for a living.

'Of course not!' he said. 'You just do this sort of thing once!' And then, he looked at me questioningly. 'Do you think we can make some kind of deal?'

'What kind of a deal?'

'You know...' He looked down at the white powder by my feet and then he shook his head, again. 'Shit! How can I trust you? You're a fucking reporter!'

'You can try,' I said, placatingly.

'Would it do any good?'

'Depends on what the deal is,' I said.

He nervously rubbed the side of his face. 'Oh, Jesus! Oh, Christ! What am I going to do?' Then, reaching down for the portfolio which he had dropped when he came in, he opened it up. 'Where the hell did I put it?' he said, rummaging around blindly with his hand.

'What are you looking for?' I asked.

'This,' he said, pulling out a gun and pointing it at my head.

My heart stopped beating. He wasn't supposed to carry a gun. After all, he was English. 'You don't want to shoot me,' I said.

'Of course I don't want to shoot you, you fucking prick! But I have to shoot you! Otherwise I'm done for, aren't I?'

'Let's think about this,' I said, trying to sound calm.

'It's too late for thinking. I should have thought before. I should have known this would happen! I should have told Van Houten to forget that stupid, fucking provo and his stupid, fucking paintings...'

'Then maybe it's Van Houten you should be shooting. Not me,' I said.

'You think Van Houten knows about this? He actually thought you could raise the price of those paintings just by getting the story into the newspapers!' He gestured to the picture next to me. 'Look at that one! What is it? A leaf someone's regurgitated? I wouldn't give you a nickel for it even if it was packaged with the greatest story ever told!'

'But you'd give more than a nickel for it now,' I said. Everything would be fine if I could keep him talking, I thought.

'Yeah,' he said. 'You're right. I've given them added value, haven't I? Let's not tell the VAT man!' He chuckled. Tears began streaming from his eyes.

I could see his hand was trembling. 'Why don't you put the gun down?' I suggested.

'I can't put it down,' he said.

'Why not?'

'Because I'm going to shoot you.'

'You're not a bloody murderer,' I told him.

His hand trembled harder as he pulled back the hammer, cocking the gun and slowly squeezing his finger against the trigger.

At that moment, I knew I was dead.

Chapter 70

A SHOT RANG out. I heard it in my brain and I felt it in my head. But first I saw something else. I saw him drop his arm. I heard him say, 'You're right, I'm not a bloody murderer.'

I heard him say that before he fell. He wasn't going to shoot me. He couldn't. But someone else could. I turned and saw who.

It was Frankie boy, the internet zapping Yank I had met at the Waag Café.

'You Limeys really like to stick your noses were they don't belong, don't you?' he said, going over to the body lying face down and turning it over with his foot.

Parkins's head flopped to the side. Eyes open wide in horror. Blood oozing from a hole in his forehead.

Frank looked down in disgust. 'I bet he never thought he'd end up like this. Dying in a pool of his own piss. Not when he was back in jolly old England.' He glanced over at me. 'What do you think, Dumont?'

'I think you're a pretty frightening man,' I said.

'Now is that any way to talk to someone who's just saved your life?' he said with a little grin. 'You guys never seem to appreciate us, even when it's your ass we're protecting.'

'He wasn't going to shoot,' I said.

'Really? Well from where I stood, it looked like he had his finger on the trigger.'

'He wasn't going to shoot,' I said, again.

'He was just playing a game of trick or treat, I guess,' said Frank. The smile had disappeared. He looked meaner.

'But I suppose you had to shoot him, didn't you?' I said. 'If he wasn't going to shoot me, that is. And probably that would have been the better option. Him shoot me and you shoot him.'

Frank turned to another man who had just stepped in the door. A man I hadn't seen till then. 'You see, Mack. You try to help someone and this is the thanks you get.'

Mack shrugged. 'What are we going to do with that stuff?' he said, motioning to the crates.

'First things first,' said Frank. 'What are we going to do with him?'

I looked at Frank. Into his eyes. I'd never seen eyes so cold and ruthless, I thought. And then I looked at the smoking gun which he still was holding and wondered how anyone could die twice in one night.

'I think Mack's right, Frankie boy. What about the stuff?'

I didn't say that. But I knew who did even before he walked in. And I'd never been so bloody pleased to see him!

'This doesn't have anything to do with you, Hugo,' said Frank, looking at him angrily. 'Get lost!'

'Well, unless this warehouse has been taken over by the United States Government, I'd say you're on my territory. Not the other way around.' Hugo's voice had lost it's jocular charm. It was forceful, firm. His eyes and Frank's were locked in a battle of animal musk.

'Don't step on my toes,' said Frank. 'Not if you know what's good for you.'

'If you knew what was good for you, you'd make your move, right now' said Hugo, reaching into his pocket.

Frank's fingers tightened round his gun.

Hugo smiled and pulled out his mobile. 'I'm not stupid, Fankie boy,' he said in a Hugoish voice again. 'There are four or five cars headed this way. They'll be here in a minute. So, if I were you, I'd be thinking how to explain this...' He gestured toward the body with his hand.

Frank looked over at Mack and then back at Hugo again and said, 'You don't know what you've gotten yourself into. It's something you'll regret.'

And then motioning to his partner, they left.

After they disappeared, Hugo looked at me and said, 'Well, he's right about that. I don't know what I've got myself into and it probably is something I'll regret.'

Chapter 71

I PULLED OUT a cigarette.

'Give me one of those filthy things!' said Hugo, holding out his hairy hand which seemed to be trembling slightly.

'That and my life's fortune,' I said, lighting him up. 'You've earned it.'

'I'll take it in cash, Sacha my friend.' He took a deep puff of smoke and slowly let it out. 'I might have to after all this is over.' Then looking down at the Parkins's body, he made a face. 'Let's get him covered up.'

We found a roll of plastic bubble wrap and used it as a shroud. Then we went out to breathe the night air, instead of the sickening odour that was rising up inside the warehouse.

I kept listening for the sound of sirens. Hearing nothing, I said, 'How soon are they coming?'

'Who?' he said.

'The reinforcements. Your police friends.'

'Oh, I never called,' he said.

'You didn't? Why not?' I looked at him in horror knowing we might both have been shot if that had been public information.

'Your message wasn't all that clear,' he said. 'I didn't know what was up.'

'I called before it happened,' I said. 'Not afterward. Besides, I thought you rang for reinforcements before you walked in.'

'I didn't know what was happening until I walked in,' he said, looking at me as if I was crazy.

We smoked our cigarettes and looked out into the inky black river. Then I turned to him and asked, 'So what's it all about?'

'I was just going to ask you that,' he said.

'I thought you knew.'

'It might help if you told me something about the guy who was shot.'

I told him who he was and I told him also about my meeting with Parkins and Van Houten and, finally, my meeting with Heinke.

He nodded. 'It's starting to make sense,' he said. 'Frankie's been hinting that there would be a big bust in New York which would make us look bad.'

'So he knew about the scam all along?'

'Knew about it?' Hugo slapped me on the back and roared. 'He probably set it up!'

'How?' I asked.

'Easy,' said Hugo. 'You have someone like Parkins. In Media and PR you say? Probably half the people he dealt with used the stuff. And he was desperate for money. An easy mark to be offered that one big job that will net him a little fortune.'

'Are you saying he was set up by the American Drugs Enforcement Agency?' I said.

'Probably not,' he said. 'Not the Agency, anyway. More likely just an Agent. Someone who wants a reputation. It's done all the time, Sacha. Half the big busts are set up like that. It's easier, less dangerous and you're in charge...'

I tried to imagine Parkins being met in New York by twenty armed men and fifty journalists. Maybe he was better off dead, I thought.

'Think of the headlines,' said Hugo. 'Dutch Art Exhibit Front For Cocaine Ring! Wouldn't that sound nice to Drug Enforcement ears? And wouldn't Amsterdam sound awful! What a feather in Frankie's cap!'

'But there has to be more to it,' I said. 'Why would Frankie shoot Parkins if Parkins didn't know he was being set up?'

'But Parkins was pointing a gun at you. Maybe Frankie saved your life. Did you ever think of that?'

'Parkins wasn't going to shoot.'

'Are you certain?'

'Yes.' I said. 'Sort of.'

The wind was blowing in from the North. A chill was in the air.

Hugo flicked the remnants of his cigarette into the river, turned to me and said, 'It's time I guess.'

'What are you going to say?' I asked.

He shrugged his heavy shoulders. 'I'll think of something. It's just a matter of creating a reasonable story. People want to believe what's reasonable, don't they?'

'That's the problem,' I said. 'What's reasonable?'

'Well, reasonable doesn't include you, Sacha, my friend. I'd rather not have you around when I'm doing the explaining.'

'Are you sure?' I said.

'I'm sure. Just leave me your smokes.'

I tossed him my pack of cigarettes and left him there on the pier smoking a fag and looking out into the jet black water.

Chapter 72

I NEARLY REACHED the windmill when I realised there was something I needed to tell him. There must have been an inventory of the paintings. And one of them would be missing - one that was possibly stuffed with cocaine. Whatever story he told, that would have to be taken into account or he, himself, might be blamed.

I doubled back to the warehouse. By the time I got there, I found the front entrance had been bolted shut, so I went around to the passage which led toward the back..

The side door was still ajar. I went inside. And then I stopped. Standing in the shadows, I saw him kneeling by the body which had been unwrapped. He was using a knife and pliers to dig the bullet out of Parkins's head. Even from a distance, I could see the ooze of brain.

Then, wiping his hands, he stood up, reached inside his jacket, pulled out a gun and moved back a pace or two. Gleaming, silvery bright, he held it out. And then he fired. One short crack.

Bits of Parkins's skull ricocheted off the wall in a shower of red. Quietly, I stepped back out the door and left.

Chapter 73

MY THROAT WAS dry. So dry I could hardly swallow. My head was throbbing. I felt sick. By the time I reached my hotel, all I wanted to do was drop myself in bed.

I opened the door and found an envelope by my foot. I reached down to pick it up and saw that my shoe had a few flakes of blood.

I went to the bath and wiped off the specks with a tissue. Then I took off all my clothes, wrapped them in a bundle and tossed them into a corner. I turned on the shower, scrubbed myself in lather and then twisted the nozzle of the shower so the water beat against my skin. I stayed like that for quite a while, fifteen minutes perhaps, until I started to feel clean again.

Then, drying myself off, I wrapped the towel around me and went to fix myself the stiffest drink I could manage.

I bolted half of it down and then picked up the envelope that I had found by the door, opened it and pulled out the pages. It was the fax from London I had been waiting for - the article that Rachel had written and that Heinke had posted me just before he was sent to jail.

I lay down in bed and began to read. It told the story of a country in desperate straits. Of a revolution failed. Of a people without work, without hope, without aid. And it told of some who had enough, who decided to exploit whatever they could muster. If the land was harsh, if the plantations had gone bust, if the tourists wouldn't come because of lousy beaches, then why not make their disadvantages work for them? Why not make assets out of their liabilities and develop products that had a market, that sold well and where part of the profits could be returned to the people?

The old plantations were overgrown. They had turned back into jungle again. The land was impossible to farm. But some of the old buildings remained. And, with effort, some bits of jungle could be cleared. Enough for a tiny landing strip for little aeroplanes.

And the buildings could be refurbished. Again with work. But what do you need to make a lab to refine the coca plants? Not much. Just some chemicals and bottles and tubs for distilling stuff in. The plants could be flown in easily from the neighbouring countries, like Colombia and Bolivia, to these hidden refineries and then, packaged and taken, clandestinely by river to a nearby harbour.

The idea, somehow, appealed to her sense of revenge. The cocaine would go to the very countries that had exploited them. It would be used to further their decline into moral barbarity. And the profits would help feed some hungry people. Besides, wouldn't it be just one more in a progression of other commodities - sugar, tobacco, coffee - all stimulants, all deeply desired, all, in their own way narcotic?

And most of all it would come from the plantations. The very place which enslaved her ancestors. The place that robbed them of their culture, their heritage and their birthright.

But then - there was the catch. The fly in the ointment. They had to deal with the dealers. And one day it occurred to her. Who were these people who came in their fancy suits? Who smoked fine cigars and complained of the heat and the insects? And where did all the money come for the heavy equipment to enlarge the air strips, and better equipment and faster boats to take their supplies up river? And who was the young Dutchman? The one with the strange mole on his hand who helped with distribution in Amsterdam. And what was his link with the American who came with him once and then disappeared but was seen again in a picture over an article about the 'Drugs for Guns' scandal being investigated by the United States Senate?

She didn't as much leave as escape. The money she had earned was confiscated by the people who really controlled the processing farms. And she arrived in Amsterdam, broke, angry and distraught. Only to meet up with the Dutchman, the one with the mole on his hand. He didn't recognise her - she was just another fucked-up woman from Suriname - but she remembered him. And one day, when he was pressing her for money for the very drugs which now were destroying both her and her son, she reminded him. And he freaked out. Not for the Suriname connection but because she implied he had been working for the narks.

She didn't say it outright and most of what she wrote was unsubstantiated rumour. But it must have frightened Troost out of his socks. Even dealers live on their reputations. And even rumours can destroy you, especially if they hit close to the mark.

I folded the pages of the fax and put them back in the envelope. Then I lay back down in bed, extremely fatigued. My body ached for sleep, for rest, to remember and forget. But what I realised, as I shut my eyes on the way to slumber land, was that if Rachel's meandering article was even partially correct, Marijke was in worse trouble than I had thought. And so was her brother Solomon, for different reasons perhaps.

Chapter 74

I WOKE UP and glanced at my watch. It was one in the afternoon. I had slept far later than I had wanted. I jumped out of bed, threw some water on my face and dressed.

Downstairs I saw Joop, the relief clerk, reading the paper. 'Hey, Sacha!' he called. 'Come look at this!'

He held out the front page for me to inspect. 'Isn't that the guy who met you here a few nights ago? His name was Hugo, wasn't it?'

I read the article. It told about an heroic Amsterdam policeman who had single-handedly cracked an American smuggling operation using as a conduit important works of Dutch art bound for international exhibition. Underneath was a photo of a smiling Hugo standing before several of Heinke's pictures.

'When did this come out?' I asked.

'Just now,' Joop replied. 'It's the early afternoon edition.'

I tried ringing Hugo but he wasn't available. I left a message saying I'd ring him later and that I needed to talk.

Then I went out. I took the tram into the centre where I made a copy of Rachel's article and did a little shopping for some food and clothes. I took the parcels up the Western Isles, retracing the route I had taken with Elisabet until I reached the alley with the derelict, abandoned house.

It was awkward, but I managed to get the stuff up the free-hanging stairway and then into the room with the mat and the ragged bedcovers and the alter over the mantelpiece he had constructed.

The little photo was gone. In its place was the painting.

I put the parcels down in front of the hearth. Then I sat down and wrote him a letter. I told him the story of the cocaine scam and what I expected was hidden in his painting. I said that it was possible he was in danger since the warehouse had been under observation. I also told him to be careful of Troost when he returned. I said I was going to Paris on the evening train to see about Marijke, and that I'd contact him on my return through Heinke, who, I suspected, would soon be out of jail.

Then I folded the letter and put it in the envelope with his mother's article. I sealed it shut and put it on the mantelpiece underneath the painting.

Chapter 75

I WENT BACK to my hotel where I reworked my article and faxed it off to Tompkins at the paper. Then I tried ringing Hugo again. This time I connected.

'Things never work out the way you expect, do they, old friend?' he said.

'Maybe that's because I don't know what to expect anymore. So I've given up expecting. But you must have had a long and busy night,' I said.

'I lead such a dull life. It's nice to have some excitement for a change. And I met some very interesting and important people,' he said.

'I guess you did. Any offers?'

'Some. But I think I'll sit on them for a while.'

'How did Frank know when to come in last night?' I asked. 'It was perfect timing, wasn't it?'

'He probably had the place wired,' said Hugo. 'He was listening to everything that was said.'

'Then someone probably heard the shot.'

'What shot?'

'Yours.'

There was a brief silence. Very unlike Hugo to be caught without a quick reply, I thought. Then he said, 'It doesn't matter. He's been reassigned. Left for the States this very day, I understand.'

'I'd be careful anyway.'

'I'm always careful, my friend.'

After I hung up the telephone, I packed my bag. Then I went downstairs to check out.

'Where are you going?' asked Kiko.

'To Paris,' I said.

'Will you be back soon?'

'I hope so. Yes.

'Give us a call. Your room will be waiting for you. And a hot bowl of miso soup!'

Chapter 76

I RANG NASSY at the museum before I left.

'I'd like to see you before I go,' I said.

'I'll be at the university mensa in about fifteen minutes,' he said.

The university dining hall wasn't far from Central Station. I grabbed my bag, hopped on the tram and in twenty minutes I was there.

Nassy was sitting at one of the long tables feasting on an unrecognisable concoction that might have been regurgitated several times before it reached his plate.

'That looks disgusting,' I said, sitting down with him after getting a cup of coffee from the coffee machine.

'It is disgusting,' he replied. 'But it's cheap. Eating here allows me to buy both food and books. Otherwise it would be either or.'

'I was sent this by Marijke,' I said, handing him the letter.

He read it quickly and then handed it back. 'So she's in Paris,' he said.

'Heinke says she's mixed up in something she doesn't understand.'

'Most of us are,' he replied.

'He thinks she's in a great deal of danger. He wants me to go there and talk with her.'

'Are you?' he asked.

I nodded. 'But I need your help.'

'What can I do?' he asked.

'I need someone I can trust. Someone who could research something. I can pay you a bit...'

'I wouldn't take money,' he said.

'Whatever,' I said. 'Would you do it?'

He nodded.

I handed him my notebook. 'Write down all your details,' I said. 'Where I can reach you day or night.'

He took the notebook and a pen. As he began writing, I noticed a young woman at a nearby table was staring at me. I glanced back at Nassy and then looked up again. She was still staring, over the top of her glasses.

Nassy finished and handed me back the notebook. 'When are you leaving?' he asked.

'I'm taking the next train,' I said.

'What would you like me to do?' he asked.

I tore a piece of paper from the notebook and wrote some things down. 'I'd like you to find out what you can about a man called Karl Troost. He used to play with a jazz group at the Boom! Boom! Club...'

As I a handed him the paper, I noticed the young woman had stood up and was now walking in our direction. She came over to our table, smiled at me and said, 'I thought you recognised me.'

I looked at her. She appeared to be just another sweet young student. And then it clicked.

Nassy seemed to grasp the idea that she wanted to say something for my ears alone. 'I'm just going to get some coffee,' he said.

She waited for him to walk off. Then she turned back to me. Her face looked worried. 'No one here knows about my work,' she said.

'Why would I say anything?' I said.

She shrugged. 'Some men would.'

'I'm not that kind of man,' I assured her.

'I'm sorry about what happened,' she said. She looked sorry, too.

'I didn't appreciate it,' I admitted.

'I'm sorry,' she said again.

I saw Nassy was coming back. 'What's your name?' I asked. 'I suppose you don't use "Suzy" here.'

'Christine,' she said.

I introduced her to Nassy when he sat back down. He glanced at the book she had placed on the table in front of her. 'Spinoza,' he said. 'Do you like him?'

222

'Oh, yes,' she replied. 'He's fascinating!'

'Really?' said Nassy.

'You don't like him then?' she said.

'Certainly. It's just I find few women your age who do...'

'I'll be off,' I said. 'I'll ring you later.'

I left them at the table talking Spinoza together.

Chapter 77

THE SUN WAS pouring through the great arched windows of Central Station as I waited for the train to Paris. And my mind wandered back to a day like this, some years ago, just before I left Amsterdam for London. As a final farewell, Heinke had taken me someplace I hadn't been, someplace he thought I should go before I departed.

It was to the Beurs, the old Amsterdam Stock Exchange, he took me that day. And we climbed to the top of the clock tower where we looked down upon the city lit up brightly by the sun.

'You don't often get a chance to see the city from above,' he said. 'We don't have skyscrapers like New York or great monuments like Paris or steep hills like Lisbon, so here you must climb up the clock towers to get a decent view...'

'But the Stock Exchange?' I said. 'I thought this would be the last place in the world you'd take me to.'

'So,' he said, 'you don't understand me at all. And you still don't understand Amsterdam. Not that you ever will because no one truly understands this place. But the Beurs, the Stock Exchange, is one of the pillars on which Amsterdam stands. Down below, inside the chamber is a mural extolling the world of trade and enterprise, the commodities and goods that flowed here from every conceivable place on earth. And there is a frieze depicting the ascent of man, from Adam, in the beginning, to the final stage of supreme evolution - the birth of the stockbroker. For more than anyplace else, the Beurs is our church, our most holy temple of temples and there are those who will sacrifice anything and everything to the gods who control it.

'But there is something else,' he said. 'Spelt out in tiles on the clock built in this very tower is a motto which reads, "Bide your time". Think of that as a motto, Sacha - "Bide your time". It means wait, be patient and if you preserver, things will come to you. "Bide your time." Imagine having that as a motto in London, Paris or Berlin!

'And there is something even more. On this building there is a stone depicting two fisherman and a dog in a very small boat. It's the story of how Amsterdam was founded. One day two fishermen were lost in a storm. When they finally washed ashore, the poor dog jumped out and puked. And legend has it that there, on the very spot he was sick, is where Amsterdam was built. So you see, Sacha, my friend, even the official myth-makers say that we started from a pile of vomit. What other city would admit such a thing, let alone glory in it?'

I looked down at the city glistening below and then I turned to him and said, 'Where would you live if you didn't live here? Paris? Rome? London?'

'Nowhere,' he said. 'This is my city. I love it.'

'Nowhere else?' I asked.

And then he looked at me and his eyes twinkled. 'Nowhere.'

I thought of this as I boarded the Paris Express. To me, Heinke was Amsterdam. And Amsterdam was his imagination.

I settled in my seat and looked out of the window as the train slowly began to move away. And then I saw him. It was Solomon. He was loping along the platform next to my carriage. As the train began to build up speed, so did he. I looked ahead. Another few yards and the platform would end. He was running so fast, I thought he would plunge over the side, over the precipice and into the jungle of metal track.

But just as he reached the edge, he stopped. He teetered, then regaining his balance, held out both arms.

I saw him through the window getting smaller and smaller, as the train moved on. His arms held out in a gesture of farewell.

But perhaps it wasn't that at all. Maybe, just maybe, he was going to fly, I thought.

BLACK APOLLO PRESS
RECENT PUBLICATIONS

A KNIGHT AT SEA
by R. J. Raskin

ISBN: 9781900355131
Pages: 264
Price: £12.00

On the 12th of April, 1955 Raymond Chandler boarded the Mauritania in New York setting sail for the England of his youth. A Knight at Sea is a fictional account of that voyage. Woven likea film noir, this is a Chandleresque tale of bizarre friendship coupled with intrigue and murder.
"Probably the best novel about Raymond Chandler ever written! Brilliant, bold, witty, political and totally absorbing!" Ozymandias

EIGHT WEEKS IN THE SUMMER OF VICTORIA'S JUBILEE
The Queeen, the Jews and a Mruder
by Bob Biderman

ISBN: 9781900355711
Pages: 267
Price: £13.95

Jubilee Summer - June 1887. Britain is deep in lavish celebration of Empire. That same month, in the East End of London, a quiet young man, recently arrived from Warsaw, is accused of murdering an Angel. Two writers at the start of their career - Z, a brilliant, Ango-Jewish novelist and Maggie, a fiery social reformer - are brought together in a remarkable encounter as they investigate a crime that would change their lives and their vision of themselves, England and the world.